JACK FROST

REBECCA F. KENNEY

1

PLAYLIST

"All the King's Horses" Karmina
"Wintersong" Marcus Warner ft. Fatma Fadel
"Last Christmas Epic Version"
"Silent Night" Epic Version by J2 Ft. Seth Bowser
"God I Hope This Year Is Better Than The Last" SYML
"Come December" Jordan Fisher
"Dance of the Sugar Plum Fairy" Lindsey Stirling
"Carry You" Ruelle, Fleurie
"Winter Things" Ariana Grande
"Jealous Gods" Poets of the Fall
"Clear Blue Sky" Poets of the Fall
"Be the One" Dua Lipa
"Do You Hear What I Hear" Idina Menzel
"All I Want For Christmas Is You" Chase Holfelder
"Walking in the Air" Karliene
"In Your Arms" Ashley Serena & Ryan Louder
"Merry Christmas Everybody" I Don't Know How But They Found Me
"Carol of the Bells" Lindsey Stirling
"Battlefield" SVRCINA
"Angelis" Libera
"Burning Heart" SVRCINA
"Underneath the Tree" Kelly Clarkson

1

BONES OF ICE

This is either a noble and dramatic way to die, or a very stupid one.

My team will probably try to soften the idiocy of my actions. They'll make it out to be something selfless—"Emery died pursuing scientific knowledge, trying to capture the beauty and terror of nature at its most primal." They won't say "Yeah, Emery was really, really dumb. She ignored all the safety protocols and hung back to take more footage—wandered too far, got separated from the group. You know, it was natural selection, honestly. The idiots die and the smart ones survive."

The idiots die.

I'm going to die. In Antarctica. In the middle of a freaking blizzard.

I can't see. If I open my eyes, even a crack, they're blasted with bits of ice as fine as sand. I've lost my goggles somewhere—no hope of finding them. Each inhale is like razor blades to my throat and lungs. I tug my hood lower, trying to shield my eyes and mouth so I can take painful sips of oxygen.

It all happened so fast.

When the winds picked up, scouring across the snowy dunes, I didn't think much of it. The sky was still fairly clear, but my team mobilized at once, prompted by Luc Garnier. He's been to Antarctica several times, and he knows the dangers.

But we had been waiting for days to get good shots of the Adelie penguins hatching from their eggs, and I didn't want to leave the nest I'd been monitoring. I've only got two days left in Antarctica. And several days out of my two-week trip have already been wasted huddling in a tent while the katabatic winds roared across the snowscape. There was absolutely nothing to do during that time, except fret about all the hours I could have been logging with my camera, all the data I should have been collecting. Our team barely slept because the wind slammed into our tents with hurricane force, shaking and snapping the heavy canvas until I thought it would dislodge and hurl away into the storm, leaving us exposed like squirming worms on a shelf of ice. The noise of the gale booming against the tent was deafening, and the cold wiggled insidious fingers into our piles of bedding.

After the misery of those days, I was not about to lose my chance to film penguin chicks cracking through their shells into the world. All that waiting, all that effort and expense—no way was I giving up my shot, my one shot, that one-of-a-kind footage I was being paid to capture.

So I pretended to pack up my equipment when Luc gave the order, and I convinced Ben to go on ahead and let me take up the rear—and then I went back to the nest.

I thought I would have time to shoot a little more video, pack up, and rejoin the group before the storm really hit.

Damn was I wrong.

The wind hurls itself against my heavy pack, nearly bowling me over. My legs tremble from the exhaustion of keeping myself upright. I'm sweating copiously under my layers of clothing, but my fingers are speared with the pain of the cold. I tug my scarf up over my nose and mouth again. Immediately I remember why I pulled it down; the snow-crusted thickness of the scarf is suffocating. But if I don't keep it over my face, I could lose my nose to frostbite. I like my nose. It's nice—and straight—why am I thinking about my damn nose right now? I should be thinking about moving forward. One foot in front of the other—except I've lost all sense of direction. I can't contact the others in this gale. I can't stay here, or I'll freeze. But if I keep moving, I might head away from base camp, out into the great Nothing of this wretchedly beautiful continent.

This is the end for me. The only question is, do I burrow into the snow and die, or keep walking and die?

The cowering might come eventually. For now, I'll try to move.

The scarf sucks to my mouth as I huff freezing air. Wind blasts against me, violent as a 230-pound linebacker crashing into my body. My eyes are oozing tears that solidify into slush on my cheekbones.

I wanted so fiercely to film those chicks hatching. And I did.

Was a few minutes of footage worth my life?

Keep going, Emery. One foot forward.

Brace against a crushing shove from the wind.

Another step.

I came here to study and film the wildlife. To make a paycheck, yes, but also to inform people about these animals. About their habitat, and how it's changing as the globe gradually warms. About what we can do to shift the dangerous trends that threaten species all over the Earth, including our own.

Is that cause worth my life? Sure. But if I had been smarter, and stayed with the team, I could live another handful of decades to fight for the planet.

This is so typical of me. Caught in the passion of the moment, ready to make the big gesture. Trying to do something huge, important, and idealistic—and failing every time, my struggle soured with regret.

Another step—not so much a step as a slow shift of my boot, but still—progress.

One more step.

Come on. You've got this, Emery.

I was taught that as long as I tried harder than everyone else, as long as I studied and struggled and clawed and climbed and never gave up—as long as my work ethic was sound and my motives pure, that I could make it. That I'd succeed. That people would listen.

What a load of shit. That has never been true for me. Okay, I'm on this trip, which was a dream come true—but the dream is rapidly morphing into a nightmare with claws like ice, shredding through all the layers I wear, blasting its chill breath over my skin.

My whole body is shaking now, and my heart throbs huge and hot in my chest. I can't keep moving; the strain is too much. I might have a heart attack if I try.

Just a few more steps.

My foot shifts forward.

The ice creaks and gives a little—but I'm already moving my other foot forward, and I can't stop it—

My weight lands on the unstable ice, and it folds under me, slanting inward. I fling up my arms, scrabbling wildly for purchase, suddenly energized; but my pack bears me down with its inexorable weight and I crash bodily through the broken ice.

For a moment there's nothing—the sucking absence of the whirling storm, and a freefall that flings my stomach into my throat, like the hideous, thrilling drop of a roller coaster. Except this roller coaster is going to end in icy shards spearing my flesh, or in a lake of lethally cold water.

My butt skims against something—snow? My boot heels graze a sheet of hardpack and I'm sliding, too far and too fast, rocketing down into the bowels of some underground cavern. There's a faint luminescence growing around me—a teal-colored haze of light licking the walls of the chasm.

The slide ends, and I crash onto an icy floor. Something in my pack crunches sickeningly upon impact. I end up belly down, with my pack crushing my spine.

Whimpering, I struggle out of the straps and heave the pack off me. I'm not sure where I am, or how stable the floor is. It feels thick and solid, but ice can be deceptive. It's a fact Luc is fond of repeating.

I try to get up—I really do. But my muscles have gone completely liquid. They will not obey me. All I can do is flip onto my back and lie still.

It's cold down here—the kind of deep, aching cold that only the poles of the Earth possess. Cold like bones and mortality, like the space between the stars. Walls of corrugated ice stretch for stories above my head, up into the dark.

I have no idea how deep this hole is.

The realization knots my stomach.

No one will ever find me.

My gloved fingers skate across my pack, searching for the pocket that holds the walkie-talkie. A quick glance confirms what I already suspected—it's broken. I'm not even sure I'd be able to use it from this far down, even if it still worked.

My breath hisses through my teeth, fast and desperate, and my chest heaves. I'm going into a full-blown panic attack in a second, down here, alone. I can't do that. I have to breathe, and think about the good things, the true things.

I rip away the scarf, dragging in ice-sharp gasps.

At least I'm alive.

The wind isn't trying to knock me flat anymore. No wind, which makes it feel slightly warmer.

I didn't impale myself on spears of ice, nor am I an Emery-popsicle bobbing in the blue deep. That's also good.

I don't think I broke any bones. I didn't hit my head.

The air is so cold it neutralizes taste and smell. But I can feel the soggy weight of my clothes. I can see the crystallized tears on my lashes. I can feel the soreness stretching through my limbs. The pain means I'm *here*. Tired, but whole.

My breathing has already slowed. I spread my arms and legs out wide, like a kid making snow angels.

All right. I need to sit up and look around. Maybe lighten my pack to the bare necessities—although it's going to kill me to leave anything behind.

Maybe I should explore first and come back for the pack later.

My hands are so stiff with cold that I have to strip off my gloves and put my fingers in my mouth for a minute before I can extract the hard-frozen energy bars from one pocket of the pack. After tucking the bars into my coat pockets, I move forward into the cavern.

It's not so much a cavern as a very long, very wide hallway. Actually it reminds me a bit of the lobby at an opera house or a museum—except without any paintings, crown molding, or chandeliers. Just ice. Strangely luminescent ice. And a few sculptures here and there, very high up the walls—

Wait, what?

My feet stop moving.

I squint up at the spot that drew my attention.

Nature did not craft the hooked fangs or sharply planed face of that creature. Nature didn't etch the graceful fairy a few yards further, or the dragonesque being that seems to cling to the icy ceiling.

The sound I make is half-laugh, half-sob.

Why are there ice sculptures down here?

I must be very close to death. Dangerously cold. Hallucinating, for sure.

Closing my eyes, I press my gloved hands over them, inhaling icy air. If only it didn't hurt so much to breathe. If only I weren't losing the feeling in my toes, and the tip of my nose.

When I look again, the ice carvings are still there.

Fine. I'm just going to keep walking and pretend they don't exist.

Forward I march, my chin set grimly under my snow-crusted scarf.

Maybe the statues were left behind by some long-lost researcher or explorer who fell into the ice and carved them just for fun before dying in this lovely death-trap.

Right. Like that makes sense.

I'm a scientist. But I'm also an artist. Weird blend, sure, but it works. It means I have a detailed understanding of the biology and life cycles of penguins while *also* knowing how to compose a shot correctly, for the best visual impact. So while I am a deeply pragmatic person, I have an even more foundational love for things that are mystically, inexplicably beautiful.

When confronted with the inexplicable, humans do one of two things— deny it or believe it.

The further I walk, the closer I edge to believing it.

It's the columns that convince me. Tall and graceful, reaching three stories high—perfectly round and smooth, like frosty white tree trunks that curve into crisply pointed arches overhead.

And then the steps—two dozen of them, blue ice shot through with swirls of white.

Have I stepped into a kids' movie here? Can I expect a blonde ice queen to sweep down the steps toward me, snowflakes unfurling from her hands? I bite back a hysterical laugh and knock the tears from my cheekbones before they can freeze and chap my skin even further.

Beyond the arches and the steps is a long hallway. I could swear this part of the—cave? castle?—is marble or stone, not ice. Or perhaps it's simply a kind of ice I'm not familiar with.

There are rooms here—wide and beautiful, with crystalline branches laced across their ceilings and furniture as clear as glass sitting untouched. A dusky blue light glimmers throughout the place—the faint echo of winter daylight. Everything feels expectant, unused. Like the whole palace is waiting for something, or someone.

I'm getting a headache. The pain splinters my consciousness, shattering my appreciation for the exquisite, impossible scenery through which I'm wandering.

The hallway expands suddenly, space opening before me—a great hall with fiercely glorious lines. Columns of ebony rock, gleaming wetly in the dim blue light, soar high above my head, meeting at a peak festooned with icicles bigger than my body and sharp as spears. The floor is lake-blue ice so clear I can see down into its depths for what feels like miles.

And there's a throne, because of course there is, because I am dreaming, or dying, or dead.

If I'm dead, or dreaming, I'm totally allowed to sit on the throne, right?

I'm so damn tired, and so cold. If I can just sit for a minute, I'll feel better. Or maybe I'll fall asleep and freeze to death.

Reluctantly I skirt around the throne. At the back of the hall there's a door—the first one I've seen in this place. What kind of fancy ice castle doesn't have doors? Although I suppose unexpected visitors aren't much of an issue here. A hysterical giggle bubbles between my lips, and its echo off the icy walls is so frightening that I clap my hand across my mouth, vowing internally not to do that again.

The door is seamed with silvery lines and has a pattern of raised white snowflakes that fit together like a clockwork mechanism.

A quick wrench to the handle reveals that this door is locked, and if the snowflake-clockwork is anything to go by, it's not meant to be easy to open.

If this is a dream, I should be able to unlock the door with my mind. If it's real, maybe a good kick would help—even ice doors have weak points, right? Too bad my mind and my muscles are at their limit. I don't think I could run for my life, even if a giant snow monster stormed into the hall, roaring for my blood.

I lean my forehead against the door and release a soft sigh. "I wish there were blankets and hot chocolate and a warm bath behind you," I murmur. "But I seriously doubt it."

My breath puffs onto the cold surface, creating a swirl of opalescent white.

A faint chattering and clicking begins, and I back away as the clockwork snowflakes spin, interlocking, the motion transferring from gear to gear until the final one pops into place, and the door handle twitches a fraction.

Gingerly I test it again.

It yields to my touch, and with a little more pressure, the door opens.

The room beyond is blue and *breathing*. The azure light inside swells and ebbs like a slow, steady heartbeat. It's a small space with a floor swathed in glittering white—and this time it's actual fabric, not snow or ice. In the center is a faceted cut-glass bedframe hung with midnight-blue curtains.

I'm so far beyond skepticism now. I exist as a flickering, fading core of curiosity—it's the only thing I have energy for, the only motivation keeping me upright.

I move clumsily forward—soggy and chilled, my hair sweat-glued to my skull under my cap and hood. With my numb fingers, I part the curtains.

2

THE FROZEN GOD

The person in the bed isn't a fairytale ice queen.

It's worse, much worse.

A man.

He is only visible from the neck up. The rest of him is coated with teal-colored ice scattered with a delicate design of snowflakes. The ice looks as if it has grown over his body, coating his limbs, spreading across the bed and down to the floor, where it climbs partially up the wall, spiking outward in glittering crystals.

What I can see of him is striking, to say the least. Harsh cheekbones. Savagely arched eyebrows, coal-black in contrast to the snowy hair swept back from his forehead. His skin is so smooth he could model for moisturizer. And despite the cutting edges and fierce lines of his face, his mouth is surprisingly wide and soft. A mouth that likes to smile, maybe.

Oh god. This is ridiculous.

Logic, Emery. The freaking scientific method. I clutch the concept with all the fading strength my mind possesses.

Time for some observation. He looks real enough, but—does he feel real? I strip off one glove and reach out, wincing, until my finger grazes his cheek. I feel nothing, of course, because my hands are practically frozen. I place three fingertips in my mouth until they start to prickle painfully, blood flow returning in an agonizing trickle.

The next time I touch him, I can feel his skin—cold yet malleable, smooth and almost silky. I bend lower, inhaling. Despite my chilled nostrils, I can smell him—a sharp, clean scent that reminds me of wind over the ocean, and of peppermint leaves.

Three senses out of the five tell me he's real. I have a lot of empirical evidence staring me in the face right now. But I also just whisked along an ice slide into the bowels of Antarctica, so it's quite possible I'm not myself at the moment. I could be experiencing a very vivid hallucination. Maybe I did hit my head after all, or maybe exhaustion is making me see things... like beautiful men sleeping in castles of ice... oh god...

Maybe I'm actually dead, and this is some weird afterlife dreamscape. Except I don't believe in an afterlife—at least, I claim that I don't. As much as I try to, I can't convince myself that after death we just *end*, and that's it. I mean, how depressing would that be, especially for people who had terrible lives?

An afterlife doesn't make sense, though, because that would require belief in supernatural entities or existence, and I can't make that compute either. Not even with this guy lying an arm's length from me, cocooned in ice like freaking Captain America.

If he is real...

If...

Then he's the only person who might be able to help me. My only chance to get out of here, to survive and get back to my team. Alien, superhero, magical ice being, dream or delusion—whatever he is, I need him to wake up.

"Hey." My voice cracks, scraped raw from the cold and wind. No wonder my laugh sounded so weird. "Hey—dude—guy—you there—" I cringe because my rasping tones sound just like my mother, an avid smoker who has never considered quitting. She tried to get me hooked on cigarettes too, but I was viciously determined never to do anything she'd done. I wouldn't even put one between my lips.

My hoarse voice conjures her in my head so vividly I can almost smell the reek of stale smoke and booze that always envelops her.

Shuddering away the memory, I speak louder. "Yo, ice guy! Wake up! I need your help."

Light surges through the ice that covers him and the walls that surround him—and then it fades again. It pulses steady and unchanged, even when I shout and flick his cheek with my finger.

Okay, this guy's not waking up. He's in a sleep as deep as any fairytale slumber.

The fleeting thought of fairytales wakes an idea in my brain.

My breath had an effect on the door—I'm not sure why—but maybe it would have a similar effect on him.

Kissing a stranger while they are sleeping wouldn't be my first choice, but in cases of magical slumber, it's totally justified. My college roommate used to go on forever about the lack of consent when Sleeping Beauty was kissed in the animated movie; but it never bothered me. The prince could either give her a gentle, chaste kiss, or leave everyone asleep for a hundred years, so yeah—the choice was kind of obvious.

Besides, I don't really have to kiss this guy. I just have to breathe on him.

Pulling my scarf out of the way, I lean forward. My head turns weirdly dizzy, and for a second I think I'm going to collapse on top of him. I'm rapidly approaching my body's final limits. I release a gasp, edged with a whimper of panic, over the man's lips.

Instantly the cold white of his mouth turns faintly lavender. A frosty exhale rushes from him, and I breathe it in, because that scent of snow and mint is the best thing I've smelled in a long time. For weeks it's been nothing but sour body odor and penguin crap, wet coats and morning breath in the confines of a canvas tent, lukewarm canned food and fishy saltwater.

The man's eyes flash open, shocked and baleful and blue, so blue.

I'm still leaning over him. Way too close.

"Nick's icy balls!" he exclaims. "What in the fresh hell are you doing?"

The icy shield across his chest begins to crack, and I lurch backward. "I—I need your help."

"You woke me up. Do you realize what you've done?"

"No?" I wince. "I'm freezing, and I'm lost, and I thought maybe you could help me."

His cold mouth quirks in a sneer. The ice around him shatters, and he sits up, sloughing off the shards. "Of course you did. Humans, always so focused on their individual needs and not the collective good. You've set me back at least a week." He rakes his hands through his hair. "Damn it. I should have switched out of human aspect before going to sleep. Then you wouldn't have been able to see me."

He stands up, brushing grains of ice from his body. He's a good foot taller than me, slim and naked from the waist up, with dark blue pants settled temptingly low on his hips. His body is stone-white—pale curves and ledges of muscle.

I'm going insane. I must be. I press my gloved hands over my eyes. My whole body is shaking uncontrollably from the cold and from exhaustion. My mouth can barely form words anymore.

"Hey. Hey there." The pale-haired man snaps his fingers in front of me. "What's wrong with you?"

"I'm freezing to death." I force the words between chattering teeth.

"Oh god." He rolls his eyes. "Come here."

"Wh-why?"

"I can make you immune to the cold. It'll just take a second."

A helpless, raw laugh breaks from me. "Okay. Yeah, that would be nice."

He grabs my hooded head in both of his long white hands and crushes his mouth to mine. His lips are sharply cold, and his breath tastes chilly and sweet. A trickle of icy sensation skims across my tongue, down my throat, along my nerves. Suddenly I'm not cold anymore. I'm not warm either, though. I'm just— fine. No shivering, no stabbing pain in my extremities, no lingering numbness.

He pulls away, examining me briefly and nodding with satisfaction. "There. I gave you the Chill. You'll be impervious to cold now. Unfortunately you'll also be able to see me even when I'm invisible to other humans. And not just me—you'll be able to perceive other supernatural entities too. True Sight is a side effect of the Chill."

"Sure, okay. Whatever you say." With the physical relief from the cold comes a hint of clarity, even though I'm still muggy-minded from exhaustion and dazed by all the very impossible things that are happening right now.

Get home first. Process later.

"I need to get back to my team," I tell him. "We're researchers. I'm a cinematographer."

"You make movies?" He lifts a disapproving eyebrow.

"About animals and nature. For documentaries. To raise awareness, help with conservation causes—you wouldn't understand."

"The hell I wouldn't. Do you know who I am? I'm—"

"No!" I slam my soggy glove across his mouth. His blue eyes widen with shock. "I don't want to know anything about you. I just want to get back to my team, up on the—the surface or whatever. And I don't want to remember any of this. Can you wipe my memory of the last several minutes?"

He knocks away my hand. "I don't mess with memories. I'm not a vampire."

"Then what are y—never mind. I don't care. Just show me the way out of here, please."

"There's no way out."

"You must have a way of leaving this place." I survey his body. "You look fleshy enough—" His frown deepens, and I hurry to correct myself. "I mean, it looks as if you eat and everything, like a normal person, so you must go out to get food. And your pants are modern-ish, so obviously you haven't been under the ice for centuries. You can get out, which means you can get me out."

"I can spiral to any place, anywhere around the globe."

"Spiral?"

"Like, um, whisking myself to a spot. Except it's kind of a whirling, windy thing—you should be able to handle it, now that I've given you the Chill—"

"Would you please stop talking about 'the Chill'?" I shrink away as he steps closer.

"Look, you're the one who came in here and woke me out of my regenerative phase, which is a really stupid thing to do, by the way. You're lucky I was over halfway through the process, or I could have died. *Died*." He leans forward, his eyes widening to emphasize the concept.

"Sorry," I mutter. "I didn't know. I was kind of desperate. And maybe you should lock your doors—"

"I did."

"Then how did I get in?"

"Good question. How *did* you get in?"

"I breathed on the door."

His eyes narrowed. "Not just any human can get through a glacial lock. What is it that you do again? Take videos or something?"

"I'm a scientist and cinematographer. I'm doing freelance work right now, but I have a job lined up when I get home, with this conservancy in Asheville—they're a non-profit."

His lips pucker as if he's trying to hide a smile. "So you're a good person. You really care about the planet, not just with lip service, but with your life."

"I—yes. That's kind of why I'm in this situation. I was too involved in my work and I didn't leave the site when I should have. I needed footage of an Adelie penguin hatching."

He grins suddenly, a huge wide smile that shows frosty white teeth. His canines are a touch longer than they should be. If he hadn't already told me that he's not a vampire, I might have panicked.

"I love those little guys," he says. "The emperor penguins are so snooty, but the Adelies—plucky as hell. Tough and stubborn as rocks, too, but in a good way. The chicks are pretty cute, yeah?"

"Yeah." An answering smile pulls at my chapped lips. "Before you whisk me back up to the surface, I need to get my pack. It's got my camera, and the footage." All that equipment was in the insulated, padded center section of the pack, so I'm hoping it will be okay, despite my wild trip down the ice slide.

"Just a minute." He disappears in a burst of white snowflakes that flutter softly to the ground.

A few seconds later he reappears with my pack slung over his shoulder. "This yours?"

"That's the one."

"Okay then. Let's get you back to your people."

"If you could drop me off close to our camp, but not right *in* the camp—I don't want to have to explain any of this to anyone."

"Understood."

"So how do we—"

He grins again, opening his arms. "Give me a hug."

"Do I have to?"

"Only if you want to get out of here."

Making a wry face, I move in and wrap my arms around his lean torso.

"Mmmm. This would be a lot nicer if you weren't wearing so many clothes," he says.

Silently I bless the layers between us. "That's harassment."

"My humblest apologies. Describe to me where your camp is, please. Any landmarks nearby?"

I give him a halting description of the location.

It seems to do the trick, because he nods. "Got it. Hold on tight now."

There's a blinding whirl of snow and wind, a sucking sensation, and a sickening feeling of disembodiment. I'm frantically clawing at the pieces of myself, willing them all to come back together—and then I'm me again, solid and whole.

The pale-haired man and I stand in a sphere of clear space, while the ongoing blizzard buffets the invisible walls of our bubble. I step back from him.

"Your camp is that way," he says, pointing. "I'll stick around to make sure you don't get lost again. Remember to wear your coat and gear during the rest of the trip, even if you can't feel the cold. Otherwise your team will get suspicious."

"Will I still be able to feel heat?"

"Sure."

"Good. I like hot baths."

"Ugh. I can't stand hot water. Even lukewarm is—yuck." A shudder runs through him.

Now that I'm out of the cavern, so close to getting my life back, I can't help a throb of curiosity. Would it be so terrible to know just one thing about this guy? Just his name?

"I'm Emery Caulfield," I venture.

"Nice to meet you, Emery. I'm Jack." He takes another step back, lifting his arms, and the blizzard responds, kicking up in snowy swirls behind him, like phantom wings. "Don't tell anyone you met me."

"I'm not stupid," I snap. "Just reckless."

"Reckless." He hisses the word with a kind of savage relish.

"I can be a little too passionate about my work, and it makes me careless," I reply. "It won't happen again."

"Oh, but it will. Reckless people simply can't help themselves. It's been a pleasure, Emery. Now I have to go and see what damage has been done while I slept. One question—any big forest fires in the world lately?"

"Are you kidding? California has been burning itself to a crisp."

"I'll head there then. Thank you!"

And he whirls away into the storm. The bubble of protection breaks, and I'm inundated with blistering ice and snow again. Even though I can't feel the cold, the wind's force is almost too much for me in my weakened state.

I stagger in the direction Jack pointed out. Within several steps, a dark shadow rises before me, its form shifting in the wind.

A tent.

3
THE
VERY NEXT DAY

Our expedition leader Luc Garnier chews me out the next day, after I've rested and eaten. He tells me, in fierce phrases punctuated with French swears, how lucky I am that I managed to find my way back to camp.

"I do not know how you did it but I am glad, because if you died, there would be the paperwork, *tu comprends*? So much of the paperwork. I do not like the paperwork, Emery. It is not fun for me. You stay alive, and I keep my job, *oui*? We have this agreement. It is not difficult. Follow the rules, because the rules are there for a reason. You think you are what, some free spirit? I say *non*, because you are not free when you are on my team. It is my job to keep you alive. From now on you walk when I say walk, and you set up the camera when I say you set up the camera, and if I say, 'Emery, we go now,' then you say *oui, monsieur.* You say, 'Yes, Luc, I will listen because you are the boss.' *Tu comprends, la?*"

"Yes, I understand." I exchange sidelong glances with my tentmate Dana, who turns away quickly and pretends to be very interested in her bland breakfast oatmeal. "I'm sorry, Luc."

"*Bien sur*, of course you are sorry. You have learned an important lesson, one that you will not forget. *Mon Dieu. Tu te tuerais pour les pingouins? Les pingouins? C'est des conneries, ça!*"

"You're absolutely right, Luc," Dana interjects. "Dying for penguins would be bullshit. I'll keep a close eye on Emery for the rest of the trip, okay?"

"*D'accord.* You watch her." He shoves his way out of the tent, then ducks back in to say, "Blue sky today. We will be filming. Get ready."

For the rest of the trip, we have good weather. I have a suspicion it's not entirely a natural phenomenon, but even though I have an interest in climate change, I'm no weather expert, so I can't say for sure that Jack is involved. After all, he said he was off to California where all the forest fires are. What on earth does he plan to do there? Can he actually help out? Use some of his magical snowy mojo to push back the fires?

That is something I'd like to see. But I'm fairly sure I'll never encounter him again.

On the last day before Dana and I fly out for the long trip home, I convince Luc to let me take a walk alone, as long as I stay within view of base camp. The sheer variety of textures in the Antarctic landscape still amazes me. There's the snow-infused ice that creaks faintly under my boots, the slick-as-glass ice I'd love to carve with a pair of skates, and the slopes that look like gleaming snow but are actually frozen hard and slippery as hell. There's the deep snow that yields in soft crevices to my steps, leaving pockets of blue shadow in my wake. There's the snow that skims, light and powdery, across the surface of the continent, shifting and eddying as if it has a mind of its own.

The thin skin of my nostrils crinkles with cold as I inhale. I'm going to miss the piercing clarity of this world, its violent beauty. Sometimes it's deceptively calm, like now, and comparatively warm—though "warm" in Antarctica is usually no milder than 30 degrees Fahrenheit. This is the continent's summer. We were lucky this year—the hatching of the penguin eggs started early enough that we could film it and still get home in time for

Christmas. The team coming in behind us will be spending Christmas in Antarctica. I've heard holidays can actually be fun at the Dumont d'Urville Station, the French research center. Luc has spent Christmas there a couple of times, because his husband is a chef who periodically serves at the base. Apparently the chef prepares quite the lavish spread. It's a different story for teams camping out in tents on the ice, though.

"Eight days 'til Christmas," I murmur aloud.

"You celebrate Christmas?" The voice is casual, conversational.

I whirl, my heart lurching.

Jack stands a few steps away, his white hair ruffling in the wind. He looks a bit more fae than he did the last time I saw him—sharply pointed ears, a crisper edge to his features, and an unnatural luminescence to his eyes.

His shirt and pants might once have been as white as his hair, but they've been singed and smoked to a dingy gray mottled with black. They're spattered with holes, too—ragged gashes exposing the pale skin underneath. He has a dark smudge along his neck and another on his cheekbone. And is that ash sifting out of his hair? When he waves at me, the sunlight winks on his silver rings; but his fingernails are stained dark. A hint of wood smoke wafts from him.

"What the hell happened to you?" I ask.

"Fire."

I wait for him to explain, but he doesn't. He merely closes his eyes and breathes deeply, as if he's bathing his smoke-stained lungs with the fresh air.

What do I say to him? I wasn't expecting to see him again, and definitely not in this tattered state.

I had almost convinced myself that he was a figment of my overworked imagination. Because magic does not exist, not in this world of gas pumps and plastic straws and carbon emissions, of viruses and volatility and death.

He's still standing there, motionless. Just breathing, with the sun gilding his eyelids and the bridge of his straight nose. He's much too pretty to be real. And I'm very suspicious of pretty boys, even the ones without magic powers. In my experience, a beautiful face on a man typically pairs with misogyny, overconfidence, and annoying cockiness. In the worst cases, the beauty masks a latent male-pattern dumbness that I just don't have time to deal with.

Okay fine—my inner sense of fairness requires the tiny caveat that not *all* hot men are like that. Just most of them. Like ninety percent of them. Ninety-five percent. Why am I mentally rambling while this guy who saved my life is standing three steps away, looking like he just got dragged headfirst through a forest fire?

Clearing my throat, I venture a semi-compassionate question. "Are—are you okay?"

"I'm tired. Thanks to a certain someone, I woke up before it was time. So I wasn't fully restored. Not to mention the fact that I was dangerously depleted before I went into regeneration mode. The last couple hundred years have been rough, I won't lie. You humans have made it tough to do my job. As if supernatural foes weren't enough, you have to pump the air full of pollutants and cause a chain effect—"

"I know about global warming," I interrupt. "How does that affect you?"

He looks at me from under hooded lids. "Seriously? I'm Jack *Frost*. I think it's fairly obvious how global *warming* would affect me."

"Jack Frost? The guy who flies around with a staff and leaves pretty snowflake designs on glass?"

He groans, rubbing the heels of his hands into his eyes. The gesture leaves more dark smudges along his cheekbones. "The ice wraiths do the frosty windowpanes thing. My role is far more important. I maintain the global balance. Ice and fire, cold and hot—you're familiar with the concepts?"

"Of course. Stop talking to me like I'm an idiot."

"I'll talk to you however I please. And while we're on the subject, how about a 'Thanks, Jack, for saving my life—sorry that the whole planet is going to burn now, but hey—at least *I* survived!' "

I stare at him. "What are you talking about? Why is the planet going to burn? Nothing you're saying makes any sense at all—"

"I have been fighting. So. Hard." The words leak through his gritted teeth, and his blue eyes sear mine. "A few weeks ago, I was exhausted. Burned out. Nearly dead. I couldn't fight anymore—I had to go under, to recover so I could regain my full power and maybe beat her for good next time. And you disturbed my rest. You wrecked my chances of gaining back the ground I've lost over the past several decades."

"So this is about some weird war thing you've got going on? You should know that I don't believe in war—"

He laughs, loud and harsh. "How nice to have that luxury. Such a privileged little idealist you are."

Heat rushes into my cheeks. "You don't know anything about me."

"Oh, I think I do." He takes two quick steps toward me. "Selfish and entitled, unconscious of all the privilege you possess, self-righteously proud of your lobbying and activism, your advocacy on behalf of the planet."

I refuse to back away, even though his height and intensity trigger fight-or-flight jitters inside me. "Some of that is probably true. But you said I was a good person, that I really care. Otherwise I couldn't have opened the lock on your door, right?"

His mouth tightens. "True. But sincerity doesn't make you blameless."

"Of course not. Which is why I work very hard to make a difference. But I don't have to defend myself to you. I wasn't the one lying around in an ice cocoon."

"I explained why I—you know what? Forget it. I'm not even sure why I'm here, talking to you."

"I'm not sure either." I cross my arms, but the gesture is less impactful since my arms are basically puffy coat sausages right now.

We're awkwardly close. My eyes are shielded with sunglasses, a protective measure against the Antarctic glare, but his eyes are naked and furious. No, not furious exactly. Pained. They hold all the angry frustration of dying hope.

A trickle of sympathy runs through me. I would much rather he just disappear, so I can pretend he doesn't exist; but with him standing here, smelling of burnt forests and despair, I can't feign ignorance, or indifference. "Can you—can you get some help for this war you're fighting?"

His anger recedes, softening into sadness. "I used to have help. I suppose maybe I could recruit someone, but—it's complicated. There's magic involved, rituals—"

"Magic." I shake my head. "This is—this is crazy."

"I find that word offensive."

"Sorry. I'm having trouble wrapping my head around all of—" I wave my hand wildly at his entire being. "I had nearly convinced myself that you were a piece of my psyche, a personality I invented to get me through the trauma of being lost in the blizzard."

"Sorry to disappoint."

"I'm not exactly disappointed." Oh god, did those words just pop out of my mouth?

Jack's face melts into a brilliant smile. "Aw, thanks. So nice to feel seen and wanted."

"I wouldn't go that far."

He flicks his hand, and a snowy armchair emerges from the ice shelf we're standing on. Jack sits sideways, legs crossed over one arm of the chair. His pants leave sooty marks on the snow. "You must have so many questions for me. What do you want to know?"

Nervously I glance over my shoulder, toward the camp. At this distance, my team members are tiny dark silhouettes against the glacial landscape. "I really should go back. We're leaving tomorrow."

"Tomorrow?"

"Yes, so all of this will be over and done with." I'm glad of it, honestly. I can't handle the continuation of actual magic in my real life. The scientist in me is ravenous for answers, but it's my affinity for logic, for crisp categories and defined data, that holds me back from asking more questions. Knowing more about Jack Frost means opening a door to a wild, uncertain reality that I don't want to face. Right now the door is only open a slim crack. I'd prefer to leave it that way. "I think the less I know about you, the better."

Jack's face settles into icy lines. "Fine."

"It's nothing personal."

"Weird, because it felt really personal when you were breathing into my mouth while I was sleeping."

My cheeks flame instantly. "I had tried everything else! You wouldn't wake up!"

"Right. That's the only reason."

"It *was* the only reason! Hot guys are all the same—you think you're so irresistible—"

"'Hot' doesn't seem like the right word for me." His teeth glitter like icicles when he smiles.

"Whatever. You're just like the rest of them."

"Hmm." He narrows his eyes at me. "When people say that, they are usually thinking of one or two specific individuals."

Declan. Sam. Their faces float in my memory, one outfitted with a cold sneer and the other contorted with anger.

"I'm not thinking of anyone in particular." But I can't help shifting my gaze from his when I say it.

"Interesting." He reaches out again, fingers rippling, and a couch surges from the ice. It's crafted with exquisite detail, from the piping along the cushions' edges to the fringe of the snow-sculpted throw pillow at one end.

"How—" I take a step toward it, intrigued, before I remember that I am not getting involved with this. No questions, no connections. "Never mind. I'm going back to base before they come looking for me. You should get rid of this ice furniture before someone sees it."

"What does it matter if they see it? They'll just reason it away, like you're trying to." Jack disappears from the chair and reappears on the couch. He looks incredibly tall draped along its length. Tucking his hands behind his head, he grins at me.

"If it doesn't matter to you, fine." I shrug. "I guess this is goodbye."

"Is it though?" He winks.

"Yes. I told you we're flying out tomorrow. So good luck with your—supernatural war thing—that is somehow connected to the climate or the forest fires—" I bite my lip to keep from asking him an actual question. "Yeah. And thanks for—you know."

"For saving your life?"

"You make it sound so dramatic. You just gave me a lift out of your ice cave after I fell into it."

"Ice cave?" He presses one hand to his heart. "Now I'm hurt. Only a heartless harpy would call my carefully-designed, aesthetically perfect ice castle a *cave*."

A twist of hot anger spirals through my chest. "Nice move, calling me a 'heartless harpy.' Now I'm even less interested in anything you have to say, or anything you do." I kick the couch as I stalk past it. Not a good idea, kicking solid ice. I keep my face impassive while I squeal inwardly at the pain. My boots protected me from the worst of the impact, but it still hurt.

"Ouch." There's an insufferable smile in Jack's voice. "See you around, Emery."

"You won't," I snap.

It's a relief, knowing I'll never encounter him again. The last thing I need is a cocky magical asshole messing with my head.

4

SILENT NIGHT

The first leg of the trip home is a helicopter ride. Then there's a voyage by boat, followed by a flight to the Charles de Gaulle airport in Paris. At last I'm on my flight from Paris, France to Charlotte, North Carolina. A two-hour drive to Asheville will bring me home to my little fifth-floor apartment. My own bed. God, I've missed it.

The seats on both sides of me are empty, but I keep my cloth mask on anyway—a precaution I take while traveling.

"I don't get sick, you know. It's a perk of being me."

My entire body jerks with shock, because Jack just appeared in the aisle seat beside me.

"Where did you come from?" I exclaim, way too loudly for our surroundings. As the words leave my mouth, I meet the eyes of the woman across the aisle from me. She gives me a suspicious glare and turns pointedly away.

I face straight in my seat and unlock my phone, typing a quick message which I then tilt toward Jack. "No one else can see you or hear you right now, can they?"

"No. You're special, remember?" He kisses his fingertips to me. "I can make myself visible, tangible, and audible if I want to—more normal-looking. I call it my human aspect. In human form, I can walk around cities and live like a normal person. But when I'm in stealth mode like this, only someone blessed with True Sight can perceive me."

"Blessed, or cursed?" I mutter. The woman across the aisle side-eyes me again. I need to shut up before she calls the attendant.

Jack reaches up and touches my hair lightly. "You're nearly as blond as me. I like this style. Short and fun. Like a Peter Pan cut, or something."

"It's called a pixie cut and why the HELL are you here?" I type into my phone.

"To hang out?" He smiles happily. Why are airplane seats so close together? His shoulder is brushing mine, and those blue eyes are overwhelming. He's wearing a cozy-looking sweater and dark jeans. If it weren't for the white hair, the feral smile, and the knife-sharp ears, he would look like your typical, average, run-of-the-mill male cover model.

"You're here. To. Hang. Out." I type furiously, hoping the glare I'm giving him translates over the top edge of my mask.

"I don't know, I just—I feel good after I talk to you. Happier. Stronger."

"Well, I don't feel happier. I feel very very unhappy right now. You were supposed to stay in Antarctica where you belong."

"Oh, you think I live there all the time? Not at all. I have a few homes, all over the world. And my work takes me literally everywhere—usually to the 'hot spots,' so to speak, but I can go anywhere I want."

"You have a family? Friends?"

"A handful of necessary acquaintances. I've only been in this role for a couple hundred years, and I've been fighting the Horae pretty much non-stop since I started, so that doesn't leave much time for socializing."

Frowning, I type more words. "The whore who?"

"No, the *Horae*. Beings from Greek mythology?"

I shake my head and type, "I never liked the old classic stuff. I usually read non-fiction. Sometimes a contemporary romance or web comic for fun."

Jack groans. "Okay. The Horae were goddesses, sort of. They were in charge of maintaining the balance of the seasons, the weather, and the hours. The cycles of nature."

"They sound great. Why are you fighting them?"

"It's a long story. Like the gods, the Horae weakened and deteriorated over millennia. Most of them turned into air sprites, fire wisps, ice wraiths, or earth shades. The work they do now is mostly useless, a shadow of their old power. You'll probably see them around occasionally now that you have True Sight."

My thumbs pound frantically on my phone. "But I don't want to see them."

"Sorry, sweetheart. It's a side effect of the Chill. I had to give it to you, or you would have died. I think a little supernatural insight is a reasonable price to pay for your life, don't you?"

I squint balefully at him over the mask, and he looks delighted. "You're adorable, you know that?"

I don't want to be adorable. I've never liked the kind of man who tells women "You're beautiful when you're angry"—even if it's true, even if the inner fire and power is appealing. "Adorable" is demeaning, and any guy who tells a woman she's beautiful when she's angry is merely finding an excuse to dodge the topic and to *not listen*.

I type, "LEAVE ME ALONE."

"Don't you want to hear more of my backstory?"

"I already said I don't want to know anything about you. I honestly don't care. Go away."

"I could keep you company. It's going to be a long flight." Uncertainty shivers in his blue eyes. He's not exactly pleading, but he's definitely asking.

"I have e-books and music on my phone. If you would shut up I could relax and enjoy them."

"Can I stay if I shut up?"

"Don't you have some Horae to fight?"

He faces forward, settling his shoulders against the seat. I cast a sidelong glance at his profile, but I dare not look at it too long or the woman across the aisle will think I'm staring at her.

"I've been working all day, and I'm tired," Jack says softly. "I need sleep, and for some reason when I'm around you, my energy replenishes faster."

"Well, that makes absolutely no sense."

"I know. But can I stay?"

I chew my lip under the mask. Then I tug it down slightly and lean close to him, until my mouth is nearly touching his ear. In my faintest whisper I say, "You will be quiet?"

"As a snowflake."

I replace the mask and relax into my own seat, conscious that his shoulder is still pressed against mine. There's no warmth from the pressure, like there would be from the body of a normal human. In fact, if I didn't have "the Chill" as he calls it, I suspect his arm would be radiating ice into mine. As it is, I can only sense a gentle coolness, not unpleasant or uncomfortable.

My sense of temperature isn't gone—that would be a problem—but it has changed. The part of the spectrum related to warmth and heat remains the same, and I can tell when a drink is cold, or the weather is chilly. But there's no physical effect of the cold on my body. I didn't shiver while I stood on the deck of the boat and watched Antarctica's broken white shoreline recede into the blue distance. There was no temporary headache when I took a giant bite of ice cream during my layover at the Paris airport. No goosebumps from an unexpected rush of air conditioning when I boarded this plane. In fact, the little nub of a vent above my seat is blasting air right on me, and I don't even mind.

I skim through the e-books loaded onto my phone, but nothing feels as compelling as the long-legged man trying to get comfortable in the seat beside me. It's comical, really, how his knees jam the back of the seat in front of him, how far his right leg extends when he stretches it out into the aisle.

"You know, you don't have to ride home in this plane," he says. "I could whisk you back home. It would be a matter of two seconds."

"Shh!" My shushing noise cracks the humming quiet of the plane. The woman across the aisle stares daggers at me.

Jack's eyes widen in mock horror and he lays a long finger across his lips.

I grit my teeth, wishing he could hear my thoughts. *You're the one who talked after you said you wouldn't.*

His offer of quick transport is tempting. But then I'd have to explain to Karyl why she doesn't need to pick me up from the Charlotte airport. And what about my luggage? I suppose Jack could get that too—

No! I can't disappear from a plane that's in mid-flight. I can't allow my normal routine to be disrupted by magic. I told him he could sit quietly beside me and that's all.

I type another message into my phone and poke him so he'll look at it. "You could never be a monk. You kept your vow of silence for all of two minutes."

While his eyes are downcast, reading the note, I examine his face. A few snowflakes have caught in the thick sweep of his dark eyelashes and they gleam there without melting.

His lashes flick upward, unveiling blue eyes dancing with humor. "You're right. I'd make a very incompetent monk." Then he winces apologetically and mimes zipping his lips. Of course the gesture only draws my attention to his mouth—wide and expressive, with a mobile softness that hints at his penchant for chatter and ridiculously broad smiles.

Quickly I look away, out the small oval window of the plane.

I manage to last another twenty minutes before I type another note. "Fine, I guess you can tell me more about what you do."

But when I glance over to get his attention, he's fast asleep.

Eventually I close the window shade and doze off too, though I'm careful not to lean against him. That would look fairly strange, me slumped against an invisible shoulder.

The plane's interior is dark when I rouse again. A few islands of golden light mark the people who are still awake, reading or working or watching a movie.

Jack shifts beside me and angles his face toward mine. In the gloom, his eyes are azure tide-pools, and his hair shimmers faintly like snow at night. He's all tousled and tempting, loose-limbed and slow-blinking in the seat beside me.

It's weirdly intimate, waking up next to him in such close quarters. I shrink toward the window, eyeing him with suspicion.

"You're awake," he says, with a soft smile. "Hello."

Panic surges in my chest because while his voice is perfectly audible to me, no one else reacts. It's the weirdest sensation.

My fingers constrict around my knees and I swallow hard, trying to breathe, trying to force my heart into a slower rhythm. I look toward the window, centering myself with its prosaic oval shape and ugly beige shade.

It was easier to believe in him when I was at the end of the world, in a wild land of snow and ice and savage beauty. But now, in this cocoon of canned air, textured plastic, and upholstery, I can't believe in magic. It's not rational, and therefore not true. None of it fits with what I know, what I believe. I'm slipping back into my original theory: that when I was wandering in the blizzard, my consciousness split into another persona, someone who could protect my mind and help me survive. That's what I'm seeing right now. And my perceived imperviousness to the cold—that's got to be a blend of acclimation and my body's psychosomatic response to stress factors.

Jack does not exist.

5

GOING HOME

"Emery?" His voice pierces my internal monologue. Or maybe it's part of my internal monologue.

I inhale sharply and close my eyes. I won't feed the illusion or indulge this persona.

"You're not real," I whisper. "I can't believe I actually thought you were real. But none of it's true, is it? I'm having some kind of breakdown."

No answer.

I open my eyes a slit and glance at the seat beside me.

He's gone.

An imaginary friend, after all. And I banished him from my brain. Hopefully he won't come back.

Stifling the odd sense of unhappiness that creeps over me, I settle back into my seat for another nap.

The next thing I'm conscious of is the shudder of the plane as the landing gear unlatch and lock into position. The seat next to me remains empty. Apparently I've retained my sanity, which is a good thing because my friend Karyl has little time for nonsense. She and I have been like sisters for four years now, ever since we were sophomore roommates in college. She hated me at first—called me a "basic white bitch" once when she didn't think I could hear her—and I thought she was a sour snob. We challenged each other's preconceptions in countless little ways over the course of the year, and by the end we were bringing each other coffee and sharing clothes—which according to Karyl was far more to my advantage than hers. I have to admit, my personal sense of style doesn't extend far beyond jeans and T-shirts, with the occasional blouse for work. I almost never wear dresses, because each time I do my mother's voice echoes in my head: "You have the knobbliest knees I ever saw, Em. So crooked. And your calves are way too thick for the rest of you. Do yourself a favor and leave the dresses to someone who can pull them off." All this while she sashayed across the living room of our mobile home in a silky ivory slip and no bra. She'd go outside like that all the time, nipples poking the thin fabric, the bones of her chest clearly defined above the pink lace edging the neckline. Smoking kept her skinny, drew pucker lines around her mouth, and put gravel in her voice. Even now, whenever I picture her, it's always with a cigarette tucked between two bony fingers, ash flicked aside by glossy red nails.

I shuffle off the plane with the other passengers. Jack may not be here anymore, but he occupies space in my head—I can't help it. It concerns me, how real and tangible the illusion was. I'll need to make an appointment with a psychologist, and soon. Can't let this kind of mental health issue get out of hand. I've got work to do.

The conservation non-profit where I'll be working is hosting a holiday benefit on Christmas Eve. I haven't been part of the planning, of course, since I've been away; but as the newbie, I'll be expected to help out with a lot of party-related errands. They offered to let me start after the holidays, so I could recover from my trip; but I wanted to be involved in the festivities. The event is a networking opportunity I can't give up. Plus, one of the non-profit's directors, Marian, wants me around so I can film a few promo clips and chat with the wealthy guests about my trip to Antarctica. It's good press for the organization, having a member of the Antarctic expedition on staff.

Laden with my backpack and duffel bag, rolling my suitcase behind me, I trudge outside to the pick-up area. I do a quick scan of the waiting cars, and there's Karyl's red Toyota. She's standing beside it, talking to some guy wearing a knit cap.

I hustle toward them. In spite of my weariness and my anxiety about the Jack thing, my mouth stretches in a huge grin. Karyl is family to me, and her very presence makes me feel better about everything.

Weird—that's how Jack said he felt around me.

"Babe!" Karyl squeals and charges me, engulfing me in a hug. "Let me look at you. You look amazing, but tired of course—we gotta get you a coffee. Not the creepy mega-chain stuff, either—we're going to Julia's Coffee & Books. It's like twenty minutes away—and don't worry, they're very environmentally and socially conscious. You coming with, Jack?"

At the name, my very bones freeze. I angle my head to peek over Karyl's shoulder, and there, standing behind her, is Jack Frost, looking very human in his knit cap, blue sweater, and leather jacket. He gives me a satisfied smirk. "Sure, I'll tag along."

I can't think of anything to say. It's obviously him, and Karyl can *see* him.

So he *is* real. He's appearing in—what did he call it?—human aspect.

Dazed, I wander to Karyl's trunk and heft my duffel bag inside while she lifts the suitcase.

"You didn't tell me about him," she whispers reproachfully. "He said you guys met in Antarctica? That he was with another research team?"

"I—yeah—"

"Damn, girl, he fine! You hit that?"

I stare at her. "No!"

"No!" She mimics my horrified tone. "You don't have to say 'no!' in that prissy little voice, babe. It's been way too long since you got some. Maybe now that you're both Stateside—and he says he's working in North Carolina, too—"

"Oh he is, is he?" Tension knots in my temple, pulsing behind my eye. Between the long days of travel and this new development, I've got the beginnings of a killer migraine. Maybe some caffeine will help. "Let's grab that coffee and he can tell us more about this 'work' he's doing in North Carolina."

As I slide into the front passenger seat, I studiously avoid Jack's gaze. Clearly he took tangible form and introduced himself to my friend so I would have no choice but to believe he's real. A smart move, because I can't reason this away. And I'm pissed, because now I have to re-adjust my entire worldview to include magic and frost-wielding men and whatever else is out there.

He stays quiet while Karyl and I discuss my trip. She asks him a few questions, like what he was studying in Antarctica, to which he replies, "Weather patterns. Did you know that Antarctica clocked a record temperature this year? 64.9 degrees Fahrenheit, or 18.2 degrees Celsius. That breaks 2015's record of 63.5 Fahrenheit."

Karyl whistled. "Global warming's a bitch, huh?"

"Yes, she is," Jack agrees fervently. Why do I get the feeling that he's talking about a specific entity, not just a global effect?

"It's weirdly cold in the car though." Karyl bumps up the vehicle's heat a couple notches. "You chilly, Emery?"

"I'm fine."

"Right, I guess you're used to the cold now."

When we reach the coffee shop, Jack leaps out of the car like a piece of bread from a hot toaster. I guess he's not a fan of warm, enclosed spaces. Too bad, because the coffee shop is also toasty warm, scented with rich coffee beans and chocolate, cluttered with overstuffed bookshelves.

Karyl and I order espressos and slices of quiche, and then I grudgingly turn to Jack. "Do you have a wallet, or money?" I mutter under my breath.

He slides a leather wallet out of his back pocket. The interior is stuffed with bills, not all of them U.S. currency. "I'll take care of it."

"That's not what I meant. I wasn't asking you to pay—I thought you might need *me* to pay for *you*. You know, since you're—" I stop, because Karyl is watching us quizzically. She's definitely within earshot. "Never mind."

Jack sidles past me and drums his fingers on the counter. Where his fingertips land, tiny circles of frost appear and then vanish, so quickly I might have imagined it.

"What's your coldest coffee?" he asks the barista.

She frowns slightly. "We have a nitro cold brew—"

"That's the one. Thanks!" He pays, stuffing a twenty in the tip jar.

Karyl catches my arm and steers me toward a table. "Good Lord. The man is certainly generous. But why do I get the feeling you don't like him too much?"

"He's—difficult. Cocky."

"Doesn't seem so to me. And I'm an excellent judge of character."

"Girl." I shake my head at her. "You're not."

"Okay, I'm not. But I'm getting a real good vibe from him. He's classy, smart, handsome, clearly got money to burn—ooh, you're gonna have *Fun. With. Him.*" She pokes my shoulder three times for emphasis.

"Yeah. Lots of fun," I say dryly.

Jack brings our drinks, and we struggle through more small talk—at least, I struggle. He and Karyl seem to find plenty to say. While observing them, I notice a pattern; anytime she swerves into a topic he's unfamiliar with, he just listens for a while, and then skillfully nudges the subject in a different direction.

Finally Karyl drains her coffee cup and rises. "All right, bathroom break before the drive to Asheville! You coming, Emery?"

"I went at the airport," I tell her.

"Girl, you just drank a ton of coffee." She waggles a finger at me. "You better not be asking me to stop half an hour into the trip."

"I won't."

She saunters away, and finally I work up the courage to look Jack straight in the eyes. "What are you doing?"

"You didn't believe I was real, so—" He spreads his hands, the corner of his mouth lifting.

"Okay, you proved your point. We're done now."

"Done?"

"Do you plan to hitch a ride to Asheville with us?"

"Not at all. My cover story is that I'm working here in Charlotte. That way I can pop over to Asheville whenever I want, and no one will suspect a thing."

"You don't need a cover story. You're not 'popping over' to Asheville. You're not involved in my life."

"Hey, I *saved* your life."

"What, so you're my stalker now?"

Jack recoils in mock offense. "Rude."

"Well, what else do you call someone who keeps showing up at random moments when they're not invited?"

"A friend?"

"No. Friends text first."

"But I don't have a phone."

45

"Sucks for you." I tip the rest of my coffee into my mouth. "Why don't you use some of your cash to buy yourself a phone?"

"I usually don't need to call anyone."

"A phone isn't just for calling. It's for games, books, news, social media—everything."

Jack props his elbows on the tiny table and leans across it, until his blue eyes are dazzlingly close to mine. "And these companies that make the phones—I assume they are every bit as conscientious about the environment as you are?"

My cheeks warm. "You know they're not. But I'm not wasteful with my tech—I don't chase new models, and I always recycle my old phones—"

"I know." His smile doesn't erase the sadness in his eyes. "You're caught in the web, like everyone else. You can't escape it completely, but at least you're struggling. I'm sorry for what I said to you back in Antarctica—calling you selfish and entitled. I was frustrated, and tired."

"Welcome to the club. I'm always frustrated and tired."

That predatory grin again. "We should try to remedy that." He moves an inch closer, his gaze dropping to my mouth.

"That's why I drink coffee," I snarl, shoving back my chair. "It's my one indulgence."

"My one indulgence is art. And now, apparently, you."

"Oh god." I snatch my purse. "Look, I don't want to be your indulgence, your rest stop, your anything, okay? I have a lot to do when I get home—I've got to get my apartment unpacked, and rest up for work on Monday, and help with the benefit. I don't have time for lonely magical strays. There are a ton of environmental activists in the world—men, women, other—and some of them are a lot prettier than me. I'm sure most of them are sincere, too. Go find one of them to be your encouragement buddy or whatever."

"But I don't know them," he says plaintively. "I know you."

He looks so pitiful that I almost relent, but Karyl returns from the bathroom at that moment. "Whatcha talking about?" she asks, looking from one of us to the other.

"I, um—I have to go." Jack smiles at her. "It was great to meet you, Karyl."

"Sure, honey. We'll meet again sometime." Karyl nudges my elbow surreptitiously and gives me a sidelong grin that's not at all subtle. "You need a ride anywhere?"

"No, I called a car. Thanks, though." His eyes meet mine briefly, and he nods. "Emery."

He strides out the door of the coffee shop, probably to find a quiet spot where he can poof himself to his next destination.

Karyl lowers her voice to mimic his tone. "Emery."

"Shut up." I elbow her.

6

SURPRISE

My Asheville apartment is a tiny pair of rooms wedged into a corner of an old building that was once some kind of factory. The place has been refurbished, and it's decent enough from what I can tell—though I only lived here for a couple of days before I left for the Antarctica trip. In the two years since graduation, I've lived in a bunch of different places, always with roommates. This is the first space I'll have all to myself, and I have plans to make it perfect.

I shove my key into the lock and push open the door. Then I sidle in clumsily, tugging my luggage with me. Karyl didn't have time to help me bring everything in—we had to stop for a couple of bathroom breaks on the way, so by the time we reached my place she had to drive straight to the hospital for her shift.

"Sorry I didn't have time to grab groceries for you, babe," she said right before driving away.

I told her that it was fine, of course, that I hadn't expected her to do that. And it's true—I didn't expect it.

Still, it's a little anticlimactic to struggle through my door into the dark, drafty apartment and flip on the light to find nothing but piles of boxes. No "Welcome Back" sign, no furniture. Not a thing except boxes, and the harsh glare of the industrial light fixture above my head, and the kitchen counter branching in a severely normal L-shape to my right.

Just a handful of days until Christmas, and I'm bone-weary and alone.

Serves me right for moving to Asheville, where I only know one person. But the conservancy project here is something I believe in, something I can be passionate about. More importantly, they were hiring. It's not much of a paycheck, but I'll make do. And I can always do freelance video work on the side, weddings and such. I've done it before.

My shoulders sag, and my bags slide to the ground with a depressing thump.

There's a bed in the other room, with sheets still on it from the two days I spent here before my trip. I'll sleep there tonight, but I need to stay awake until at least ten. It's the best way to combat the jet lag—to force myself into the schedule of this time zone.

Collecting my bags again, I lug them into the bedroom. It's the half-sandwich to the front room's whole—a strip of square footage barely large enough for a double bed. The only other bits of space in this apartment are a small bathroom and a shallow closet.

I kneel on the floor and open my suitcase, removing the bag of dirty clothes. They smell wretched. Guess it's laundry day tomorrow. I'd do it tonight, but I don't have quarters for the machines downstairs.

Something crashes in the kitchen, and I nearly leap out of my skin. Frantically I fumble in the suitcase until my hand closes around my flashlight. It's longish, and heavy. I can hit the intruder over the head with it.

My hand is shaking so hard I nearly drop the flashlight as I peer out of the bedroom doorway into the kitchen.

Jack is standing there, holding one overstuffed paper bag of groceries. The bag's lower half is dark with moisture and flecked with snowflakes. He clutches the remnants of a second paper bag in his other hand, but apparently the bottom fell out of that one, because its contents lie in a jumble on the vinyl flooring.

"Damn it," he says. "I wanted to surprise you."

"Congratulations," I gasp. "You succeeded. How did you find my place?"

"I asked Karyl where you lived. I told her I wanted to bring you some stuff—"

"Clearly we need to have a discussion about boundaries, and spiraling yourself into other people's homes without knocking, and also inserting your presence where it's not wanted."

"The eggs didn't break," he says hopefully—and then the other bag gives way, and its contents dribble out the bottom onto the floor.

Jack looks so dumbfounded—I want to stay mad, to fuss and fume at him, but I can't help it—laughter bubbles up inside me. I clap my hand over my mouth to stifle the sound—but then he surveys the half-crunched groceries and says slowly, "Aw, shit," and I lose my control. Peal after peal of hysterical, overtired, uncontrollable laughter rolls out of me. I'm laughing so hard I can't keep standing, so I slide to the floor and hold my stomach while tears ooze from the corners of my eyes.

How long has it been since I laughed like this? Months, at least.

Jack is laughing too, but mostly he looks shocked and thrilled at the effect his grocery problems had on me.

Finally I slump against the wall, doubly exhausted now, but also strangely relieved, as if a knot that had been winding tighter and tighter in my gut has now unspooled.

"Oh god." I wipe my eyes. "You're an idiot."

"Yeah. I guess the bags didn't appreciate being spiraled, with the snow and all."

"I guess not."

"It was stupid." His mouth twists wryly.

"Stupid and sweet. And very stalker-ish."

"Sorry." He pokes at the mess. "I think most of this is salvageable. I'll sort through it—you got a trash can for the stuff I can't save?"

"Under the sink. There's a little tub for recyclables in there too."

He picks through the groceries while I shove boxes around, looking for one that has a "Kitchen" label. But of course I don't have a knife, or scissors, or anything to cut the tape that holds it shut—layers and layers of tape, because I'm an anxious person with very little to her name and I was bound and determined that none of it would be damaged. Curse my excellent packing skills!

"Here, let me." Jack leans over, producing a blade of gleaming ice from thin air. He slices the tape with it, then lays the knife in my palm. It's chilly, but not unbearable, thanks to my new resistance to cold. "It won't vanish until I leave. Use it as much as you want."

I should kick him out. I should yell at him for coming into my private space unannounced, for acting like we are long-time best friends instead of very recent acquaintances. But I press my lips together, and I don't say anything, because truthfully I'm glad he's here. The place is brighter and warmer with him in it. Not literally warmer, of course. Every time he opens the fridge, frost creeps over its handle.

"You got a frying pan?" he asks. "The eggs are cracked, but salvageable. We could use them right now. I'll make you an omelet."

"Don't you have fiery battles to fight?"

A twinge of resistance crosses his face. "I've been fighting for two hundred years. I deserve a break." He sets the egg carton on the counter a little too hard, and something crunches inside it. "Besides, it's a hopeless attempt. She's stronger than me. I can't hold her back."

"She? I thought there were several of these Horae."

"If you let me cook you dinner, I'll tell you more."

I tilt my head, eyeing him reproachfully.

He nods. "Right. You're not interested. I'll cook, and then I'll leave."

I don't contradict him, because I'm struggling, debating internally, vacillating between what my logical scientist brain tells me to do and what my risk-taking, story-loving artist brain wants to do. So I keep unpacking, unwrapping paper from dishes and stowing them in cupboards, hunting down the implements Jack requests and handing them over. A small cutting board. Knives for chopping mushrooms, tomatoes, peppers, onions. A spatula. A cheese grater, because of course he didn't buy the bagged cheese.

"I'm surprised you know how to cook," I say, eyeing his progress. "You don't seem like the type to enjoy a warm meal."

"I always let my meals cool to room temperature before I eat them. To me that's hot enough. And you're right, I prefer cold foods. Doesn't mean I want to eat everything raw, though." He quirks an eyebrow at me. "So yeah, I cook."

"The ice castle has a kitchen?"

"It does. Would you like to see it sometime?"

"Wait—we could go back to Antarctica? Just like that?" It's hard for me to conceive of such rapid, easy travel. It took months of applications, approvals, planning, and training before I got to join that expedition—and even then, I only snagged the spot because a couple of other candidates became ill and weren't allowed to travel.

Now Jack is offering to take me back there, easy as snapping his fingers.

"It's the most convenient perk of being me," he says with a shrug.

"You can go anywhere? Literally anywhere? Like Rome, or Prague, or Hawaii, or Tokyo?"

"Anywhere." He grins. "Thinking about keeping me around?"

"Considering it." I turn my back to him and start tearing the packing paper off a stack of plates. I can feel his gaze on me, like a cool breath along my spine. "Careful, or you'll burn my food."

"Damn." There's a clatter and scrape behind me as he flips the omelet. My lips pull into a smile again. Why am I smiling so much? I must be tired. I should kick him out so I can eat and then go to bed in peace.

"Your dinner, my lady." Jack sets a plate atop an unopened box. The omelet is so enormous that its ends are hanging off the plate, oozing cheese. And no wonder—he used a dozen eggs to make the thing.

"I'll be going then," he says, backing toward the door. We both know very well that he could vanish instantly, spiral himself to wherever he wants to go. He's lingering, hoping I'll change my mind.

Why am I changing my mind?

"This thing is ridiculously huge," I tell him. "I can't possibly eat all of it."

He frowns. "Hmm, that's a problem."

"It sure is. A problem you created, so it's only right that you solve it. Get a plate, and a couple of forks and sit your ass down. I'd offer you a chair, but—" I gesture at the roomful of cardboard boxes.

"I don't mind." Jack snatches the forks and a plate and folds his long legs under himself. His knee brushes my thigh, and I shift away from the contact.

He slices the omelet in half, slides a portion onto his plate, and sets it aside to cool. Then he watches me closely as I take my first bite.

It's all I can do not to let my eyes roll up in my head. The warm, gooey cheese in its blanket of salty egg, the burst of tomato on my tongue, the flavor of the mushrooms and peppers—it's all so perfect, so satisfying that I want to cry.

But I won't cry, because I am an adult, a bold explorer of the Antarctic, a crusader for the planet. Not some emotionally overwrought girl brought to the brink of tears by a well-turned serving of breakfast for dinner.

"Well?"

The damn ice-boy is fishing for compliments. "It's fine." But my voice quivers.

"Are you—are you okay?"

"Mmm-fine," I mutter. "Stop grinning like an idiot."

"Can't help it," he says. "You make me happy."

The raw admission sends a twist of stress through my stomach. "Why do you keep saying things like that? It's so weird. Stop it."

His brows contract slightly. "Why?"

"It makes me uncomfortable. You don't know me that well—not at all, really. People don't say those things to each other."

"Maybe they should. Maybe if more people expressed honest emotion, especially positive emotion, the world would be a more pleasant place." He takes a bite of his omelet and winces. "Ugh. Too warm." He shoves the plate away again. "Can you be honest with yourself about what you like? What you want?"

"Sure." Of course I can be honest. Easy. "I want to get unpacked and organized. I want to go to work on Monday and get acclimated, and be useful. They've been keeping me in the loop via email, and there's a lot to do before the benefit."

"No. Not good enough. Those are all items from a to-do list. They don't tap into your deepest desires and motives." He scoots closer. Warily I slant my body away from his. "What do you *want*, right now? What do you enjoy about this moment?"

My mouth is suddenly dry. "I'm getting cups. You want some water?"

Jack sighs, defeated. "You have ice?"

"There's an ice maker in the freezer. But can't you just chill the water yourself?"

"I can, but I don't always want to expend the energy. Like you can make coffee at home, but sometimes you want to get it from a coffee shop. It's a matter of convenience, or doing something different."

"So you have like, an energy meter that goes down over time. And then you have to rest to recharge it."

"Yes. I can recharge in small ways, through regular sleep and down time. But eventually, when my energy 'meter' gets too low, I have to go into a dormant state, and that dormant state must happen at a focal point of natural potency, where I can siphon power that matches my element. If I don't successfully refill the well, so to speak, I run the risk of dissipating, and turning into an ice wraith. If that happens there will be no one to stand against Auxesia."

"Auxesia," I repeat, handing him a cup of ice water. "Is she one of the Horae you mentioned?"

"The worst of the bunch." He eyes me as I sit down a careful distance away from him. "I thought you didn't want to know anything else about them, or about me."

I take another bite of omelet and chew slowly, savoring the interwoven flavors. "I suppose you could tell me about the Horae. The short version."

His face lights up like winter sunshine. "Short versions are my favorite kind of version."

The way his grin makes my stomach flip over is completely unacceptable. My life is too full of changes and new things already—I do not have time for a guy. Especially not this particular guy, with his invisibility and spiraling and ice powers. There's nothing I want less than a magical boyfriend—not that he wants to be my boyfriend—oh god, I shouldn't have let him stay for dinner. I shouldn't have let him cook for me. Savagely I carve out another bite of eggs and cheese. "You have until I finish my omelet. Then you leave."

His smile crumples at the edges, but he nods. "As I told you, the Horae were created by the gods to maintain the balance of the seasons and the climate. The gods couldn't be bothered to keep everything running—too busy starting wars and spawning illegitimate half-human children. The Horae were essentially the maintenance workers for the planet, and they did their job reasonably well, even after the decline of the gods began. But with the Industrial Revolution, the increased use of coal, and the explosion of the world's population, pollution and waste and general filth became more of a problem. The Horae grew weary of trying to keep the world functional for swarms of dirty humans who didn't seem to give a damn. Yet still they kept performing their duties, even as many of them lost their inner spirit, their energy, and faded into wraiths and wisps.

"The one who recruited and trained me was called Kheima, the last remaining goddess of cold and of winter. She had always been the most powerful of the frost Horae—their leader—and she survived longer than the rest of them. But despite Kheima's strength, she was slowly dissolving too, losing form and force. That's why she chose me. I was a sculptor and painter, afflicted with tuberculosis, and she offered me a chance to survive. She promised me eternal life, immunity from illness, centuries of leisure time to practice my art."

Jack's jaw tensed. "Of course, she was lying. She turned me into an eternal warrior for the planet, one with little time for anything else. I've managed to create a few things over the years, but any time for art comes at the expense of my regeneration days. Sure, I can make ice sculptures in minutes, but I like to use other media too, and really do it right. But lately I've had even less time away from the fight."

"And who are you fighting, exactly?"

"Two hundred years ago, right before I was recruited, three of the Horae were living in Japan, on Sakurajima."

"Wait, that's an active supervolcano."

"Exactly. These Horae were linked to summer, fire, and heat, so they drew energy from the volcano, since it is a direct channel to the molten core of the earth. They grew very powerful, but they disagreed about how they should use their power. They turned volatile, angry, using their heat energy to battle each other. They caused eruptions and fires in various parts of the world. That's why Kheima recruited me, because she couldn't handle them alone. She needed someone else to help her hold them in check, before they scorched the entire globe.

"After I was transformed and trained, Kheima began to fade faster. She was tired, and she had lost her will to keep struggling, especially when humans did not seem to care what they did to the world and its resources. When she dissipated into a frost wraith, I was left alone, to hold back the fiery tide all by myself."

"That's not fair."

"No, it isn't. But Kheima was too old and weary to care how I felt about it." Jack sighs heavily.

For a moment I consider squeezing his hand, or his shoulder, but I don't. I fold my hands in my lap and wait for him to continue.

"With Kheima gone, one of the three fire Horae decided it was time to make her move against the others. Her name was Auxesia, goddess of increase. She imprisoned the other two, Damia and Pherusa, inside separate volcanoes, while she herself moved to Mount Etna. Until a few decades ago, she kept Damia and Pherusa alive. Each time they regained enough energy to be a threat to her, Auxesia would drain them nearly dry. In the process, with all those repeated influxes of stolen energy, she has become the most powerful Horae to ever exist in the world. Twenty years ago she drained both her sisters for the last time, until they disintegrated into fire wisps. And ever since then, I've been struggling to hold her back. The bushfires in Australia, the forest fires in California and the mid-Western United States—the changes in weather that have produced so many tornadoes and hurricanes—she's partly responsible for it all."

"But some of those events were our fault," I say, frowning. "Human greed and consumption, failure to take global warming seriously. A lack of funds for forest management."

"Much of it is a human problem, yes. In fact, Auxesia is only on this rampage because she believes humans unworthy of the world. She wants to burn it all to the ground and start over, with a new chain of evolution that will yield a completely different species of higher life form."

"But that's ridiculous. And impossible."

"Not to her." Jack downs most of his ice water in a few gulps. There's a weary slouch to his shoulders that I recognize—I too have been worn down low before, depressed at the lack of impact from my best efforts. But in his case, the stakes are far higher than anything I've ever faced.

He unfolds his long frame from the floor, rising to his full height and looking down at me. "You've indulged me long enough. I'll go."

A burst of snowflakes flutters around him, but I scramble to my feet. "Wait!"

The cold wind slackens, and he cocks an eyebrow at me.

"You look like you could use a drink. I have a bottle of wine somewhere in one of these boxes—a gift from a friend before I moved to Asheville. We could hunt it down and open it."

I regret the words almost instantly. What am I doing, offering wine to this guy? He's going to think I'm hinting at a hookup.

My tension eases when Jack shakes his head. "I don't usually drink. Alcohol has a very strange effect on me."

"What kind of effect?"

"I become an uncontrollable showoff. Trust me, unless you want your building transformed into an ice palace, and a series of snow sculptures parading along the street outside, you should not encourage me to drink."

The last thing I want is magical mayhem that people can trace back to me. "Okay, then. Well—goodbye, and thank you for dinner." Inwardly I curse myself for the prim, awkward delivery of those words.

Jack doesn't seem to notice anything stiff in my attitude. His blue eyes soften, his lashes sinking lower. He comes a step closer, and then another. There's something sensual about the angles of his body as he approaches me, a feral carnality in the loose parting of his lips. He's so close I can smell his sweet, cool breath.

"Bye," I whisper, and I step back into my bedroom and slam the door in his face.

I press my back to the door, my heart kicking wild against my ribs. Was it my imagination, or was he about to kiss me?

7

FAIRY DANCE

The next morning I'm up early—thanks, jet lag—unpacking more boxes. Jack's ice knife dissipated after he left last night, but I have my kitchen knives available now, so I use those to slit the tape.

After an hour or so, the stacks of boxes have morphed into piles of unpacked but homeless items. I had a dresser and a bookcase at my last place, but they were both borrowed from my roommate. I need some furniture of my own that's not plastic stackable drawers left over from my dorm days. At this point, with most of my current funds going towards college debt or future travel plans, my best bet is a thrift store. Surely I can snag a decent dresser from somewhere. But I won't be able to fit one inside the trunk of my Ford Fusion. Karyl doesn't have a truck, and she's probably zonked out after her long shift at work.

Maybe Jack could help me—

No. No no no, absolutely not.

After I slammed the door in his face last night, I doubt he'll come back. I can just rent a truck or something. Or order a cheap dresser on Amazon.

Speaking of which, I need to get my TV hooked up and mounted, set up my computer and get the internet activated in this place, and do laundry. The amount of stuff I need to do before I start work tomorrow is overwhelming.

Why did I convince myself that one day was enough down time between my return and my first day of work? In what world would that be enough time?

Coffee. If I'm going to get any of this done, I will need the very strongest coffee.

I twist my hair into a knot and inspect myself in the bathroom mirror. I look weary and pale, but at least my skin is clear. I swipe on a little mascara and adjust the ratty gray sweatshirt I'm wearing over my leggings. It will have to do.

Snatching my purse, I stride to the door and open it—only to be greeted by a rush of frigid air and a smiling Jack Frost.

He's holding two cups of coffee—one iced and one hot. At least, I assume it was once hot. Now there are flecks of frost creeping along the paper cup's surface.

Words flit through my head—angry ones, grateful ones, confused ones—I can't seem to settle on anything, so I just stand there, with my mouth open.

"I thought you might need some help today," he says.

The mischievous tilt of his mouth looses my tongue, and a tide of defensive phrases comes pouring out. "Me, need help? Hell no. I'm fine. I love a challenge. Nothing I like better than a to-do list to check things off of. Thanks for the coffee, but I'm all good here."

I grab the coffee cup and try to push the door closed, but ice has suddenly grown along its lower edge, cementing it open.

"So you've escalated from stalking to breaking and entering," I growl. "Nice."

"Hey, I waited outside this time. Give me some credit. I could have spiraled inside, but I didn't."

Eyeing him suspiciously, I jerk on the door again. The ice splinters a little. "You didn't spiral because you didn't want to spill the coffee."

"Damn. You know me so well." He grins. I swear this man does nothing but grin at me and show up at unexpected moments. "Look, you said you don't know anyone here, and you've got tons to do—let me help you."

"No. You go save the world or whatever."

Frustration flashes into his eyes. "I can't! Not alone. Auxesia is too strong. I did what I could after you woke me, and I can't do any more right now."

"Can't, or won't?"

He lowers his voice. "I never wanted this. This isn't what I signed up for. Why should I give up everything and everyone I want for a world of people who don't give a damn?"

"I'm pretty sure the people whose homes are being burned *give a damn*," I hiss at him. "Why don't you think about them and go do your job?"

His gaze freezes over, turning icy and inscrutable. "That's what you want me to do?"

"Yes."

"Then if it's you asking, I'll do it."

"What's that supposed to mean?"

But he's already gone. A few stray snowflakes flutter down onto the faded carpet of the hallway. I swear loudly at them, until a door yanks open a little way down the hall and a red-faced woman pokes her head out and squawks, "Hey! It's Sunday morning, bitch! Keep your voice down!"

She slams the door loudly enough to wake anyone else on this floor who may have been trying to sleep.

Sometimes I really hate humans.

My to-do list takes me all day, but I manage to get most of the things done. Instead of buying a dresser, I stack the empty boxes into makeshift cubbies as a temporary solution. So basically I unpacked and then repacked things in a different orientation—but at least everything is accessible now, and the floor is mostly clear.

I collapse into bed that night, exhausted but satisfied. I have clean clothes, internet, a working TV, and a decently arranged living space. Tomorrow, I'll start my new job. It won't involve the outdoors and cinematography right away, but there will be tasks I know how to do—contacting guests, running errands, making plans, and whatever else needs doing. Eventually, after the holidays, I'll be able to get deeper into the workings of the organization, to do more science-related stuff. Part of my job description involves capturing footage of the Southern Appalachians and Blue Ridge Mountains for use in workshops and community portals. And I'll be a member of the teams that monitor the trails, remove invasive species, and identify threats to the spaces the conservancy protects.

It's the ideal role for me, at least for now. Eventually I hope to move on to something bigger, something more vital—a position where I can effect greater change. The Blue Ridge area is important, but there's a big world out there, with so many regions in serious peril.

What if I never get the chance to make a real difference?

What if my trip to Antarctica, my bit of egg-hatching footage, is the largest contribution I'll ever make to science?

There's a sour, creeping suspicion in my mind that I've already peaked, that I've attained an important goal too early in life, and it's the most I'm capable of achieving.

Now that I'm here in Asheville, I'll probably stay. I'll get comfortable with my job, grow complacent, maybe even become dissatisfied with the low pay at the non-profit. What if I sell out one day and join some mega-company's marketing department, lured by the promise of paid vacation days and an upper-middle-class lifestyle?

What if I stop caring?

Jack's beautiful, despairing eyes appear in my mind. Maybe he hasn't stopped caring, but he has begun to believe that nothing he does is worthwhile. He is close to giving up, like his mentor Kheima did.

I'm not exactly sure what it is that he does. Change weather patterns? Help put out fires? Salvage melting icebergs? Stop volcanoes from erupting? Probably all of that and more. The toll that would take on a single person is immense. The stress of it all must be unbearable.

And now I feel bad for brushing him off this morning.

My legs thrash in the sheets as I flip from one side to the other, trying to banish Jack from my brain. My thoughts won't stop circling around, from his plight to my own fears to the global crisis and then back again.

Somehow I must get to sleep, because I have to get up for work at six-thirty and I can't just live on coffee and willpower.

I need to purge this guilt and anxiety from my body. Maybe I should go for a run. Before the Antarctica trip, I used to run all the time. I even worked out at a gym for months leading up to our departure, so I'd be strong enough to carry my massive pack and other equipment across the icy landscape from our camp to the penguins' nesting area.

I press my phone to light it up. 12:30 a.m. Probably not the best time to go for a run. But I can't exercise in the building at night, not with these creaky floors, or my neighbors will really begin to hate me.

The area around here seems safe enough from what I've seen. There's a little park with a playground nearby, several businesses, no bars or nightclubs in the immediate vicinity. I should be fine, especially if I bring along my pepper spray and my whistle.

Quickly I dress in a tight sports top and leggings. My gray sweatshirt goes over it all, with my key, phone, and pepper spray in the big front pocket. The whistle goes around my neck.

When I step out the front doors of the apartment building, my mood lightens instantly. The bite of the December air would be a painful shock to anyone else, but to me it's invigorating. A few tiny stars glitter like snowflakes against the black sky. In Antarctica, where light pollution does not exist, the stars were a crystalline spray across the heavens. I had never seen so many of them. Sometimes it looked as if the entire brilliant Milky Way was near enough to touch.

Here, the stars are rare treasures, faded or blotted out entirely by the perpetual glow of streetlights, stoplights, windows, and cell towers.

I quicken my pace to a jog, my breath ghosting in the cold air. Despite Asheville's location in the mountains of North Carolina, there's no snow. Karyl said they've had some flurries, but nothing stuck. I'm not one of those people who salivates over white Christmases. Sure, they make things pretty, but I grew up in a trailer in rural Alabama, so I'm used to having beige Christmases. Besides, Christmas was always more of a disappointment than anything else. Every year I hoped it would be different, and every year I ended up sobbing quietly in a bathroom or closet, hiding from my mother's sharp nails or the harsh voices of her latest boyfriends. She always had a carousel of men revolving in and out of our lives—most of them bearded rednecks with "Don't Tread on Me" stickers plastered onto the back windshields of their rusty pickups. Now and then, just to shake things up, she'd snag a businessman, some owner of two or three janky motels or diners, with frayed business cards poking out of his pocket. About ten years ago, when I was fourteen, there was a self-proclaimed indie rock star who insisted on wearing leather vests without a shirt and then complained loudly about his chafed nipples. He had tattoos everywhere, most of them blurry and poorly done. Once, when my mother was passed out drunk, he tried to get me to sit on his lap. I told my mother the next day, and she smashed the records he'd given her over his head and kicked his ass out. It's the one time I can remember being proud of her.

That was her one rule. Her boyfriends could yell at me, boss me around, throw cutting phrases and nasty names my way, but they weren't allowed to lay a hand on me. For a long time I was grateful to her for that—until I realized it was the bare minimum of what a mother should do for her daughter. I just didn't know any better.

I'm different now. A different person, one that *I* created, with my own hard work, my sweat and tears and toil.

She can't take the credit for who I've become.

My sneakers scuff the pavement as I run faster. I started working before I was legally old enough, and I saved every penny I could. I skipped parties and lunch dates; I wore thrifted clothes until they were peppered with holes. With clunky vintage cameras from the pawn shop and stacks of magazines from the library, I taught myself how to take good photos. I studied, applied for scholarships, scraped along through college, took every opportunity that came my way. Sometimes I look back and wonder how I managed it. It's exhausting, just thinking about what it took to get here. But it's also deeply encouraging to remember how far I've climbed on my own.

I've been running straight down the street for a while now, but it tees into another street, so I take a left. A little way down the new street lies a shabby strip mall, its parking lot littered with wrappers and crumpled cans, its single streetlight buzzing and flickering. There's a hair care place, a laundromat, and a dingy restaurant that advertises tacos, teriyaki, sushi, and subs—very confusing. The place on the end is a card game shop, the kind where people might go to play Dungeons & Dragons or Magic the Gathering.

Something blue and wispy darts across the window of the game store.

My heart jerks, and I slow my pace, glancing back over my shoulder. It had to be my imagination, right?

There it is again. A wispy, glowing, azure shape, dancing along the shop windows.

Jack said that I have True Sight now, that I'd be able to see other supernatural creatures—wisps, wraiths, whatever. Maybe this is one of them.

I walk toward the creature, step after tentative step, like a child sneaking up on a squirrel. That's when I see the second ice wraith, flitting down from the eaves of the building to trace lacy white frills along the window of the hair-care place.

The wraiths are about the size of a child's doll—maybe the length of my forearm from fingertip to elbow. They are vaguely human-shaped, but with an incorporeal translucency to their bodies. Frosty air swirls around them in shifting ribbons. There's a soft joy in the way they move, floating and twirling in the air, drawing delicate frost-pictures on the glass.

They're so pretty. My fingers twitch toward my phone, longing to capture the moment, but the wraiths probably wouldn't show up in a video to anyone without the Chill or True Sight or whatever.

I slink closer, easing the soles of my sneakers down so as not to make a sound. But my shoe grazes the edge of a stray can, causing a rasp of metal on pavement. The ice wraiths spin around and hiss with alarm.

"Wait!" I hold out both hands. "I'm not going to hurt you. I was just watching. It's very beautiful, what you're doing."

The wraiths glance at each other. Their elfin faces are bluish ice, carved into the semblance of features, with frosty patches along the cheeks. They're like little ice fairies, and I can't help being enchanted.

They float toward me, uncertain but curious. Their whispers are faint as smoke, and even if they were speaking English I'm not sure I could make it out.

I hold out one hand, as I might to a stray dog or a skittish horse—though honestly I feel more like kneeling in awe. One of the wraiths trails its sharp icicle fingers along my palm, and my skin frosts over briefly, but it doesn't hurt.

The touch and my answering smile apparently convince them that I'm not a threat, and they begin dancing around me, stirring up sprays of snowflakes. They're laughing, or singing, high and thin and far away. A wondering laugh slips from me, too. Why was I so vehemently against the idea of seeing these creatures? Of course they make no scientific sense, but the delight I feel in their presence is all too real.

A harsh voice breaks through the tinkling song of the wraiths, disturbing the delicate spiral of their dance.

"Hey there, girlie!" It's a male voice, slow and stupid and growly with drink. "Whatcha doin'? You looking for somebody?"

"No, I'm—just out for a run." I slide one hand into the pocket of my sweatshirt, finding the familiar shape of my phone. The wraiths rise into the sky, but they don't leave. They spin slowly, watching us.

"You were laughin'." The man sidles nearer. He's a big guy, young and rawboned, with reddish hair and a goatee. He's wearing dress slacks and a collared shirt.

"I—um—I was talking to a friend." I waggle my phone in the air.

"I forgot my phone. And they took my keys." He starts digging his fingers into his pockets.

"You need me to call you a ride home?"

He just stares at me, swaying a little. "You live around here?"

"Listen, I'm going to call someone for you." The police are my best bet, I think—I don't want to saddle some poor lift driver with this drunken dude.

When I raise the phone to my ear, he lunges forward and knocks it away. It bounces and skims across the pavement, and I grit my teeth, willing the screen not to break.

"That wasn't nice," I tell the guy firmly. "I'm trying to help you, but if you can't behave, then I won't, okay?"

"Okay." He nods.

Backing slowly away, I lean over to pick up my phone. The protective cover did its job, and there doesn't seem to be any damage. Maybe a small scrape.

The ice wraiths are still hovering, watching.

"How much you charge?" mutters the guy.

"What do you mean?" I blow the dirt off the screen and trace the unlock pattern on my phone again.

"That's rude. Lookin' at your phone when someone's trying to ask you a question." He lurches toward me again, but my grip on the phone is better this time.

I knock his hand away. "Okay, that's it. You have a nice night."

I back up swiftly, then turn and walk toward the street. I'll go around the corner and call someone from there. This man is probably decent when he's sober, and I don't want him stumbling into traffic or anything in this state.

A hand grips my upper arm, jerking me around. "I said, how much?"

"I'm not a hooker." I reach toward my pocket for the pepper spray, but the man seizes my other wrist. Swiftly I drive a knee upward to his crotch, but he pivots aside. There's a gleam in his eye that sparks panic in my stomach. Maybe he isn't as drunk as I thought. Maybe this situation is getting more serious.

8

CARRY YOU

I twist and duck under the drunken man's elbow, throwing my back against his arm and breaking his grip. This time I don't try to be firm, or polite, or helpful—I run.

The man's steps pound after me, chasing me toward the street, but a few seconds later I hear a heavy thump and a grunt, as if all the breath was blown out of his chest—and at the same moment a fragrance of sea-ice, mint, and wood-smoke suffuses the air.

When I turn, my pursuer is trying to scramble to his feet, but his shiny dress shoes can't get any purchase on the sheet of gleaming ice that now covers half the parking lot. Several feet away lies a figure with pale hair, one hand splayed clawlike against the pavement. From that hand races a jagged ridge of living ice that crawls up my attacker's shoes, ankles, and calves, locking him firmly in place. He's caught in a sort of runner's starting position, his hands seamed to the ice-covered lot and his back arched, one leg bent and the other splayed out. His screams echo across the parking spaces until one of the ice wraiths darts down and paints his mouth shut with a gorgeous spray of frost.

I'm equal parts grateful and horrified. But I'm more concerned with why Jack doesn't get up.

"Jack?" I hurry toward him. "What are you—oh my god."

His clothes have been partly scorched off, and the skin under them is mottled with red and black burns. His skin is steaming; tendrils of smoke curl from his blistered feet and hands. Smears of soot mark his face, and ash is caked through his hair. The whites of his blue eyes are pink from smoke exposure.

"I went to your place," he croaks. "You weren't there."

"What happened to you?" I don't know where to touch him without causing him pain. "What can I do to help? 911—I can call 911."

"Sure, you do that. I'm sure they know exactly how to care for supernatural beings like me."

"But you need a doctor." I stare at him in helpless horror.

The wraiths descend to Jack, stroking his cheeks and chest with their tiny hands. He sighs, as if the cold touch is a relief.

"Can they fix you?" I ask.

"No, but they can help a little. When I couldn't find you, I went to the nearest wraiths I could sense—and here you were." He coughs, ragged and shuddering. "Making new friends, huh?"

"These two are delightful. That one, not so much." I jerk my head toward the partly frozen man.

"I could freeze his dick for you," Jack wheezes. "He'd be peeing snowflakes for a week, if he managed not to break himself off." His shoulders jerk with painful laughter. "Break himself off—get it?"

"You're foul."

"I really am. You love it."

"I absolutely do *not*, and you shouldn't be making jokes right now! Can you spiral yourself to Antarctica? Seal yourself up in that ice cocoon to heal?"

"I'd be out for weeks. No. We need a different solution."

"Okay, so then—can you spiral us to my apartment? If you won't go to a hospital, you at least need a bed."

"A bathtub full of ice would be better."

I chew my lip, nodding. "I think I can make that happen. Will the wraiths come along?"

"They don't like being indoors, but they will if I ask them. Oh hell." His face contorts, breath hissing between his teeth. "This is the worst it's been yet. But I drove her back for a while, I think. Not for long. Not long enough."

"Jack, focus." I place my hands along his ribs, over the remnants of his tattered shirt. His stomach contracts, each muscle hardening in a paroxysm of pain. "Jack, take us to my place. Right now."

"Hold me tighter," he whispers.

Gingerly I slide my arms farther under him. "I don't want to hurt you."

"I already feel better, being near you."

"That doesn't make any sense. Shut up and spiral already."

The world spins away, devolving into a storm of snow and I am nothing again, except that I can feel Jack this time, the core of him, the soul of him, shining with impossible force. Then he shudders, flickers. Almost fades.

If he fades now, in this liminal space of transference, we will both die.

I can't scream because in this particulate form I have no mouth, but I thrust everything that I am toward him, twisting my will with his, shoring it up. His energy resurfaces with a bright pulse, and then we're sprawling onto the floor of my living room, a tangle of cold faces and smoke-seared limbs and the stickiness of wounds.

The wraiths came with us, but they look smaller and unhappier now. They mewl anxiously in their tiny faraway voices.

Jack is unresponsive, so I drag his tall form foot by foot toward the bathroom, cursing loudly because why couldn't he have just spiraled himself into the tub and why do I have to play nurse when I have my first day of work in just a handful of hours? I'm getting no sleep tonight. And what if he—

I look down at the wreck of him, at the pale expanse of his skin blotched with glistening red flesh and blackened edges. His face is whiter than ever, and there's a translucency to his features that scares me. His nose and cheekbones look sharper, like thinning shards of ice.

He's going to make it. He will be just fine.

Finally I manage to haul him into the tub. I arrange his limbs as best I can and fill the tub partway with cold water. "Do what you can for him," I tell the wraiths. "I'm going to get some ice."

Later I return, staggering under the weight of as many bags of ice as I can carry. I dump it into the tub with Jack, bag after bag, and then I hurry back to the car for more. The wraiths don't seem to have accomplished much beyond icing over the shower walls and turning the mirror into a piece of frosty artwork, but I don't fuss at them for it. Maybe their presence helps him in ways I can't understand—like mine does. I still don't get how just being around me gives him an energy boost; it's weird, and sounds like an excuse that a sorcerous stalker would give, if magical lurkers were a commonplace occurrence and not just one extraordinary man whose death would place the entire world in terrible jeopardy...

And I'm responsible for keeping him alive.

I can do this. I eat challenges for breakfast. And this is my chance to pay him back for saving my life. I won't owe him anymore; he won't be able to use the life-saving debt as an excuse to hang around and cook for me. We'll be even.

Of course he did kind of save me from the man in the parking lot—but that doesn't count because I could have gotten clear of that situation on my own. I was definitely faster than that guy; I'd have made it to the street, called someone—I would have been fine without Jack's icy interference.

Did the ice melt off the man as soon as Jack and I spiraled away? Judging from the way the ice box-cutter vanished after he left, I'll bet it did. So the guy would have been free to stumble out of there and find a way home. If he does tell anyone what he saw, they'll think he was just drunk out of his mind and seeing things. No problem there.

I'm not wasting another thought on that loser, or his acrid breath, or the spastic grip of his hands on my wrists. I will not imagine what could have happened, because it didn't. Nothing really happened, right? So why am I curled in on myself beside the tub, shaking so hard I have to clench my teeth to keep them from knocking together? It's not the cold; it's the aftershock of the trauma, flooding my system. Right now, I want nothing more than to crawl into someone's arms and be held.

My trembling hand inches over the lip of the tub. I fumble through the icy slurry for Jack's hand and lift it out by the wrist—but it's too blistered to hold. A wave of sympathy so forceful it's almost pain washes over me. Gently I release his hand, letting it sink back into the ice.

I suppose I could crawl in there with him. I have the Chill, so I won't go hypothermic. But snuggling up to him without his permission wouldn't be right—even though I'm fairly sure he'd give me enthusiastic consent if he were awake.

There's no one to hold me, or to help me.

I tug my phone out of my sweatshirt pocket. My camera equipment survived Jack's spiraling thing remarkably well back in Antarctica, and the phone seems to be perfectly functional, too. After setting an alarm, I wedge myself tighter into the corner by the tub and wait.

When my alarm chimes, I startle awake. My mouth tastes gross and fuzzy, and I have to pee. The ice wraiths are gone, and Jack is still unconscious, but he looks more solid now. His edges aren't so weirdly translucent anymore. Hopefully the danger of him fading into a wraith has passed.

Tugging the shower curtain across the bathtub space, I use the toilet and prepare for the day. Jack will have to be all right on his own while I'm at work, because I can't miss my first day. I think I've done my duty by him anyway.

9

WINTER THINGS

When I get home that evening, I'm so exhausted and shaky I can barely insert the key properly into the lock on my apartment door. I've been running on leftover adrenaline and copious infusions of coffee all day, while various new coworkers trotted me around the offices and showed me what's what. Then I picked up an order of place-cards for the benefit and called around to some key potential guests who still haven't RSVP-ed. I got a soft confirmation from several of them, so that was good. And I helped double-check the inventory list and the appraised value of the items donated for the auction.

It was almost more than I could handle for a first day at work, operating on zero sleep. And it felt odd to be doing those small bits of busywork when just a few days ago I was in freaking Antarctica, so close to Adelie penguins that I could have touched them. No one here really gets how indomitable those little creatures are—the sturdy, gritty, sassy attitude that carries them through life in such a harsh climate. During lunch with a few of my new colleagues, I tried to explain my passion for the Adelies—but I've never been great with words, at least not in person. I can write a decent grant letter, an informative article. I've waxed passionate in emails and opinion pieces. But I'm better with my camera. Even now, in my exhausted state, I have the itch to go through some of the footage and photos I took on the trip; I've turned some of it in to my sponsors already, but there's more to review.

Or maybe I'll just have a sandwich and some wine and go to bed.

After I check on my patient.

The key finally fits into the lock. It's a good thing, too, because somebody on this floor is cooking, and the savory fragrance of sizzling onions permeates the hall, turning my knees weak. I'm not strictly a vegetarian, though I don't eat a lot of meat, and I try to avoid anything that isn't free-range—but this scent is so divine that I'm ready to beg for a mouthful from whoever is cooking it, without even asking if it's been locally or sustainably sourced. Sleep deprivation has reduced my brain function to primal needs only.

When I push through the apartment door, the aroma billows around me, drawing me in to warmth and light. I hesitate, afraid for a second that I've entered the wrong apartment. This is like something out of a movie, or out of someone else's life—someone with a family who might welcome them back from work with a home-cooked meal.

Jack stands as far as he can from the stove, poking at something in a skillet. His hands are encased in oven mitts, so I can't tell how much they've healed. He has discarded the charred scraps of his clothes, and he's wearing—oh god, he's wearing my robe—a light jersey garment that clings to the curves of his butt far too nicely and leaves most of his strong legs exposed.

He looks over his shoulder, with a smile that sends my heart flying somewhere far into the sky. It's a sensation I've had before, with two other boys.

Both of them were pretty.

Both of them dropped me after a while, claiming I was too driven, too picky, too obsessed, too focused on my studies and my work. I mean of *course* I communicated my passion for protecting the planet. Of *course* I tried to convince them to reduce, reuse, and recycle. Of course I blew off the occasional "Netflix and chill" because I wanted to hear a climatologist's talk or join a rally. But it was too much for Declan. Too much for Sam. Each of them wanted someone to bone, someone to be a pretty sidekick, someone to help them pass on their genes. I don't even want to bring kids into this crappy world, honestly.

I had such magnificent flutters with Sam when I first met him. Same with Declan—magical, thrilling, disgusting flutters.

The same thing is happening with Jack, and I hate it, because there's only one way it can end—with another part of me breaking away, like a chunk from an iceberg. I'll be left smaller, and weaker, and less able to do my part in the world.

I have to shut down the flutters I'm feeling right now for the beautiful, smiling ice god in the jersey bathrobe and oven mitts.

"How was your day?" he asks me.

It's such a horribly typical, human thing to say. Like he is inserting himself into a role he's pictured—carving himself a place in my life. I can't stand it.

"What is wrong with you?" I snap, throwing down my bag. "You shouldn't be up. You almost died."

"I'm healed, see?" He slides off his oven mitts and parts the robe a little, exposing his upper chest, smooth and ice-white as ever. "My energy is still low, but my body is better than ever, thanks to you. I'm telling you, Emery, you've got a magic of your own."

"No. I don't have any magic. I'm tired, I'm starving, and I probably don't smell too great because I couldn't shower this morning because someone was occupying part of my bathroom."

"You wanna shower now, or eat first? Because it's almost ready."

I want to resist, but my muscles are practically melting with desire for the source of that magnificent smell. "Eat first," I murmur. "What did you cook?"

"Nothing much. Just some onions, potatoes, garlic, butter, flank steak, spices—"

"Oh god." I sink to the floor, onto a cushion. Jack has placed two pillows on the living room carpet, in roughly the same spots where we sat and ate our omelets last night. There's a towel spread out between them by way of a tablecloth.

"I need to buy an actual table. And chairs." I'm so tired I feel as if a very long tunnel connects my brain to my mouth—it's hard to keep the words intact as they make the journey from one point to the other.

"I don't mind the floor." Jack flashes me another smile. His sharp canines give the expression a wicked glint. "It's kind of fun."

"Of course you'd think that." I ease my arms out of my coat. I wore it just for show, not because I need it as a barrier anymore. But I figured if I went to work in a thin blouse when it's freezing outside, people might notice, and wonder.

There's a chilly breeze in the room, and when I glance up at the thermostat on the wall, I see that Jack has set it to 50 degrees Fahrenheit. My electric bill is going to be ridiculous this month if he sticks around. Which he shouldn't. Now that he's healed, I have to get him out of here, away from me. Back to his usual haunts, and his ongoing battle.

He did almost die, though. And if he died, what would happen? This invisible battle of supernatural forces is clearly intertwined with human carelessness, and it's all having a devastating effect on the planet. With Jack out of the picture, unable to hold back the fire goddess and the effects of global warming, would the world really end?

Jack is standing beside me, holding two plates and staring down at me. A faint flush colors his pale cheeks.

"What?" I frown at him.

"Nothing." He swallows, sets a plate in front of me, then seats himself on the other cushion. "You look good."

I glance down at myself, confused—and then I realize that I removed my blouse as well as my coat, and I'm sitting there in my tank top. It's what I usually do when I get home; I must have done it without thinking. The tank top is thin, but I'm wearing a bra under it. Still, it definitely sags at the neckline, and when he was standing above me the view of my breasts must have been a generous one.

Without meaning to, I glance at his crotch area. Does he have actual man parts? I mean, he's a frost elemental, so technically he wouldn't need them. The robe he's wearing shifts tantalizingly as he gets comfortable on the cushion, opening to expose part of his inner thigh—white carved muscle like a marble statue. If it would only open a little more—a little higher—

A swirl of frosty blue and white glides between us, blocking my view of Jack. The dainty ice wraith touches my cheek lightly, and though the cold doesn't hurt, my skin stiffens, frozen for a second. A second wraith whisks above my head, showering me with snowflakes.

Their touches are clearly a greeting. Elated, I smile at them. "Hey there, pretty things. Did you take good care of Jack for me?"

I've barely finished the question when two more wraiths glide straight through the closed window into my apartment. They hang back for a second until the first pair draws them forward to meet me. As they dance around me, Jack snatches my steaming plate of food out of the way of the drifting snowflakes.

There are subtle differences between the wraiths—slightly longer hair on one, larger eyes on another, tiny blue horns on a third. According to Jack's tale, each one of them used to be a powerful goddess of ice and frost.

"Okay, girls. That's enough." Jack waves his hand dismissively, and they swirl around him briefly before sailing through my living room window into the night. Jack hands me my plate, shaking his head, but his wide mouth curves in a half-repressed smile. "They don't often get to meet new people. They're excited."

"So they've met others that you've—that you've—"

"There have been one or two others to whom I've given the Chill, as a life-saving thing. But so far I'd say you're the favorite. They sense it too. There's something different about you."

"Hm." I snort. "So I'm 'not like other girls'?"

He tilts his head, eyeing me. "What do you want to hear? That you're just like everyone else? That you're not special, or unique, or important? That you mean no more to me than any other girl? That I would have the same connection with any other man or woman who had stumbled into my castle and breathed me awake?"

The bite I just took sticks in my throat. Of course I want to believe that I'm unique, and special. "There's only one *you*," as the children's books say. I want to believe—to *know*—that I'm not just one of the milling crowd. That I could be important. But it seems self-centered to admit that, so I don't.

Jack hasn't moved—he still sits cross-legged, hands splayed against the carpet—but his entire body is rigid, his jaw set and his eyes blazing at me like blue stars. He looks like a white tiger, tense and ferocious, ready to pounce.

I force down the bite of flank steak. "I don't know what you're talking about," I rasp. "You helped me out, and I helped you out. There's no connection, just the facts, and what unfolded out of necessity."

But my entire body is playing traitor to my words. My skin and nerves are practically vibrating, and my blood races hot through my veins, impelled by my throbbing heart.

Jack glares at me until I lower my gaze to my food. It's too tasty to ignore, and I try to enjoy it despite the tempest of emotion inside me. I'm not even sure what I'm feeling right now. Confusion, irritation, anxiety—those I know. We're old friends. But there's a trembling, aching soreness too—a twinge of pain so sharp it's almost a thrill—it's both and neither, unidentifiable and dreadful and delightful. I had silly flutters with my exes, sure, but I never felt *this*. This is something deep and raw, waking up, surging toward the surface. I don't dare look it in the face because I want so badly for it to be beautiful and real but what if it's hideous and false?

When I finally dare to peek at Jack again, he has veiled the blaze of those blue eyes. They're resigned now, almost sad. "How's the food?" he asks softly, like an apology.

I reply with an "mmm" that seems to satisfy him.

Slowly, bit by bit, I tell him about my day, until we've both relaxed into the flow of conversation. When we're done eating, I collect the plates and head for the sink, intending to clean up. It's only fair, after he cooked for me. And then I have to figure out how to kick a supernatural stalker out of my apartment so I can get some sleep.

"What do you think you're doing?" Jack's frosty breath ghosts across the back of my neck.

"Cleaning up."

"I'd like to take care of that for you." His soft, cool voice slithers right into my core, tingling in all the little places I haven't touched in way too long. My heartbeat goes quick and crooked.

Gritting my teeth, I turn on the water and squeeze soap across the plates. Jack's hand slips over my right one, attempting to steal the sponge, but I smack him away. "Go rest some more."

He snaps his fingers, and with a scintillating flash the water streaming out of the faucet freezes into a thick icicle stretching from spout to drain. The plates are encased in a thin sheet of ice, impossible to wash.

Savagely I wrench the faucet further to the "hot" side, grab the sprayer, and turn it on Jack. The blast of hot water catches him full in the chest, and he yelps, darting across the room. "Ow!"

His skin is barely pink from the heat, so he's not badly hurt; but his expression is one of such profound and dramatic offense that I can't help a giggle. I pinch my lips together to cut it short.

"That is the cutest sound I've heard you make." Jack's eyes glitter as he stalks toward me. The air stirs around him, six-pointed crystalline flakes fluttering along his limbs. My breath catches, because he looked and acted so human this evening that I almost forgot how powerful he is. The breeze flows outward from him, across my cheeks and through the ends of my hair. He's an arm's length away now—closer, closer—I'm trapped in the corner by the sink, caged between the counter and Jack's body.

His eyes are a beautiful compulsion, a pressure so overwhelming that I have to avert my own. My gaze drifts down his throat, across the T-shape of his clavicles and breastbone, down to the groove that runs between his abs. The robe he's wearing is so thin, and the knot looks so temptingly loose—my fingers dart for the long end, and with one quick tug the knot is undone, and the robe falls open.

His scent wafts to me—mint and evergreen, sea ice and the clean, crisp fragrance of snow. There's a faint azure tint to his skin in places, like under his pecs and along the slanted muscles of his abdomen.

And he's fully equipped. More than adequate for anything we might want to do—which is nothing. Absolutely nothing, because sex with a frost god would be ridiculous and weird and—

He hauls me toward him, his hand cupping the back of my skull, and I meet his mouth eagerly, my mind going blessedly blank for a moment as I simply *feel*. I feel everything—my skin sparkling with the delicious chill of him, my pulse pounding in my throat, his arm wrapped hard and fierce around my body.

With other men, moments like this have always consisted of heat and heavy limbs, the sweat and smell of all-too human bodies. But Jack—oh, Jack— he is all litheness and lean muscle and smooth, ocean-scented skin. His lips are marvelously soft, and the sweetness of his breath in my mouth refreshes my entire being, revitalizes me from tongue to toes in a way no espresso ever could.

But the niggling, gnawing voice of anxiety in my head won't shut up, won't let me enjoy the moment. I probably smell awful. I'm over-tired and overwrought. I shouldn't be kissing him back this desperately—shouldn't be doing this when I don't really want him in my life. I've always had trouble with anything being "just sex." For me, actions have intention, and meaning, and consequences, emotional and otherwise. I need to stop this. Now.

But—

One more kiss.

One more salacious sweep of his tongue through my mouth. One more moment in which I am pressed against every bit of his gorgeous, solid, perfectly naked body.

And then I force myself to push him away, to shape words that will put distance between us. "I need to shower, and sleep. You should go."

He blinks snow-flecked lashes at me, slow and dazed, the exhilaration in his eyes fading to comprehension.

A tremor races through me, because I *did* make the first move. I unfastened his robe, and I kissed him back. And I know that sometimes, once a woman brings a man this far, he won't stop, even if she asks.

But Jack pulls the robe's edges together and ties the belt carefully in place. "Of course. I'll go home and rest as well. I hope you don't mind if I return the robe later?"

"Sure."

"All right then. Good night, Emery."

He vanishes in a spray of icy wind, leaving behind more snow than usual.

10

JEALOUS GODS

The next morning I'm walking from my car toward the conservancy offices, sipping my coffee, when Jack pops up at my elbow. I startle violently, dropping the cup, which he catches and tucks back into my hand.

"Sorry about that." He grins an apology. "Did you sleep well?"

"I did, thank you." Though not until after I took care of certain physical cravings in my own way. Jack does *not* need to know how horny he made me.

"Glad to hear it." He keeps walking at my side.

"Um, Jack? What do you think you're doing?"

"Going to work with you."

"You can't do that. You don't work here."

"Don't worry, I'm invisible to everyone but you right now. No one will know I'm here."

"But *I* will know."

"And that's a problem because..."

"Because you'll distract me! I won't be able to focus!"

"But I'm so curious about what they do here. I will be quiet, I promise. Silent as a frozen corpse."

"Ew. No, you can't come with me. And don't give me those pathetic puppy eyes." The entrance to my building is just a few strides away. "I'm ignoring you now. Shoo!"

I breeze into the building with a smile plastered onto my face and a "good morning" for Janet, the woman at the front desk. When I glance casually over my shoulder, Jack is gone. Relieved, I continue to the office I share with three others. One of them is out sick today, and the other coworker, Alice, who seems to assume that she's also my boss, assigns me to more RSVP follow-ups and some check-in calls with the caterer and other vendors.

Around mid-morning, Alice leaves for a meeting about an upcoming excursion into the mountains. It sounds like a fascinating session, but I haven't been invited. I suppose I'm too new. Sighing, I swivel in my chair, surveying the empty office. Three plain desks, plus we have the distinction of hosting the copier. There's a box of auction lists beside my desk, which I'm supposed to fold. "Before lunch, preferably," Alice told me with a stiff smile. I get the feeling she doesn't like me much, although I can't imagine why. I was nothing but amenable yesterday. Okay, maybe I talked about my Antarctica trip in too much detail at lunch, but I've had no one but Karyl to talk to. Mysterious frost gods don't count.

I plop a stack of auction lists on my desk and take the first one, setting its edges together and running my fingertip along the fold to create a crisp edge.

"Well, this is a lot less exciting than I imagined."

My body jerks in response to Jack's voice. "Oh. My. God. You have to stop doing that, you absolute asshole!"

He's sitting on the edge of Alice's desk with his boots propped on her chair. I'm learning the differences between his two forms—when he's imperceptible to humans, there's a snowy splendor about him, a faint frostiness to his skin, and an icy sharpness to his features. In human form, his ears are rounded instead of pointed, and though his hair is still white and his face is still flawless, he looks slightly—earthier. More physical, less ethereal. Right now, he's flaunting his icy, unearthly gorgeousness.

Jack crosses his boots at the ankles, and crusts of snow dribble off them onto Alice's chair cushion. "I've been wandering around this place, and it really feels like your average human company. Lots of busywork being done, very little actually accomplished. And you—you're...folding paper?"

"Auction lists," I snap. "So people know what's available, and the numbers, and everything."

"Seems like something you could do digitally, and save paper."

"That's what I thought, but I'm the newbie here. I didn't make the decision, did I? At this point, it is what it is."

Jack kicks the chair expertly, making it spin around on one wheel twice before settling his boots back on it.

"You're getting snow on the seat," I point out. "Alice is going to think I spilled something on her chair."

"I'll dry it off before I leave. A quick blast of wind, and it'll be fine." His blue eyes arrest mine. "Does this feel important to you, Emery? Does it feel like you're making a difference in the world? Helping the planet?"

"I mean, sure. This kind of work isn't glamorous. It's slow and painful. It's contacting people with power, developing allies, legislating change. The upcoming benefit will raise money for those efforts, give the conservancy the funds it needs to keep protecting and managing natural spaces."

"Managing natural spaces," Jack repeats slowly.

"Yes, and we have just a couple days left until the benefit, so at this point, we have to make sure that everything is in place and that we've thought of every detail."

"You've already got the rhetoric down." His wry tone carries a tinge of sadness. "You'll fit in well here."

I fling aside the paper I was about to fold. "What else do you expect us to do? We're human, Jack. We don't have special woo-woo powers like you do, that can alter temperatures and weather patterns. We do the best we can with what we've got. And unfortunately, for humans, that's a lot of red tape and networking."

His mouth tightens as if he's trying to hide a smile, and his eyes sparkle. "Special woo-woo powers?"

"Yes." Blushing, I collect the discarded paper and resume my careful folding. At least when I'm doing that, I don't have to look at his stupid beautiful face.

"Would you like to have 'special woo-woo powers' of your own?"

A shudder runs through me, shock and alarm. "What do you mean?"

He takes in my apprehension, his eyes narrowing. "Never mind. It's nothing you'd ever want. Forget it."

"Forget it? How am I supposed to forget that? Why did you even mention—"

A shadow falls across my office doorway and I shut my mouth immediately, remembering that I'm the only one who can hear and see Jack right now. Being caught talking to myself wouldn't be great for my reputation among my new colleagues.

A slim man with brown hair and a placid, pleasant face raps on the doorframe. "Hello in there!" He smiles widely, showing teeth that I'd guess were recently bleached—they're painfully resplendent. "I'm one of the directors here. Minnick. Newt Minnick."

He says it like "Bond, James Bond," and Jack guffaws. Obviously he has found at least a little time for pop culture during his two centuries as an immortal ice warrior.

I rise, holding out my hand to Newt Minnick. "I'm Emery Caulfield."

"A pleasure. A real pleasure." Newt captures my hand in both of his. The moist heat of his palms makes me uncomfortable; I want to snatch my hand away, but he might take offense. "I saw you making the rounds yesterday with Alice, but I was just swamped with work—you know how it is. So I thought I would come by and introduce myself. I hear you just came back from a fantastic trip!"

"Yes, I did—"

"Let's you and I have dinner. You can tell me all about it."

"Oh, well, I—I'm—"

"Just for fun, okay? No pressure, nothing like that." The smile and the humid hand-holding and his mellow voice are like a dense cloud, fogging my senses. "You're new in town so you need someone to show you the best spots, right? You like Southern home cooking? Well, you're in for a treat. I'll take you to Sallie Mae's and we'll have ourselves a good old time, maybe invite a few others, make it a party, okay? We can leave from here around six and take my car, it's no trouble at all, and I'll bring you back here after dinner to pick up your car, okay? Okay! You be good now. Get lots of work done." With a final press of his palms, he releases me and walks out of my office, still smiling.

Jack stalks around me and peers into my face. "Amazing. I thought humans didn't possess any magical powers, but this one seems to have the ability to render you speechless. Incredible."

"Wish he'd try it on *you* sometime," I snarl, returning to my chair.

"So you have a date." Jack bites out the last word. "That's nice. Excited? Want me to help you choose an outfit?"

"It's not a date, and I have Karyl to help me choose outfits."

"Karyl, yes. I like her. Do you see her much?"

"Not as much since college. She works a lot. Has a wife. They just adopted a baby, so we can't hang out like we used to." Why am I telling him this?

"And she's the only person you know in Asheville."

"Until I met the other people here at the conservancy."

"And Minnick. Newt Minnick. Don't forget about him. I think he's got the makings of a very close friend." There's ice in Jack's tone, and not the pretty frosty kind; this ice has razor edges. He glares down at me, the collar of his blue dress shirt shifting with his quick breath. His wide mouth hitches up in a sneer, revealing one of those sharp eyeteeth.

"Oh my god. You're jealous."

"The hell I am."

"You are. Even though you have no right to be, because you and I are barely acquaintances."

His voice turns low and husky. "You kiss all your acquaintances like that?"

One step forward, and I'd be touching him. Every inch of my skin buzzes with awareness, with the memory of how he felt against me.

"That," I whisper, "was an unfortunate error in judgment on my part. I was exhausted. Not thinking straight. You—you're not good for me. You mess things up and make them even more complicated. The world is complicated enough, Jack. I don't need this magical angle skewing my perspective and my goals. I don't want it. I need something solid and human, something that makes sense."

"Like Newt Minnick." Jack stalks away from me, toward the copier.

"He's a director. A relationship with him would be inappropriate."

"That's what he wants, though."

"No, he said there will be others at dinner. He's just being nice, welcoming a new employee."

Jack lays a hand on the copier and watches frost creep outward from his fingers, glazing the machine. "He wants to fuck you, Emery. And you know it."

At those words from his mouth, my face turns hot, and warmth pools deep inside me.

"Why wouldn't he?" Jack continues, without looking at me. "You're more than gorgeous. You're clever and honest, sharp and transparent as ice. You sparkle even when you don't mean to."

I can't speak. My pulse throbs hot in my throat.

"Want me to come along tonight?" Jack removes his hand from the copier, and the frost recedes.

"Why would I want that?" I'm still breathless from what he just said to me. "You think I need protection? I can handle myself."

"Of course you can. But even the most capable person—man, woman, or otherwise—needs backup on occasion. Like the other night, with that horny drunk."

"I would have been fine. You're the one who showed up looking half-dead. Scratch that—seventy-five percent dead. What exactly happened that night?"

"I pushed Auxesia hard, and she pushed back. Unfortunately she did more damage to me than I did to her. She'll take a little time to recharge, and then she'll be back, enflaming more of the world. Right now she's testing the limits, starting different fires in various places, noting how the humans respond, and how fast I react. Soon she'll start a major onslaught—I can feel it coming."

"Is that how you know where to go? You can feel the fires?"

"I can sense a shift, yes." He runs his fingers through his silky white hair. "It's like I have very fine threads in my mind, and those threads run all over the world. I can feel the ones that are being strained and scorched. The sense is stronger when my energy is full, but the lower it gets, the weaker my instinct is."

"That's why you asked me if I'd heard about any big fires, when we first met." I plop into my seat and scoop up another paper to fold.

He nods. "I was still a little disoriented, and not fully recharged, so I couldn't tell."

"Yes, yes, I woke you up too early, I know."

"It's fine. I'm glad I could help you. Meeting you has been the highlight of my life as Jack Frost."

My heart thumps tenderly in response, but I stifle the swelling emotion and retort, "Just the highlight of your life as Jack Frost? Not of your entire existence? Damn. You must have known some gorgeous, accomplished women during your human life."

"Of course I did." I don't look up from my folding, but I can hear the smirk in Jack's voice as he continues. "I was a skilled and handsome sculptor, very popular in the art community, and a tragic figure because of my impending and inevitable demise."

"And then, like a beneficent vampire, Kheima arrived to offer you eternal life." Which is another reason why I cannot and will not allow myself to slip into a relationship with this beautiful, magical man. I won't be the cliche, the young human woman who falls for the immortal guy. I won't. I refuse.

"Eternal life, yes. What she cleverly left out of the deal was her intent to withdraw and let herself fade, while I took on the war alone. I had to shoulder the responsibility of an entire planet's safety, when all I wanted to do was make beautiful art."

"We don't all have the privilege of indulging our best talents all the time." I glance morosely at the box of papers. "I wish I could be out in the mountains with a camera instead of doing this. But here I am. Besides, you shouldn't be complaining. Most climate activists would kill to have power on your level—the ability to actually *make change happen*. Don't you realize how valuable that is? Don't you care about the world?"

"Of course I do! Maybe I didn't at first, but since I transformed, I've come to realize its beauty and complexity on a level no human could ever understand."

My gaze snaps to his. "Oh really? Arrogant much?"

"It's not arrogance. When you're one of us, one of the elemental gods, you experience everything differently. It's a fact."

Jealousy coils inside me, but I don't have time to bark a retort or press for details, because my coworker Alice walks back into the office. "Still not done with those, Emery?" She clucks her tongue. "I guess you can take a later lunch then. I'll go now with Jocelyn and Phineas, and you can have the one o'clock shift."

"Great!" I bare my clenched teeth in a smile.

When Alice leaves, I glance around for Jack, but he's gone.

11

CLEAR BLUE SKY

Jack doesn't reappear until one o'clock precisely, when he strides into the office wearing jeans and a red sweater, looking less frosty and distinctly more human. Alice can see him, because she clears her throat, flushing, and rises from her desk with a flutter of her lashes and a throaty "Can I help you?"

"I'm here to pick Emery up for lunch." Jack gives me a scintillating grin.

"Oh." Alice casts me a look that's part admiration and part envy. Great. The last thing I need is another reason for her to dislike me. "Just one hour, Emery. We have a lot to get done this afternoon."

"Sure." With my foot, I shove the box of folded auction lists toward her desk. "These are done. Maybe next time we can find an app to use, instead of wasting the paper."

"It's *recycled* paper," she says crisply. "And we'll have recycling bins available for proper disposal. Don't worry, I'm not new to this. *I* have experience with these events."

Jack drags me out of the office before I can respond, which is probably a good thing. When I got this job, I didn't expect to be entering a popularity contest, or experiencing high-school-esque drama. I thought, for some naive reason, that we'd all be friends—a big happy team working together to protect the environment. So far, working at the conservancy is nothing like I expected.

Mark that down as another disappointment on the long obituary of Emery's idealistic dreams.

I'm still seething when I realize that Jack is pulling me toward the end of the hall. There's nothing down here except a supply closet. "Jack, what are you doing?"

"Taking you to lunch."

"In the closet?"

"Yes, Emery, in the closet. It's bigger on the inside, and there's a lovely cafe with twinkle lights—of course not in the closet. I just need privacy, so I can whisk you off somewhere else."

"I have one hour for lunch, Jack. One hour."

"So I heard." He opens the closet door and hustles me inside. I stumble over a mop handle and curse, while he slips in after me and shuts the door.

"This is dumb," I hiss. "They're going to think we're—you know—"

"What?" His cool breath wafts across my cheek, and I flinch away from his presence even as my heartbeat accelerates.

"If anyone sees us they'll think we were *doing it* in here."

"Doing. What?" There's a smile in his voice. He's just trying to make me say it. I'm not a prude; I can say it. I *can*. But I don't want to, not with the chill of him whispering over my skin, and that fragrance of pine and sea air suffusing the cramped space.

Jack slides his hands along my waist, his palms cool through my thin blouse. "What will they think we're doing, Emery?"

"Having sex," I murmur.

"And that's something we'd never do."

"No."

"Why not?"

"For many reasons, the first of which is that I'm not the type of girl to bang her boyfriend at work—"

His voice drifts across my ear. "But I'm not your boyfriend."

"I never said you were. Look, are we getting food, or—"

"Hang on tight." Wind kicks up in the closet, and I have barely enough time to cinch my arms around his body before we swirl into nothing, into particles of mind and matter and magic, whirling across the world to some distant point. I can feel us approaching the destination, coalescing again—and then we land on solid ground, under a brilliant sun.

No, it's not ground—it's ice. A glorious sweep of ice, a shelf of it, rearing out of the ocean. I can feel the cold, as I might sense it through layers of coats, but I'm not actually cold. I'm awestruck, speechless before the mighty bulk of the iceberg, chiseled into gleaming splendor by the vagaries of the blue water in which it drifts. I've only seen such blue in one place.

Antarctica.

"Did you take me back to Antarctica?" I whisper, edging out of Jack's arms.

"I did." He points to a lumpy black heap on the ice. It's two sets of scuba diving gear. "I thought we could go for a swim. Have you used one of these before?"

"Twice, for a cinematography course. We practiced shooting underwater. But I've never—are you serious about this?"

"Why not? You have the Chill now. You won't get cold. And if anything happens, I'll spiral us out of there quick as that." He snaps his fingers. "Come on, Emery. It's the most beautiful thing you've ever seen, I promise."

"Oh my god yes!" I dart for the scuba gear. "Jack, for once I might be happy to know you."

His smile wavers a little, but he only says, "Lucky me."

"If only I had the right camera along—the footage I could get—"

"I'll bring you again sometime, with the right equipment. For now, just enjoy yourself."

"With the right equipment? Ha! Not likely. It's super expensive."

"I have money."

"How?" I rock back on my heels, still clutching the gear. "How do you have money?"

"The Horae and the other elemental gods and goddesses have treasures of the Old World—things they stole, or made, or were given by worshipers. There's a lot of it still lying around the treasury in the Antarctic palace, and more at my apartment in Prague. So whenever I need money, I just sell something, either on eBay or through one of my fences."

"Fences? As in creepy guys who fence stolen goods?"

Jack shrugs. "Immortal warriors can't be too picky in their dealings, especially when they need money for food and toilet paper."

"I guess you would need those things. You know, for a while I wasn't sure if you had—parts."

"I eat and drink, don't I? How else would I eliminate waste? Unfortunately my eliminations tend to clog up human toilets—but they usually flush just fine after everything thaws out." He grins so widely I can't tell if he's joking or not. "Now take your clothes off and put on that dive skin. You only have an hour, and we've already wasted seven minutes of that."

"Turn around," I order.

Jack obeys, grumbling about how I've already seen him naked and it's only fair that he sees me naked, and so on. Of course I don't strip completely, Chill or no Chill, but I take off everything but the underwear and pull on the dive skin. Jack gets into his own gear and then checks mine with the skilled nonchalance of an expert. Clearly he's done this many times. He shows me the pressure gauge, depth gauge, compass—I try to listen but I'm so excited I can hardly stand it.

Finally he cocks his head and says, "Basically just breathe and follow me. Okay? Ready?"

I can't answer through my gear and mask, but I nod, and when he finishes adjusting his own gear and dives from the edge of the iceberg, I follow him.

He must have known exactly where to jump, because we sink straight under, without grazing any of the jagged ridges of ice hidden beneath the rippling water. I focus on breathing carefully, smoothly, while I follow Jack through a gurgling world of blue and green beauty.

I think what surprises me most is the colors. I didn't expect the water to be so pristinely, achingly clear, or the light to turn the ice the most beautiful shades of azure and jade. We swim further, beneath the ice floes. With the sun shining through them, the floes resemble thick slabs of frosted glass, marked with lines and shadows and slim cracks. We dive deeper, past slopes and shelves of submerged ice, textured in millions of wavy lines.

My heart is going to burst with the sheer beauty of it all, with the wonder that I'm here, I'm *here*, doing something that I never thought I'd be able to do. Except for those two classes, I wasn't trained for underwater photography— certainly not in this environment, so no one would have paid for me to do it professionally, and I could never have afforded this on my own. But Jack Frost brought me here. He gave me this gift, because he knew what it would mean to me.

I can't cry because of the whole regulator and mask deal, but I want to, because it's so heartbreakingly lovely down here. If I could kiss that ridiculous ice god swimming ahead of me, I think I would.

The swim is over all too soon. When we resurface, Jack spirals us back to the top of the iceberg where we left our clothes. This time I don't ask him to turn away. After stripping off my dive skin, I stand in my underwear for a moment, bared to the sun, my arms spread to feel the flow of the Antarctic wind.

He's watching me. I can feel it—the pressure of his gaze on my skin. But he doesn't speak, or try to touch me. When I pick up my clothes, I risk a glance at him, and the raw *want* in his eyes rips the breath from my lungs.

I've seen lust before, too many times. This is lust, yes, but it's also something more, a craving for all of me, a hunger for something deeper and broader and higher than I'm willing to give.

I pull on my slacks and button my blouse, my fingers trembling, not from cold, but from the power of that longing.

Why does he have to look at me that way?

"I have ten minutes left," I say, trying to sound casual. "Where's the lunch you promised?"

"Artists can subsist on beauty alone."

I snort. "Not this artist."

Jack grins and tugs a cooler pouch from some crevice in the ice. After unzipping it, he reaches inside and tosses me a foil-wrapped packet. "Sandwich. Avocado, bacon, egg, other stuff."

I tear open the packet and sink my teeth in. "Oh. My. God. This is incredible."

Jack prims up his mouth and splays his fingers against his chest. "Goodness me, Miss Emery—you really should swallow your food before you try to talk."

"I can't take breaks for talking. It's too good."

With our sandwiches devoured, Jack wraps me in his arms and whirls us back into the supply closet.

"What about the gear we left on the iceberg?" I whisper.

"I'll go back and get it now."

"Oh. Right. Yes, you should go. I really need to focus on work this afternoon." I squirm in his arms; he hasn't loosened his grip at all. "And I should stop by the bathroom. My hair is probably wild right now."

Still Jack holds me, his breath whisking quick and cold past my cheek. There's a desperation in the way he clings to me, a vibrating tension of power held forcibly in check. My skin tingles and glows along every point of pressure between his body and mine.

My voice is barely a whisper. "Jack?"

A shuddering inhale quakes through him, and then he says, low, "I'm sure your hair is fine."

"Thank you," I tell him; and I know he understands that I'm grateful for more than the reassurance.

Carefully I disengage myself and slip into the hallway. Thankfully no one is there to see me emerging from the closet. A quiet swish of wind lets me know that Jack has spiraled away.

103

Alice disappears fifteen minutes before five o'clock—not that I care. The benefit is the day after tomorrow, on Christmas Eve, and from what I can tell, we're in good shape for it. I have a list of minor to-do's for tomorrow, and then I'll need to find out what kind of footage they want me to take at the party. After that I'll have a week of vacation, which I plan to spend editing all the photos and videos I took in Antarctica. I'm also going to write a couple pieces about my time there and see if I can sell one to a magazine. I can always use the extra money—camera accessories aren't cheap, and the tech keeps changing at a pace that I can't keep up with. I have to stay semi-relevant, though, or I'll lose the professional ground I've gained.

As I'm heading for the front doors of the office, someone reaches in front of me and pushes the handle. It's Newt Minnick. His pseudo-gallant gesture places him uncomfortably close to me; I practically have to brush against his chest to get out the door.

"Thanks," I mutter.

"Ready for some good Southern cooking?" He flares that too-white smile again.

"Sure. Who else is coming?"

"Oh, um—no one else could make it. Too busy with pre-holiday prep— you know." He smirks at me.

My stomach sinks. Jack was right—this guy is a sleazeball looking for a lay. He didn't actually invite anyone else.

"My car is this way." Minnick points to a parking spot near the front doors.

I hesitate, trying to think up an excuse. I should be able to simply say, "I don't want to go to dinner with you;" but society has come up with ridiculous rules about not hurting other people's feelings. Why should I care about this smarmy asshole's feelings? I care about not having to spend an extremely awkward evening countering his clumsy attempts to flirt me into bed.

But he *is* one of my bosses. He could make things difficult for me if he thinks I'm being rude, or difficult, or cold. Maybe I should just go along with it, despite the warning that burns in my gut.

A chilly breeze whisks past my left shoulder, and I smother a relieved smile, because I know who it is before he steps forward. Jack advances on Minnick with a carnivorous grin, holding out one pale, long-fingered hand. "Hi there. I'm Jack. I'll be joining you for dinner."

"Oh. How—how nice." Minnick shakes Jack's hand. His expression is the poster child for foiled plans.

"It's okay, isn't it?" I ask. "You said a group, so I invited him."

"It's fine, of course," Minnick replies, absently patting his own hair, a helmet of acorn-brown parted crisply along the right side and solidified with hairspray.

"Why don't you ride with Mr. Minnick?" Jack says, turning to me. "I'll drive your car and meet you there."

That is *not* what I had in mind. In fact, I'd love to take *myself* to dinner and leave the two of them out of the picture completely. But I suppose we should throw Minnick a bone, since he won't be getting anything else bone-related tonight. I can endure a short car ride with him.

Gritting my teeth, I toss Jack my keys. "Not a scratch." Not that I would know if he scratched it. My poor old car is already latticed with scratches and dappled with dings.

"I swear," says Jack, crossing his heart. After Minnick gives him the name of the restaurant, he jaunts away across the parking lot, tossing my keys into the air. They twirl upward in a cloud of glittering snowflakes before floating back down to his palm. Quickly I glance at Minnick to see if he noticed, but he's frowning at his phone, skimming through Twitter or something. He glances at his phone at every red light on the way to the restaurant, and he's still scrolling when the server arrives to take our drink order and tell us the specials, which primarily consist of heavily fried things. Fried chicken, fried fish, fried shrimp, fried okra, fried freaking pickles.

Jack taps his menu. "What do you have that's cold?"

"I'm sorry?" The server chuckles nervously and sweeps his shaggy brown hair behind his ear. "You want something cold? We have ice cream."

"Any dinner foods that are cold? Like, freezing cold?"

I jam Jack's ribs with my elbow, and he coughs.

"We have salads? Maybe that will work for you?" The server's attitude toward Jack is rapidly shifting from admiration to annoyance. I can't blame the guy, really. I myself seem to be transforming into a pendulum that swings from "Jack is so sweet and handsome" to "oh my god he's driving me crazy"—sometimes within the space of two seconds.

"Sure. I'll take a look at the salads," Jack replies.

"And you, sir?" The server says loudly to Minnick.

"Hm? Oh yeah. Um, sweet tea," Minnick says, without taking his eyes off his phone.

And that's how the entire evening goes. Now that Jack's in the picture, Newt Minnick seems to have completely lost interest in me, as a professional or otherwise. He spends most of the time scrolling through social media, texting, or half-heartedly answering my questions about the conservancy's strategies for next year and beyond.

When I interviewed for this job virtually, through a Zoom call, I spoke with a different director, Marian, and another man named Jerry—both of whom

I've seen very little of since my arrival. They at least seemed passionate and dedicated, with intelligent plans for the conservancy's role in the region. Maybe if I can stick it out with this job, I'll eventually get to work more closely with those two, instead of enduring Alice and Minnick.

Jack quietly picks up the bill when the awkward meal has concluded, and Minnick concedes a nod of thanks. With a perfunctory, "See you at work," he leaves the restaurant while Jack and I are still rising from the table.

"Nice guy." Jack moves ahead of me to hold one of the doors open.

"Don't do that," I snap, pushing the other door open. "I'm perfectly capable of doing it myself."

"All right then." He barges through the second set of doors, letting them swing shut behind him. The doors nearly hit me in the face, but I bite back a protest, because I kind of asked for that.

"So that was a lovely evening." Jack shoves his hands into his pockets and tips his head up to the night sky, drawing in a deep breath of cold air. "I'll accept your gratitude now."

"Gratitude?"

"Yes, I believe I saved you from a night of innuendo with a side of sly groping. And that's best-case scenario. Worst case, he would have gotten you drunk and persuaded you to go home with him."

"Don't pretend to be walking the moral high ground," I snap. "You want the same thing he does." I stalk to my car and yank on the handle, but it's locked, of course. "Give me my keys."

Jack dangles the keys from his fingers, his eyes burning blue under the snowfall of his white hair. "I do *not* want the same thing he does."

"Oh really? So if I asked you to come home with me right now, you'd say no?"

"He doesn't care about you like I do." Jack collects my hand and presses the keys into my palm, cupping his fingers over them. The cold, wild scent of him flows around me, teasing my lips and making my breasts peak through my blouse. I should have worn a thicker bra—

"My coat," I whisper. "I left my coat in Minnick's car."

Jack's gaze trails across my breasts for a moment before returning to my face. His reply is as soft as a touch. "Well, it's not like you need it."

He bends, bringing his face closer to mine, but his lips hover temptingly without touching me. I can taste the sweetness of his breath on my tongue. His eyes are like blue oceans, begging me to dive into something new.

I could give in and kiss him. But what would that *mean*? What would happen next? This year, next year, ten or twenty years from now?

No, I can't do this—I just want to be alone, to be *me* for a while, without any complications or decisions.

Slamming both hands against his chest, I shove him away. "Stop it. Go back to your ice palace or whatever. And don't follow me, or I'll call the police."

"Okay, okay. But you know calling the police wouldn't do any good. I'd just go invisible. Like this." His appearance changes, his ears stretching into sharp points and his eyes glittering brighter blue. His cheekbones are crisp as an iceberg's edges, his fingernails icicle-sharp, and his lashes frosted with snow. Wind rises around him, and he rises with it, lifted into the air by its force. Snow collects at his back, taking the shape of frosty, effervescent wings.

Maybe he thinks he's going to impress me with his powers, but the display only cements in my mind just how different he is, how much he doesn't belong in my life.

"Showoff." I jerk open the car door and duck inside.

12

STALKER ICE GOD

My dreams are fitful that night, and in one of them I'm naked and twisted up with my ex, Sam, while Jack watches from the shadows, his eyes shards of blue ice. I reach for him, trying to crawl out of the bed, but he's freezing over, fast and faster, and I can't touch him before he's entirely encased in thick ice. I breathe on the ice, knock on it until my knuckles bleed, drag my nails along it and scream, but Jack recedes farther and farther away, endless layers of ice separating us.

"It's all right," says my ex, but he has Minnick's face now. "You're with me."

I wake with a cry, jolted out of the nightmare by the chiming of my phone alarm.

It wasn't real.

I didn't have sex with Sam again. And I'm not stuck with Minnick.

Jack is not buried in ice.

But my throat is raw. I think I was screaming for real.

Still trembling, I swing my legs out of bed and hurry to the shower, eager to wash away the clinging mental scum of the nightmare.

As the hot water floods my face and hair, I breathe deeply. My shoulders relax, tension easing from my spine.

"Did you sleep well?" The all-too-familiar voice comes from the other side of the shower curtain. "Any hot dreams of Newt Minnick?"

I yelp and cover my breasts with my arms, even though the curtain is opaque and Jack can't see me. "What the hell, pervert? You're spiraling into my *bathroom* now?"

"I could have appeared right in the shower with you, but I did not, because I have *standards.*"

"Whatever. You're afraid of the hot water."

Silence. I grin in spite of myself.

"Fine," Jack growls. "I hate hot water. But I also respect you as a woman."

"If you respected me as a woman, you would respect my request for you to quit popping up everywhere. You crossed a line this time, and I'm sick of you messing with me, getting into my head, bothering me constantly—you need to get out of my apartment and leave me alone."

"You want me to leave you alone for good? Permanently?"

"Yes," I say before thinking—and then my heart seizes up with a kind of senseless panic.

No reply.

"Jack?"

Nothing.

I drag aside the shower curtain, folding my body behind its edge and scanning the bathroom. He's nowhere in sight.

He'll reappear any minute.

Quickly I finish my shower and dress. Add a little makeup. Brush my teeth. I hurry into the kitchen, expecting him to be perched on the counter, or busying himself at the stove.

But he isn't. And he doesn't appear while I'm inhaling a microwaved breakfast burrito, or when I snatch my purse and keys and leave the apartment. As I lock the door, I feel a puff of chilly air on my neck and I spin around, my heart tripping—but it's only a neighbor letting in a draft from the stairway door.

"Good morning." I wave, smiling absently, while my lungs tighten.

Jack's not invisible to me. If he were here, I would see him.

He really left.

Good. Great. That's what I wanted.

I march to the stairway and descend to the first floor, my jaw set and my eyes burning—because I'm *happy* he's gone, because I'm relieved to no longer have a supernatural stalker.

Without Jack's presence, I should be able to focus and get a ton of work done; but an uneasy heaviness settles in my bones, slowing my fingers as I type emails and assemble some research that Alice requested. My brain itches with low-key anxiety—not because of Jack, but because I'm concerned about worsening reports of the fires out west, and I'm worried about the benefit, and I'm concerned that I've made a mistake, taking this job.

Lunch is a quiet affair at a bland chain restaurant that skimps on their sandwich fixings. I scroll through social media on my phone until my anxiety dips into full-fledged despondency at the state of my country in particular and the human race in general.

To soothe myself, I type in "Antarctica" and skim through photos of the breathtaking scenery—black rock jutting from pale beaches, regal arches of ice carved by wind and water, shelves of white with undersides of misty azure.

I almost died in that place. Why do I crave it? I'm entranced by the landscape, lured in like an unwary little fish wriggling nearer to the bioluminescence of a deepwater predator. Or maybe I'm only looking at the pictures because they remind me of a certain stalker ice god.

The afternoon is as dull and productive as the morning. By the time five o'clock rolls around, I've had it. I'm done with myself and my own attitude and Alice's snide remarks about how my 'special friend' didn't show up today.

I don't care. I'm *fine*. Okay, a guy walked out of my life because I asked him to—that's a good thing. It should not bother me this much, shouldn't suck the joy out of my world like this.

So what if he's gone for good? Mentally I subtract him from my days, my weeks—my life. I remove him from all future meals and evenings. All the surprise encounters are over and done with. I will not see him again, for months, for years, for the rest of forever.

It's fine. Now my life can get back to being clear and simple, with one primary goal—the preservation of the planet and its life forms, in as whole and healthy an environment as possible.

Unfortunately Jack's existence makes that goal more complex, because he's woven into the very fabric of what I'm trying to accomplish. His powers and my connection with him offer a unique opportunity, to do more good than I ever dreamed. Obviously humans have to do their part to conserve, recycle, etc. But having some magical help along the way? Not a bad thing at all.

Jack said I was helping him, just by letting him hang around me. Sure, I was serving in a supportive, secondary role, which I'm not a fan of—but hey, I'm always working as an employee for someone or other. I might as well help out one of Earth's magical god-beings, right? Especially if it achieves actual, visible good. This paper-pushing and lobbying and protesting I've been doing for years hasn't yielded many tangible results. And while my current busywork may be an important part of the process—*damn* do I want tangible results.

It's too late, though. Instead of working it out with Jack, setting boundaries and figuring out an acceptable way to coexist, I kicked him out of my life completely. What bothers me the most is the loss of a potential teammate in the fight against global warming. That's why my mind is sluggish and my heart is heavy. Not because I miss anyone's sparkling blue eyes and quick smile and inappropriate jokes.

We could have had such a successful *business* partnership.

When I pull into the apartment parking lot, I blow out a sigh because of course, someone has taken my numbered parking spot. Resignedly I drive to the back of the lot, hitch my bag over my shoulder, and slide out of the car.

"What if I left you for good?"

My breath catches, and everything inside me freezes.

Jack is sitting on the trunk of my car, one long leg hitched up and the other one swinging. He tilts his head, lifting his eyebrows. "What if I took you seriously and never came back? What would you do?"

I can't speak, because my throat is swelling, and the backs of my eyes are burning, sparking hot tears that swim across my irises before I can force them back.

Why am I crying? People don't cry about the return of their potential business partners.

"Emery?" Alarm lights his eyes, but it shifts quickly to a wicked satisfaction. "You missed me."

"Shut up," I choke.

"Emery." He slides off the car and wraps me in a fierce hug. I crumple against him for a moment, savoring his scent, and the chill hardness of his body, and the strength of his arms. There's a hint of wood smoke about him—he must have been working today.

"I was just thinking—" I sniff loudly and blink away more incoming tears— "that you and I could have a sort of—business arrangement. You say it helps you regenerate, when you're around me—so that's fine if you want to—hang out—sometimes. And I want to go with you to work sometime, to see what you do."

"A business arrangement."

"Yeah."

"If that's what you need."

I twist out of his arms. "It's what *you* need. I'm helping you out, doing you a favor."

"Sure, but you can't come with me when I'm working, Emery. I move fast, from point to point all over the globe, and when I'm in an area with wildfires, it's too dangerous."

"I could watch from a distance."

"It would have to be an extremely far distance. The smoke and ash affects the air for miles and miles around."

"I need to see it, Jack."

He rubs his jaw. "Fine. Sometime. But for now, don't worry about it. You have the day off tomorrow, right? Christmas Eve? I was thinking of taking you somewhere—"

But I shake my head. "I have to help out with prep for the benefit. I'll be busy most of the day. They'll give me a little time off in the afternoon, so I can get ready, but other than that—" I clap my hand to my mouth. "Oh my god. I don't have a dress! It's a formal occasion, and I completely forgot to buy something to wear! How could I be so stupid?"

"It's okay. You've been traveling, and they've kept you busy—"

"There's no excuse. It's sheer stupidity. And there's no time to find something now—"

"Hey." Jack catches my chin in his hand. "Do you trust me?"

"No."

He rolls his eyes. "Damn it, Emery. Do you trust anyone?"

"Maybe Karyl. That's pretty much it. People will screw you over the minute it's in their best interest. Even if you think they're your friends, they'll let you slide right out of their lives as soon as you become inconvenient."

His stare is half shock, half sorrow. "Is that what you think I would do?"

"I know it is. You're an immortal god-thing with a job to do—and if you don't die first, you'll get tired of fluttering around me."

His jaw flexes, hardening. "I guess I'll just have to prove you wrong, then. In the meantime, leave the dress problem to me. I'll need your measurements, though."

"I don't know them off-hand."

"Good." Eagerness sparkles in his eyes. "Then I'll get to measure you."

He's not kidding about the measurement thing. As soon as we reach my apartment, he creates a frosty measuring tape from thin air and orders me to stand still. I could object, of course, but I don't, and I refuse to let myself think about why I'm allowing Jack to do this.

"I should—take off some things—so you get more accurate measurements." I try to sound matter-of-fact, but my voice shakes on the last word.

"It's up to you."

My heart thunders as I unbutton my blouse and lay it aside. I slip off the dress pants too, reminding myself firmly that Jack has already seen me in my underwear and that it's *no big deal*.

While I'm undressing, Jack looks everywhere but at me, his cheeks flushed a delicate pink, like the petals of a pale tea rose. How long has it been since he was with someone?

"Ready," I tell him.

His eyes look a little glazed, but he approaches me calmly enough. He measures the breadth of my shoulders first, then the circumference of my upper arms. Next he takes the distance from my shoulder to my knee, and from my shoulder to my toes.

"Lift your arms, please." He glances up at me from under that shock of pale hair.

Breathless, I obey.

Jack wraps the cold tape around my waist first. It's fine. I can handle this. I'm not blushing at all, not one bit.

"May I?" Jack says, and I nod.

He holds my gaze while he sweeps the frosty ribbon under my arms and around my back, pinning it across my chest. My breasts react instantly to the touch, and an urgent craving races through me, tingling in my core.

He's so close I could kiss that pretty nose of his, or those eyelids rimmed with inky lashes. His eyebrows furrow slightly as he focuses on the measuring tape.

This is taking too long. I need to say something.

"How will you remember all the numbers?" Oh hell, why does my voice sound so wispy?

His gaze flicks up to mine. "Trust me, I'll remember." Is it my imagination, or is his voice a little huskier than usual, too? "Just one more thing."

The tape encircles my hips at their widest point, and his fingers, where he holds it together, are much too close to the crevice between my legs.

I can hardly stand still.

When he appeared on the trunk of my car, a door opened inside me. I think it was already open a crack, but it swung wider, clearing the way into a wild space of desire and delirium. I could step through it now—I could seize Jack by the collar of his frosty white shirt and haul him against me. But I'm still terrified of what he wants from me. Something he asked before—whether I want powers of my own—it nags at the back of my brain. What did he mean? What would that entail? Would I ever consider such a thing, even if it were possible?

The measuring tape vanishes, and Jack's fingertips graze my hip as he straightens. "I think I have everything I need now. I'll go place the order." Snow kicks up around him as he prepares to spiral.

"You're not staying for dinner?"

He turns back, and the snow settles onto my carpet. "Do you want me to stay?"

"Well, I—you popped up again, so I figured—"

"Emery." His fingers curve around my shoulder. "Do you want me to stay?"

"Does it matter?"

"It's the only thing that matters."

My heart jumps. "Like I said, I think we should discuss a business partnership. An arrangement where you spend time here, so your energy can replenish faster."

"I wish I knew why your presence has this effect on me," he says, and I turn hot all over at the words. He must notice my blush, because he smiles faintly. "Not *that* effect. The energy thing. It's similar to what I feel when I'm around the ice wraiths. You know they used to be like me and like Kheima, the one who made me. They have some residual energy, so they can help me a little with healing, like tiny batteries. But you—you're like a generator." He approaches and lays a hand on my chest, left of center, over my heart. I'm helpless and hot, thrilled and tense, while he closes his eyes and tilts his head like he's listening. Finally he shakes his head. "I don't know. I can't figure it out. Who were your parents?"

"I never knew my dad," I tell him. "But I'm sure he was nobody special. And my mother—she's anything but magical."

"Hm. I wonder if it's just *you*. Your passion, your drive. That intensity about you—" Suddenly he seems to realize where his hand is. I don't know what he sees in my face—confusion, embarrassment, craving—but he pulls away. "I'm sorry."

"It's fine." I'm not used to feeling all these emotions together. They block my internal channels, like chunks of ice clogging a waterway, and my usual reaction is to push away anyone who causes such an inconvenience. Maybe that's why so many people push me away in return. I squirm under the realization; it's more than I can dissect right now.

My own toxic behavior patterns aside—Jack's absence today showed me how much I like having him around, annoying though he can sometimes be. And somehow I find the courage to speak.

"Jack, I want you to stay for dinner. We can maybe watch something on TV, too. I like documentaries and travel shows, but other stuff is good too—crime shows, legal dramas—"

He presses cold white fingers across my mouth. "Anything you want. But first, let me put in the order for your dress. You can order us some food, okay?"

"Okay—"

But he's already gone.

I snatch my phone and hunt for an Italian place with good reviews, and I order him chilled gazpacho and chicken salad in lettuce cups, with creamy alfredo pasta for me. Then I race to the bathroom and wipe the shine of the day off my skin. Back to the bedroom again to scavenge my scanty wardrobe for something Karyl might label as *cute*. There's an off-the-shoulder top she bought for me, and a pair of thin, soft pants—comfy but sexy, too, because they hang low on my hips and cling to my butt.

The food arrives, but still no Jack. I place his portion carefully in the fridge and stalk the confines of the living room, chewing my thumb nail. I need to convince the ice god to get a phone.

When he finally whirls into the room, his hair is wild and his eyes stricken. "I can't stay," he gasps. "I have to go. The fire—it jumped the Continental Divide—she's back, and the humans are no match for her. I have to go help them."

"Take me with you!"

"Too dangerous." He's already disappearing again, and without thinking I fling myself forward and latch onto his waist. It's too late for him to shake me off, and I'm sucked away with him to some other part of the world.

13
A
STAR IN THE NIGHT

"The *hell*, Emery! I told you it was too dangerous!" Jack shakes me off, and I tumble into the scrubby bushes. The hill we landed on is dark, but the sky is alive, a dreadful ombre sweep of angry red and raw orange fading into gray and ebony. "You stay here. Stay. Do you understand? I'll come for you when I can, gods-damn you." He grips my arm and drags me to my feet, pulling me against him for a hard kiss. Then he whirls into the air, and the frosty wings appear at his back again. They don't look strong enough to carry him on their own, but a powerful current of wind and cold surges around him, buoying him upward. He sails into the night, a single frosty star in a world of wicked flame.

I want to scream after him, to tell him to be careful.

But now that he's gone, the terrible violence of what I'm witnessing overwhelms me. I sink down and crawl to the edge of the hilltop, where I can see the foothills and mountainsides swathed in fire. In some places the flames are low, muttering lines of orange creeping closer to homes and businesses; but further away, in the thick of the forest, the flames shoot high as multi-story buildings. Clouds of smoke, like massive heaping thunderheads, billow from the inferno, staining the night sky a sickening gray.

All those *trees*. All those houses full of carefully selected furniture, and treasured toys, and favorite clothes, and memories. The gardens tended with care. The playgrounds. The businesses, each one a dream, a plan, a future. The wild animals and the pets. The pain of it, the brutality—it crushes my soul.

Against the sheets of flame, figures move in the distance—firefighters like ants wielding thread-thin hoses, standing beside matchbox fire trucks. Their small streams of water are nothing to the raging blaze—nothing at all. A helicopter passes over a section of the fire, its belly releasing a flood of water. A small portion of the flames goes dark, but it's like cutting the big toe off a giant. They can't stop it.

Here and there, among the firefighters, misty blue-and-white dots appear, darting around in a frenzy. Ice wraiths. Maybe they're drawn to the fire by the memory of who they used to be, the balance they once helped to sustain. They are echoes of what they were, but at least they're here. At least they care. And when three tiny glowing entities separate from the inferno and charge a nearby gas station, the ice wraiths interfere, clashing with the fire wisps and pushing them back.

Off to my right, another flicker of movement catches my eye. The fire is bellying outward, eating toward a cluster of homes, and only a few firefighters are holding that part of the line. They don't notice a slim figure with frosty wings darting above them like an icy moth. But I can see him.

Jack Frost.

I wish I had binoculars—I need to get closer. I want to see what he's doing.

There's a ridge a little further to the right that juts out closer to the fire. I can climb over there and get a better view without being in too much danger.

Before I can make a move, the swelling bulge of the fire sucks inward suddenly, blown backward by an icy blast of wind from Jack.

I want to cheer and scream. I want to *help*. But I can't.

An ice wraith zooms directly in front of me, and I yelp, clutching my chest. "Oh my god. You scared me."

The wraith circles me, whispering mournfully. Another joins it, and another, and then three more. They flit past my back, swirl over my shoulders, and trail their icicle fingertips along my arms and across my cheeks.

It's oddly flattering that they are drawn to me like this. They clearly sensed my presence here and wanted to greet me, to be near me.

"You should help Jack," I tell them.

They sigh and whisper, ignoring my directive.

"Fine. I'm going to get a better view. You can stay or go, or whatever."

I struggle through the scrubby bushes and trees, down into a cleft and then up again. The shale and roots scratch my bare feet as I climb. Once I reach the higher ridge, I'm nearer to the inferno. Nearer to Jack.

He's whirling above the wildfire, icy rain spraying from his hands. Now and then he lands in front of the wall of flame and slams both hands forward, generating blasts of frigid wind that force back the blaze. I don't know what the firemen think of this invisible aid, if they even notice it. If they do suspect supernatural assistance, they probably keep their thoughts to themselves, or speak of it only in whispers to each other. No one wants to end up in a mental health facility for claiming that an invisible ice creature helps them fight fires.

Jack soars further away, hovering over the conflagration. And then he dives straight down into it.

A scream sticks in my throat.

What is he doing?

This man who hates hot water—he just plunged right into a towering thicket of flame.

An explosion of ice and snow shoots outward from the point where he vanished. A dark quenched spot spreads wider and wider, walls of ice driving ever outward. It's not just cutting off a toe—it's a severe wound to the body of the giant. Now there's only a ribbon of flame between the space Jack cleared and the threatened neighborhoods. Another helicopter passes along that strip of flame, quenching it with a deluge.

"Yes!" I hiss triumphantly, and the ice wraiths, who followed me up to the cliff, let out a twittering burst of song.

But then I look to my left again, and I raise my eyes to the mountains. The sheer scope of this inferno is baffling, incalculable. The firefighters will never be able to put it all out, not unless they get a full day or two of hard rain.

Jack keeps working, darting from one spot to another, shearing off the limbs of the fire with his walls of ice and blades of wind. He's like a dancer, soaring and diving and circling. But his dance is terrifying for me, because as much as I want him to protect the firefighters and the towns, I also want him to be safe, and whole. What if he gets scorched and charred again? What if he fades away into a wraith? The very thought sears my soul like a brand.

I sit on the lip of the ridge between the prickly bushes, my soft pants riddled with mulchy bits from the forest floor, my eyes stinging with smoke and my lungs aching almost as much as my heart. My knees hurt because every time Jack vanishes into the fire, I dig my fingernails into my kneecaps, tortured with unbearable desperation until he reappears.

And then he whirls into a particularly savage knot of flame, and he doesn't come out again.

Gnawing my lip, I lean forward, eyes fixed on the spot where I last saw him. "Where is he?" I say to the wraiths. "Can you see him?"

They echo my anguished tone, flitting around me.

"Go out there and *do* something!" I scream at them, and they recoil, blown backward by the force of my anger. Their whimpers waken a tremor of guilt in my heart, even as they dart away, toward the fires.

"They can't help," says Jack's voice from behind me.

I spring up and dart toward him—but then I pause. He's blackened with smoke, bracing himself against a tree as if he can barely stand. Where his sleeves have burned away, I can see bubbled skin and glistening red wounds. Just like last time.

"You're killing yourself." My voice is choked with tears.

"I have no choice."

"It's not fair. You need help."

"That's why I'm here. I can feel you, even when I'm out there." He jerks his head toward the blaze. "I think if I can be with you for a few minutes, I'll get some of my strength back."

"I don't want to be your generator. I want to help fight the fires."

"But you can't, without powers." He glances away as if there's something else he wants to say, but he's holding back.

Of course he's right. I'd be worse than useless out there. All I can do right now is support him, and although my feminist self revolts at the idea of playing the backup role, I care about him too much to let my pride get in the way. After all, everyone needs help sometimes. Jack and I seem to take turns assisting each other, and right now he needs me. It's my turn to do something for him.

"What should I do?" I look down at my hands.

"Just—sit with me." He sinks down to the earth, with his back against the tree.

Awkwardly I sit beside him, scooting in until my thigh touches his.

Jack closes his eyes and exhales deeply.

How is he still gorgeous, even with his soot-coated face? Tentatively I trace the angle of his cheekbone, leaving a white line in the wake of my fingertip. His lashes flutter open, and he looks at me with pain-glazed blue eyes.

My heart cracks. In all the world I want nothing more than to ease his pain.

Softly I place both hands on his shoulders, careful of the burns, and I lean in.

His lips taste like embers and ashes and smoke. I kiss him delicately, twice. He sighs, nearly a whimper, helpless and wanting; so the third time I kiss him harder, and I slip my tongue into his mouth. Past the bitterness of the ash is the sweetness and coolness I remember—the essence of him. The taste prickles through me like the tiny points of snowflakes, a tickling, teasing desire waking in all the hollows of my being. I am blue snow glowing white in the starlight, ice turned glittering and transparent under the moon. Eyes closed, heart open, I press my fingers to Jack's cheek and I kiss him with all my soul.

Sometime later, I realize that I'm kneeling between his legs, cupping his jaw with one hand while the other drifts down his chest. Where my knee presses to his crotch, there's an unmistakable hardness.

Flushing, I draw back. He asked me to sit with him, to lend him my energy; and like the nonsensical idiot I am, I decided it was time for a make-out session, and I turned him on in the process.

"I'm sorry," I mutter.

"Emery." He stretches out his arm. "Look."

He's still wounded, but the worst of the burns are no longer raw. They've scabbed over, as if he's days into the healing process. He grins at me. "You have magic."

"No, I don't."

"Humans can't do that, Emery. I've kissed a few since I changed, and they couldn't do this for me."

"Who did you kiss?" I ask, and then I shake my head. "Never mind. I don't have magic, Jack. I'm human."

"Right." He hauls himself upright again, tugging at the tightened crotch of his pants with a smirk. "Well. I should get back to work."

"Like *that*?" I wince at the bulge he's sporting.

"Are you offering to take care of it right now? Here? On the edge of a horrible forest fire where homes, lives, and workplaces are being threatened? I don't know about you, but to me that seems wildly inappropriate."

"No—I just—"

"Your concern is appreciated. I'll be fine. *For now*." At the last two words, his eyes flash with a raw desire that turns me hot. "You're blushing, sweetheart," he says, as snow erupts around his feet again. He ascends, sweeping the frosty wings that have reappeared at his back. "See you soon."

I hurry to the edge of the cliff so I can watch him sail into the fray again; and though I'm delighted that I was able to help him, I'm terrified, too. Terrified that he won't come back. Terrified because this is actual proof that something about me is different. Something inside me reacts with him, has a tangible effect beyond the obvious hard-on. It's weird, and scary, and fascinating.

As I watch the fire roar and advance, and writhe and retreat, I have to admire the skill of the humans who are fighting it. They have no supernatural powers, but they understand the movement of the hungry flames, and they counter as skillfully as possible, determined soldiers in a war against the roaring maw of nature itself. They've done a couple of controlled burns, and now they are working to keep the oncoming inferno from leaping those burnt strips. Jack assists with blasts of icy wind and sprays of sleet.

But behind it all, on the slopes of the mountains, the wildfire rises like a dreadful symphony, orange flames sucking upward into the sky, wavering and dancing and snapping like living figures.

There's a soft crunch behind me, a whispering crackle, and a wisp of wood smoke.

I whirl, scrambling for some way to explain to the approaching forest ranger or firefighter why I'm up here.

But the person emerging from the trees is not human.

14
THE
FIRE GODDESS

The being advancing toward me is woman-shaped, her lovely features highlighted in the glow of the distant fire. Her feet are bare, and wherever her soles press, the earth smolders. Her fingernails flicker with iridescent light, and her eyes shine ruby-red. She's naked, except for the flames that encircle her limbs, licking across her skin and lacing through her smoky hair.

Auxesia. It must be.

"Splendid, isn't it?" Her voice has the sinuous charm of flame, but there's a smoky rasp to it, too. She sweeps a hand outward, indicating the flames—an artist, proudly showing her work. "There is an incomparable purity to flame. I've not found anything so honest on this entire planet. The fire does not dissimilate, or flatter, or feign. It does not even desire. It simply consumes. That is its nature. And in its dark wake, life begins anew."

My body is frozen at the edge of the cliff, my every nerve tight with terror. *Run, run.* But there's nowhere to run.

Through my fear-cracked throat, I speak. "What about the life that is destroyed?"

"Unworthy life. Twisted and tainted by greed. Think about your race for a moment—really *think*. What are they but a squirming mess of parasites, consuming all that is good and soiling themselves where they sit? They are constantly seeking out conflict—wars at home, wars with words, blood and bombs and guns. Even the ones who claim to promote peace and tolerance are blinded by self-interest, salivating for newly imagined enemies so they can debate endlessly while the Earth is drained to the dregs. And you think I should pity this flabby, drowsy, dimwitted populace? That I should mourn as I expunge them from the surface of the planet? No."

"You want to wipe the slate clean, and see what results."

"Precisely." She smiles at me, and her teeth are like hot coals. "You have a flicker of understanding, at least. I can see why he likes you. I knew there must be someone—he has not battled me with so much energy and purpose for decades. Little Jack Frost, always so sad, so lonely, so determined. There was a fight, weeks ago, when I thought I had finished him. He cried, actually sobbed, begged me for a reprieve. Tried to advocate for his precious lost world. Sweet, foolish boy. He is a babe of two hundred years, while I have been watching this disease of humanity spread for millennia. Children cannot understand the choices that parents must make. They may seem cruel at the time, but there is always a good reason behind them."

"What of Jack?" My voice shakes. "If you burn the whole world, won't he die?"

She arches an ashy brow. "Of course."

"But without him, how can you hope to maintain the balance of your new world? Once the fires die, you will need someone to be your counterpart, to stir the weather and bring the seasons. You can't do everything with fire."

Her features shift oddly, like the ever-changing shape of flame. "The new world will have no need of seasons. There will be heat and warmth, always. The beings that rise from the ashes will be shaped to sustain life in the new reality."

"You want a world made in your image."

"And why not? I have waited, while all my brothers and sisters left the planet or remained at their posts only to fade away. I have consumed those who were too weak to take decisive action. And now, I am the only one left. The one true Goddess of this world."

My fists curl tight at my sides. My stomach is trembling and my lungs are spasming on the verge of true panic, but I lift my chin when I retort. "You're not the only one left. There's Jack."

"Yes, and *you*, it would seem." Her gaze turns malevolent. She's still a dozen feet away, but as she prowls a few steps nearer, the heat of her washes over me like a blistering tide. "If I take away his new toy, how long will the frost-boy last, I wonder?"

She cups her hands, crafting a ball of golden flame, hued amber at the edges. It's meant to kill me, but I can't help admiring it.

"It's beautiful," I murmur.

Auxesia looks up, startled. "Yes, it is."

I look straight into her eyes. "A shame that something so lovely should cause so much destruction."

The flames around her body lick higher for an instant. "Flattery, my love? You think I will spare you for the sake of pretty words?"

So she is susceptible. Lonely, and probably aching for companionship and admiration. Fine, I can play along.

"Jack has a human form," I reply. "I would love to see yours before I die, if you'll allow me."

Auxesia glances past me, out at the fires. "The boy is occupied—I suppose it couldn't hurt."

Her fire recedes, absorbed into her body, and suddenly she's a beautiful, curvy woman, perfectly proportioned, with full breasts, creamy thighs, and the face of a Greek goddess. Her dark hair flows rich and glossy down to her waist.

She's beautiful, yes. But there's a raging light in her eyes, the aching fury of a thousand years, and it sours the sight. She doesn't realize that she is as damaged as the humans she despises—more so, because she uses her incredible power to act on her hate.

"You could do so much good," I tell her softly. "Not all humans are worthless warmongers—some of us truly want change."

"But you've never been willing to yield your individual comfort for the good of all. The only thing humans care about is themselves."

"Not all—"

"Not all! Not *all*!" She spits a glob of fiery saliva onto the grass. To my relief, it dies out after a brief surge of flame—there's enough rock and earth around to prevent its spread. "I am sick of words. Sick of exceptions and excuses. I will have *change*, expansive and entire, and I will have it now."

A glimmer of blue light behind Auxesia catches my eye. Three of the ice wraiths have returned, their frosty garments tattered and smoking. Their fragile ice-blue faces are infinitely sad. Despite the way I shouted at them, they're coming to me for companionship and comfort—they don't seem to notice Auxesia standing there in human form.

Until she flares into flame again and grips two of them by their necks as they pass by.

The frost fairies scream for me, reaching out thin icicle-fingers, but Auxesia squeezes, and they burst into blue mist before I can voice a protest, before I can beg her for their lives.

The third wraith darts over to me, whimpering.

"Get Jack," I hiss to the wraith. "Go."

The creature shoots away into the smoky night.

"Clever girl," snarls Auxesia. "Pretending to care, to understand. All you want is your own agenda, your own pleasure. Have you let the frost-god put his icicle inside you yet? Have you convinced yourself that he cares for you? Trust me, little human, he has had dozens of others before you. He grows bored easily. Not much of an attention span, that one, once he's gotten what he wants."

"It's different with me," I whisper.

"Is that what you tell yourself?" Auxesia laughs. "No matter. You're dead anyway. I can't have you hanging around the boy, giving him hope."

She forms a globe of flame in her hands again. Maybe I can dodge it, but the next one, and the next? No way.

Yeah, I'm going to die.

Auxesia draws back her arm and hurls the fireball.

I weave my upper body aside, barely avoiding it. The skin of my shoulder feels raw and hot where the blaze shot past me.

Auxesia growls with displeasure and sends a flurry of sparks from her fingers, lighting the twiggy shrubs nearby and the dry grass at my feet. She molds a second fireball, winds up, and throws the streaking comet straight for my chest.

And then Jack is there, gliding between us, skating along an icy pathway that unrolls before him like a silver carpet. He slams a shield of solid ice against the oncoming fireball, and both the missile and the shield explode into shards and steam.

Icicles, sharp as death, shoot from Jack's arms and his chest and his hands, streaking toward Auxesia—it's terrifying, because I didn't know he could do that and my whole body is shaking, vibrating with the dread certainty that I almost *died.*

Auxesia blasts several of Jack's icicles into steam, but two of them shear through her body, leaving dark smoking holes. With a scream, she erupts into violent flame. She's a molten figure now, a shrieking inhuman torch streaming smoke. She melts his walls of ice as fast as he can throw them up against her onslaught. Jack circles her, flinging discs of ice with jagged edges, one after another, almost faster than sight. Most of them hiss into nothing as they strike, but one slices the side of her neck, and blood pours from her like lava.

Auxesia claps her blazing hand to the wound, and with the other hand she unfurls a twisting whip of fire that snakes through the acrid air toward me. I'm already coughing and singed, struggling to extract oxygen from the smoky air; I see the whip coming, and all I can do is dive for the ground and roll—

I roll right off the cliff.

Air whips around me and my guts turn weightless while I plunge down, down—I have a brief flash of my future self broken and splayed and spattered on the ground below—

A blast of frozen wind, a whirl of snow, and I'm crashing onto the carpeted floor of my apartment, with Jack's cold body a blessed weight on top of mine.

I'm gasping, and he's sobbing, kissing me frantically through his icy tears, feeling my face and my arms as if to reassure himself that I'm all there.

"Jack. Jack." I twist my fingers into his snowy hair, pulling his face up to mine. "I'm okay. You saved me. We're alive."

The agony on his face tears me apart inside. He groans, deep and broken, and only then do I realize that smoke is rolling from his back, and that I can hear the horrible sizzle of flesh.

"Jack!" I slither out from under him, and he collapses face-down.

The frosty wings that he generates for himself are gone—I think he can make another pair, so that's not what worries me. No, what turns my stomach is the blackened, bloodied mess of his flesh, from the nape of his neck to the base of his spine. In two places I can see the white of his vertebrae. When he dove off the ridge to rescue me, Auxesia must have blasted him with fire. She burnt him to the bone.

For a minute I feel like shrieking, panicking, melting into a flood of tears. But I can't. If I panic, if I let myself lose control, Jack will fade and die.

I have to be strong. I have to think clearly, and act quickly.

I drag him to the tub, stuff in the plug, and seat him under the shower head, with the cold water running. Thank goodness the water from the faucet is pretty near freezing on this winter night. It rushes over his back while he slumps, half-insensible, against the shower wall. It's easy to scrape off the tattered remnants of his shirt; I stuff the ash-covered rags into the bathroom trash can.

I have two extra bags of ice in the freezer, left over from the last time, so I dump those in with Jack. Then I strip down to my underwear and climb into the tub.

Sitting face to face with him, I settle myself astride his lap, with my body as close to his as possible. I kiss his forehead, his temple, his eyelids, his mouth. One kiss to the blackened tip of his poor scorched ear. A long line of kisses down his neck, to the cleft of his throat. I have never kissed anyone like this before, never. I've never felt this tender pain, this sweet ache that links my heart and my wellbeing to his.

When did this happen? How did this happen?

When did I fall in love with Jack Frost?

Maybe love is a moment of realization.

Maybe love is layers, paper-thin and sweet, accumulating like delicate honey-glazed sheets of baklava, until it's luscious and cloying, aromatic and irresistible.

Or maybe love is charred skin, and white bone, and torment.

When the tub is nearly brimming, I reach around Jack and turn off the water. Gently I wash his forehead, his cheeks, his jawline. I don't dare touch his back. Eventually I work out a position where he's lying nearly full-length on his back in the tub, with his long legs bent at the knees so he'll fit; and I sit at one end, cradling his head.

I can't kiss his mouth from this angle, but I stroke his forehead and face with one hand while my other hand cups his head. He's completely unconscious now, his face smooth and tinged with azure shadows.

"You should count yourself lucky," I whisper. "I'm not usually the cuddly kind of girl. I've never been one to snuggle after sex, either. More of a 'get it done and go' person. Although maybe that had less to do with me, and more to do with the kinds of guys I chose, and the overall experience." Why am I blushing? It's not as if he can hear me right now.

"I need you to get better," I murmur. "I think you might be my best friend. Don't tell Karyl, she'll be pissed. Although I think her wife is *her* best friend, so maybe she'd just be happy for me."

I trace the outline of his other ear, the undamaged one. It's beautiful, with pale blue hollows inside and a nearly translucent tip.

From time to time I adjust our position as my legs cramp under me. I don't dare leave him, but I manage to find a position where I can lean into the corner of the shower and catch a little sleep.

When I wake up, I'm uncomfortably clammy. Without the Chill I'd probably be borderline hypothermic from sitting in a bathtub of ice water most of the night; but as it is, I'm just damp and unhappy. I want to be warm, and dressed in dry clothes.

Slowly I shift Jack's head a little. He's breathing, slow and deep. When I move, his face turns inward, his parted mouth lightly grazing my breast through the bra. The sight of that proximity sends a ripple of want deep into my body.

Enough of that. Once again I'm faced with a long and challenging day of work after a night of monitoring a half-burnt ice god. This can't go on. Jack needs help—backup, followers, friends, a team—it's ridiculous that he expects to be able to do this on his own. I wonder if he's ever tried to recruit anyone. I wonder if it's even possible for him to create someone like him.

A couple of times, I've suspected that he wants *me* to join him like that— to become what he is. But he won't come out and say it, maybe because he thinks I don't like him all that much. Or maybe he doesn't like me well enough to want me around for centuries.

Maybe he's only interested in me because I can help with his power reserves, and his healing. And he's horny, obviously—who wouldn't be, living the kind of lonely life he endures?

It seems so painfully clear now. He's not in love with me. Why on earth would he ever love me? No, he wants sex, and an energy boost. I'm a useful tool and a stimulating diversion to him. Like Auxesia said—he's had dozens of others, and where are they now? He got bored and left them, and he'll do the same again.

Except that he took an almost-lethal fire-blast to the spine for me. And when we got back to the apartment—the way he cried and kissed my face—

He could have been crying from the agony of the burn. And he only risked his life to save his precious energy source. I'll bet he was kissing me to salve the pain from his own wound.

My reasoning carries the sour, familiar reek of truth. Did I really think, for even a moment, that someone as magnificent and breathtaking as Jack Frost could love me—*me*, an averagely pretty human woman of average intelligence and average talent, with boatloads of crummy family baggage and such a laser-focused one-track mind that I can't hold onto more than a couple friends at a time?

I am such an idiot. And *he's* an idiot. We're both idiots.

I climb out of the tub, dripping water. After tossing a towel onto the floor to sop up the puddles, I use the toilet and strip off my soggy underwear. I brush my teeth, but I barely apply any makeup, since I'll be coming back here to prepare for the party. My stomach flutters momentarily at the memory of Jack measuring me for the dress. I wonder what sort of dress it will be, or if he'll even feel like going to fetch it from wherever he placed the order. I'd better have a backup plan just in case. Maybe I can borrow Karyl's faux-fur wrap and put it over a sundress—but I know she'd kill me just for thinking it. Even I know that's a massive fashion error. I need a formal dress appropriate for December.

I cast a glance over my shoulder at Jack's limp form. He could wake up any minute; I should probably put some clothes on.

15

ALL I WANT

Alice keeps me busy toting boxes back and forth from our offices to the venue, helping with decorations, running out on last-minute errands. Halfway through the afternoon she disappears, but I keep working until our manager Sal tells me to go get ready. She's a nice enough woman, but I suspect my office-mate has given Sal the impression that we're sharing the workload, when in fact Alice keeps shoving most of it onto me. It's the kind of workplace dynamic that I would have expected from a regular business, but at a non-profit like ours, it seems particularly unforgivable. Shouldn't we all be pulling our weight, working together seamlessly as a team?

There I go, being an idealist again. Shaking my head at my own naiveté, I shove my way into my apartment.

The air inside doesn't have that Jack Frost chill to it, and when I step into the bathroom, he isn't there. The wet towel has been hung neatly over the shower curtain rod, along with the clothes I left on the floor. The pungent smell of smoke still hangs in the tiny space.

Trudging to my bedroom, I flip on the light and freeze.

On the bed lies a slim indigo dress, floor-length, its structured bodice frosted with silvery snowflakes and twining leaves. Along the hemline, more silvery flakes are sprinkled, interspersed with hints of sea-green beading. A strapless bra lies beside the dress, and a pair of strappy silver heels sit by the bed. On my pillow there's a soft gray wrap, like a wearable cloud; and beside it, a box.

Holding my breath, I approach the box and tip the lid open.

Inside, on navy velvet, lies a pendant shaped like an icicle, studded with tiny white gems, with earrings to match.

These look like actual diamonds. Genuine. Not crystal, or cubic zirconia.

I have never owned a diamond. Never even borrowed one to wear.

There are no designer names on any of the items, but the quality is undeniable. This is a very expensive ensemble, created just for me.

Limply I plop onto the edge of the bed. My fingers find Karyl's number almost automatically, and I lift the phone to my ear, still dazed.

Karyl's voice greets me. "Hey girl. You got that thing tonight, right? The benefit? Need me to do your hair and makeup?"

"I—maybe?"

"You okay?"

"Maybe?"

"Okay, yeah, I'm coming over. Be there in fifteen. What time is the party deal?"

"I need to be there a little before eight."

"Cool, we got time."

"But—" My brain is recovering, starting to form rational thoughts again. "You're going to do my hair? You haven't done my hair and makeup since college. Besides, you have a wife and a baby. You don't have time—"

"Hey. I've been busy, sure, but that doesn't mean you're off my radar, babe. You're family as far as I'm concerned. Speaking of which, you coming for

Christmas? Wait, scratch that—it's not a question. You're coming over here for Christmas. And I'll see you in fifteen for your makeover."

" 'Kay." I drop the phone and run my fingertips over the silky surface of the dress. Never in my life did I imagine wearing something this lovely, with such elegant accessories.

I'm still staring at the outfit, wondering why Jack would do this and what it means, when Karyl knocks at the door. I always know it's her—she does this crisp staccato rap, five beats in sharp succession.

The first thing out of her mouth is, "What are you wearing tonight?"

Without answering, I sweep my hand toward the bedroom.

Karyl gasps when she sees the outfit. "Damn girl! I didn't know trips to Antarctica paid that much!"

"They don't. This is from Jack."

"Jack? The pasty pretty dude from the airport? The one we had coffee with?"

"Pasty—that's not very nice. Sure he's pale, but—"

"So it *is* from him." She whistles. "What is he, a model? App creator? Bitcoin banker?"

"He's got family money." It's the best excuse I can think of.

"Okay. Okay." She turns to face me, her dark eyes piercing right into my soul. "He obviously likes you. More than likes you, I'd say. He's taking you to this thing tonight?"

"I—I don't know."

"Text him, girl!"

"He doesn't have a—his phone is broken."

Karyl frowns. "So the boy can buy designer rags, but he doesn't have a working phone?"

I give her an apologetic smile.

"Here's what we're gonna do." She places both hands on her hips. "I'm going to do your face and shape up that pixie cut of yours, and we're gonna talk about this boy."

I can't answer all her questions, especially not with her daubing and lining makeup all over my face, but I do my best, giving vague replies to anything I don't know, which is a lot. Guilt settles in my stomach, because I haven't really asked Jack much about himself—his likes or dislikes, the family he used to have. We mostly talk about me, or about magic.

"I can tell you like him." Karyl squeezes the straightener around a wisp of my hair, then tucks the stray lock deftly into place. "You keep turning all pink and fluttery."

"I do not. I'm not that kind of girl."

"Not 'til now."

My stomach thrills. Okay, maybe I am that kind of girl now. That doesn't change the fact that I'm still not sure how Jack feels about me, or how I would fit into his life.

Also why am I even thinking about fitting into his life? I barely know him!

"Don't laugh at what I'm going to say, please." I hold up a reproving hand to Karyl. "I'm only asking because I have literally no one else to ask."

"Well, now I feel real special." She grins wryly. "Go on."

"Is it possible to fall in love with someone in a few days?"

Her smile broadens, but then she reins it in. "Baby, I fell in love with Sarah in a few hours. It can take years to know some people, to get down to the depths of their heart, the nice and the nasty. With others—doesn't take long at all. And sometimes the universe steps in with a challenge, and people get a chance to show you who they really are, right off the bat. The way I see it, you can't help who you love, or how fast. The only thing you get to choose is whether or not to act on it." After a few final tweaks to my hair, she adds a spritz of hairspray to keep it in place. "Now for that dress."

The strapless bra fits perfectly. Jack must have checked the size on the one I left in the bathroom, and maybe he also consulted with someone who knows women's bodies. It's snug enough to be secure, but not so tight that I can't breathe properly. The dress glides over my body as if I was born to wear it, and once the necklace and earrings are added, I feel like a literal ice princess. Even the silver shoes fit me well, with a little adjustment to the straps.

When I walk out into the living room, Karyl claps. "Cinderella off to the damn ball! Now where's your Prince Charming?"

Suddenly I'm terrified that Jack will come swirling into the apartment and give himself away. "I'm just going to meet him there. You should go—thank you so much—"

She feigns a frown. "So I've completed my task as your best friend, and now you're shooing me out? I see how it is. A little makeup, a little advice, then out the door."

"You know you mean more to me than that." My throat tightens.

"I do. I'm just playing with you, babe." She squeezes my hand. "Well, this has been a nice break from mama duty, but I should get back. It's our first Christmas Eve with Darla. You best have a gift for that baby when you come tomorrow."

"I have gifts for all three of you." I've never been so grateful to my past self for planning ahead and buying the presents before I went on the Antarctic trip. "See you tomorrow. Merry Christmas."

143

"Merry Christmas, my love." She gives me a very careful hug, so as not to damage my look—though honestly it feels fairly sturdy—and then she slips out the door.

A relieved sigh wafts from me. Now Jack can't sweep in and scare the pants off my dearest friend.

The door pops open again, and Karyl leans in. "Um, Emery—somebody here for you." She stares at me very hard and mouths the word "gorgeous" before disappearing into the hallway. "Good to see you, Jack."

"Same to you, Karyl."

At Jack's husky voice, my stomach thrills again.

He appears in the doorway, his tall frame filling the space. He's wearing a sweeping dark blue coat that flows behind him, flashing glimpses of silver lining. His dress shirt is crisply white, with a faint glimmering pattern of snowflakes across the material. It looks designer-level pricey to me, as do the black pants encasing his slim legs. His boots have a ridiculous number of straps and buckles—they must take forever to put on. But I have to admit the overall effect is pretty damn sexy. It's also a little odd for a formal benefit. But I suppose no one will care, as long as he contributes cash.

And he's doing the rom-com freeze. Where the guy stares at the girl when he sees her in a fancy dress for the first time? Yeah. That's exactly the way Jack is looking at me, and I have to admit—I love it. I never went to a prom, and my exes never took me anywhere fancier than an Olive Garden restaurant.

"I imagined you in that dress." Jack's voice sounds raw, probably from smoke inhalation, but his face looks as flawless as ever. "But my imagination was obviously lacking, because you—you're so—you're sublime."

"Sublime?" I giggle.

"Beautiful isn't a strong enough word." He steps forward, and suddenly I'm burning up inside the dress, and my lungs draw tighter with every breath. Those eyes of his—they're mesmerizing, like the azure sweep of Antarctic ice. "You look glamorous," he says, "and graceful."

"Stop it," I whisper, because I'm blushing hotter and I don't want to sweat in this beautiful dress—

His hands slide over my bare shoulders, cool and soothing. "Relax. You'll do great at this thing. Everyone will be watching you now, admiring you."

Oh god. "Maybe I don't want that?" Maybe I'm going to have an anxiety attack, right now, in this exquisite dress, with this exquisite man standing in front of me, calling me *sublime*, of all things—

Jack examines my face for a second. "Okay then. Take the gown off and go put on those smoky clothes from last night—those pants that hug that cute little butt of yours, and the shirt that slides off your shoulders—did you think I didn't notice?" He winks. "You looked just as enticing in that as you do in this. Although, speaking objectively, this ensemble might be more socially appropriate for the event we're about to attend. Can you turn around? I want to see how your ass looks in this dr—" His words cut off as I smack him in the face with a pillow.

"I'm getting my camera," I growl, stalking into the bedroom. But I can't help the big stupid grin on my face, because he gets me. He switched from romantic earnestness to inappropriate teasing, and that's exactly what I needed—to be piqued just enough that my anxiety eased.

I love him.

Oh hell. I love him so much.

No. No. I can't think about this right now.

Focus on the benefit. Professional. Poised. Taking videos, networking. Eyes on the future.

With a deep breath, I return to the living room, where Jack is waiting with mischief in his eyes. "Emery, darling, would you kiss me again? I forgot my lipstick and I thought maybe I could borrow some of yours—"

"Hush." I sweep past him, out into the hall.

"Good goddess, look at that view," he crows. "I think I'll walk behind you all night."

"Do I need to hit you again?"

"Please. It's very exciting. Or if you have a knife handy, you could hold it to my throat. I hear that's considered romantic in some circles."

I stare over my shoulder at him. "What the hell circles do you hang out in?"

"The fun ones?"

Auxesia's word flit through my mind: *Dozens of women before you. He tired of them quickly.* When I speak, my voice is stiff as hard-frozen snow. "And which of your dozens of previous girlfriends—or boyfriends—held knives to your throat?"

"Dozens? No. Three girls, and no boyfriends."

I spin around, glaring. "Auxesia said you'd been with dozens of women. You expect me to believe you've only been with *three* women in your two-hundred-plus years?"

"Yes." His expression is open, honest, clear as the sea beneath the ice floes.

A door down the hall opens. Jack and I move toward the stairs together, our silence a mutual agreement to discuss this later.

146

He has a car ready—a sleek BMW, brand-new and all-electric. When I slide inside, I feel as if I've stepped into a spaceship instead of a car. I don't think I've ever ridden in something this fancy before. The sheer excess of the vehicle causes me a twinge of guilt. How much energy, how many resources went into its creation? But I quiet my own inner protest, reminding myself that at least it's electric. Cleaner. A step in the right direction.

Jack hops into the driver's side. "I'll drive there, but you get to drive back, okay?"

"What? Oh, no. I'm not driving this thing. What if I wreck it?"

"Insurance, baby." He slaps the dash. "No problem."

We glide out of the parking lot, heading for the benefit venue downtown, and Jack picks up the conversation as if we never ended it. "Now then, to answer your question in a little more detail—I've kissed about a dozen women, but I've only slept with three, all of them before my transformation. Even when I'm in my human aspect, there are telltale signs I can't disguise. I can't have sex with humans without them noticing that I'm different."

"So you must be—pretty horny then." I look out the window to hide my blush.

"I have two hands, don't I? I can take care of myself well enough." Maybe he means it to sound casual, rakish, but there's a hollowness to his tone that pierces my heart. "But I won't lie, I do miss being touched, or touching someone who won't fear me or give me away. Not that anyone would believe them if they tried to tell my secret—but they'd probably end up institutionalized and I'd feel guilty for ruining their lives. It's a whole thing." He laughs, short and mirthless.

I pity him, I do—but I won't sleep with him out of pity, or a one-sided love. If we're going to do this, I need to know what he feels for me, beyond the shadow of a doubt. How on earth am I going to figure that out?

Wait a second. I'm a scientist as well as a cinematographer. We figure things out all the time. Hypothesis, theory, control factors—then testing and observation. I've got this. All I need to do is apply science to matters of the heart.

Easy.

"I'm not going to sleep with you," I tell him. "Not ever."

His profile doesn't change, other than a faint tensing of his jaw. "I didn't really expect you to."

So far, so good. Time to hit the next pressure point. "I know you're only hanging around me to siphon my energy or whatever."

He sucks in a sharp breath. "Is that what you think?"

"Red light, Jack!"

He slams on the brakes and the car grinds to a stop just in time. Jack glares at me, breathing hard. "That's what you think of me? That I'm hanging around you wanting sex and healing energy, like some kind of incubus?"

"Aren't you?"

"No, damn it! Maybe a little, at first, but then—I thought we had something—that we were becoming closer friends. You said you wanted to work together—you *kissed* me, Emery. Not just once, either. I don't know what game you're playing right now, but it's not funny."

I've never seen him this angry. Is he mad because I shut down the idea of us having sex, or have I really hurt his feelings by questioning his motives?

So much for the scientific method. My test to discern his intentions only left me with more questions.

Silence drapes the interior of the car during the rest of the drive to the benefit. We're early, so the valet parking isn't happening yet. Jack finds a spot in the parking garage and stalks defiantly around the car to open the door for me.

I let him do it. Once I'm out, he slams the car door shut and faces me, his eyes flaming blue.

"Tell me you don't care about me," he says, low and fierce.

Blood pounds in my ears, fresh from my thundering heart. I didn't expect this. I know how I feel for him, but I can't say it out loud. Not yet. It would be too silly, too soon—speaking the words might shatter the emotion. And if I fear its fragility so deeply, how true can it really be?

I angle my face away from his. "I feel bad for you—"

"No! That's not it."

"I know we could work together, to help the planet—"

"No. Wrong again. Forget all that for a second. How do *you* feel, about me?"

Emotions churn inside me, unbearably powerful and confusing. "How dare you do this to me right before the benefit?" I shove him away with all my strength, and he stumbles back. "You know I'm anxious about tonight—how dare you add this stress to my plate? You think buying me a fancy dress gives you the right to pressure me? Back off!"

He tilts back his head and clenches his fists, groaning in frustration. "Okay, fair enough. I'm sorry. I meant for this to be a lovely night—I wanted to help you through it. Damn it—" He ruffles his pale hair wildly. "I screwed up, all right? Can you—can we just table this, for later? For now, we can be a couple of friends enjoying a nice event."

Desperation shines in his eyes, and the sight of it quells my anger. Slowly I exhale, nodding. "All right. Friends. But no more pressure."

"No pressure." He holds up both hands, palms out. "I'll be good, I promise."

But he still looks distressed, and I want the sparkle of mischief back in his eye. That's what I need tonight—confident, playful Jack—not desperate, passionate Jack.

I link my arm with his. "I never said you had to be good. Just don't ask me any hard questions."

"You got it." He sweeps his cool hand over my fingers where they rest on his arm. "Whatever you need."

16
THE
PEOPLE FAR BELOW

When we approach the entrance to the venue, I worry briefly about how I am going to explain my plus one and find a spot for him—but Jack has already secured himself a place on the list. In fact, he's been assigned a spot at one of the VIP tables, which means he has made a significant contribution to the benefit—and he somehow arranged for me to be seated next to him. I'm not sure how he got all that done in the limited time he had, without me knowing about it; but I suppose someone like him, with money and a couple centuries of varied experience, could make it happen.

I place my clutch on my assigned seat and take my camera out of its bag, eager to get some photos of the decorated room. The theme of the gala is "Winter Wonderland"—not original at all, but unfailingly pretty nonetheless. The round tables are festooned with frosty tulle, faceted crystal, and tall vases holding sprays of white twiggy branches and silver ferns. Strings of pearly beads and imitation crystals drape from the ceiling, twinkling in the light, and the string ensemble in the corner plays airy holiday music.

Jack inhales deeply, as if he's breathing it all in. "I love Christmas, don't you?"

"Uh-huh." I don't feel like explaining why the holiday doesn't hold the same charm for me that it does for others. "I've got to wander, and video, and network. Will you be okay?"

"You're going to leave me here to watch your purse?"

"Um—yes?"

"I'd rather circulate with you. I can be your arm candy." His smile, white and brilliant, proves his point for him. "And I'll help carry your camera bag, hold your equipment, whatever you need."

"Fine. Come along."

Alice bustles up to me, glittering in a red gown. "Emery, we've got a problem in the prep room. You need to go in the back and—" She hesitates, eyeing my gown. "You need to go and mop up. Could get a little messy."

Jack's knuckles graze the back of my arm, and I glean confidence from the subtle touch. "Actually, I was asked to take some video of the event," I tell her. "And I'm also supposed to network, meet people, and talk about my Antarctic trip to donors. So I'm afraid you'll have to take care of the cleanup yourself, Alice."

Gracefully I sweep away from her.

"Savage," Jack whispers.

"I don't understand why she hates me."

"She's jealous. You're talented, beautiful—you've traveled to fascinating places—you've got passion and interesting things to say, and she doesn't."

I want to protest that women aren't that petty, that he's stereotyping or assuming—but I know, deep down, that sometimes it's really that simple. Sometimes it boils down to pure jealousy, both professional and primal, in this case. And while I'd love to think that the human race has evolved beyond that, the sad truth is that we're as petty and ridiculous as ever. Despite Auxesia's flawed solution to the problem, she does have a point. The world is full of careless, ignorant, vindictive people.

The more I circulate and chat throughout the evening, the more disgruntled I become. I feel like a judgy Ebenezer Scrooge, outwardly smiling and conversing, while inwardly I grouse at the finery and the endless little excesses of the people around me. The guests must care about the preservation of natural resources, or they wouldn't be here, would they? Or are they only attending because it makes them look good, because it salves their guilt, because they need a tax write-off, or because they wanted to attend a fancy party on Christmas Eve?

"You're beginning to look dour," Jack says in my ear as we glide away from greeting yet another cluster of guests. "Anything I can do?"

"I'm just hungry."

"Well, you're in luck, because I believe they're going to start serving. Shall we sit?"

Two other couples share our table—a pair of charming businessmen who wear matching wedding bands, and a paunchy older fellow with a woman younger than me. The older guy keeps playing with the young woman's hand, touching her wrist and her palm, even reaching under the table once or twice while he leers suggestively. The rest of us pretend not to notice. Clearly the man paid well to be here, and I suppose his money is as good as anyone else's, even if he has the foul manners of one of my mother's boyfriends.

The food, at least, is delightful. And while most of the auctioning has been done silently, there's still the live auction to look forward to. Something about the competition and the high stakes of a live auction has always excited me.

I'm savoring the last bite of my cheesecake when Newt Minnick approaches our table. He nods curtly to Jack and lays his humid hand on my bare shoulder. "We're about to start the live auction," he says. "I'll do a short presentation first, so be sure to get some footage of that. You don't need to film the auction itself, though. Okay?" He squeezes my shoulder.

"I understand."

"Good. Enjoying yourself?" His hand slides along my skin, just a fraction—too slight a shift for anyone else to notice.

"It's all very nice, thanks." I shift away from his touch, but he follows the movement, maintaining contact.

"Wonderful. And you look stunning tonight, by the way. Just the person we need at the conservancy. A pretty face helps draw in them ducats! I had my doubts when Marian chose you—there were a couple other candidates on the table, with more experience—but she said we needed somebody young and photogenic around the place. Has she talked to you about posing for the website photos?"

"I—no."

"Ah, she'll probably talk to you about it after the holidays. Too expensive to hire models, you see. Better to use someone in-house." With a final caressing squeeze, he releases my shoulder. "Enjoy the rest of the evening."

My face burns, and I stare at my plate while Minnick saunters away.

I thought they hired me because of my skill with a camera and my passion for the cause. Not for my face. Tears sting the corners of my eyes.

Jack's hand presses against the small of my back, rubbing gently.

The two businessmen are off chatting at another table, and the older man is too enchanted with his date to notice Jack and me, so I let a tear or two fall quietly onto the crumbled crust of the cheesecake.

This clearly isn't the job for me. But if I leave right away, how will that look on my resume? I should try to stick it out for at least a year—endure

Alice's subtle needling and Minnick's not-so-subtle lusting. If I were braver, I'd leave right away. I wouldn't put up with any of it. But where would I go? What would I do? I need this paycheck.

"Emery."

I flick away the tears and drag my gaze up to Jack's face.

His mouth twists in a devilish smile, but his eyes are wells of sympathy. "Want me to freeze Minnick's dick for you?"

I choke on a laugh. "What is it with you wanting to freeze people's privates?"

He shrugs. "It's fun?"

"Have you ever actually done that to a guy?"

"No."

"Just as I thought. You talk a big game, but you're too nice inside." I tap his chest, over the crisp white shirt.

He catches my hand, his expression turning serious. "Emery, I want you to know—"

"Happy holidays, everyone!" Newt Minnick's voice booms through the microphone at the head of the room, startling me.

"I've got to film his little welcome speech," I whisper to Jack. "I'll be back."

Minnick's presentation takes about forty minutes and includes a good deal of ass-kissing and sly praise for himself under the guise of lauding the conservancy's accomplishments over the past year. By the time he winds down, guests are shifting restlessly in their seats.

Once Minnick is done, his co-director Marian steps up to introduce the auctioneer and the pieces for the live auction. I return to my seat to find Jack gripping his water glass, white-knuckled.

"Careful!" I stroke his fingers until they loosen. "You'll break it. What's wrong?"

"Nothing. I'm just excited about the auction."

Under the table, his knee is jiggling up and down wildly. The tablecloth is turning stiff and icy where his fingers rest on it.

"Jack!" I hiss at him. "Calm down. Geez."

A luxurious spa package goes first, followed by a two-day retreat in a mountain cabin. Then Marian steps forward again, while three men roll out a massive something, covered by a huge white sheet.

"This piece was donated just a couple days ago by a North Carolina artist who happens to be with us tonight. He presented this sculpture as an exclusive, one-of-a-kind tribute—" she consults a notecard— "dedicated to the adventurers whose passion and courage make the world a brighter place. Thank you, Mr. Jack Snowden, for your generous donation." She indicates our table, and Jack rises partway out of his seat to wave as the guests break into polite applause.

A wild thrill turns my insides to jelly. A sculpture? Donated by Jack?

"We will unveil the piece and give you a moment before we start the bidding." Marian moves back, and the men grip the covering over the sculpture.

As the sheet slides away, a collective gasp ripples over the room.

I don't know what kind of stone it is—marble, maybe? White, swirled with smoky blue in places. The figure is a woman on one knee, leaning forward, eagerness in every line of her body. She holds a camera with a long lens, but instead of looking through it, she's looking over the top of it, her eyes fixed on a distant point. There's strength in her face—a fierce purpose—but she's half-smiling, too, as if what she sees is wondrous beyond belief. The stony folds of her clothing sweep across her body as if wind is blowing them, hugging her curves without highlighting them. Her short hair is wind-blown as well, and so beautifully crafted that it looks real. Touchable.

The woman is me.

I know it when I look into her face, and the thought is confirmed when both Minnick's and Alice's heads swivel my way.

I don't know when Jack had time to create this. He must have been working on it since the day I fell into his cave and woke him up; and it's quite likely that he used magic to speed the process along.

I'm glad he did, because now I have the answers I was searching for earlier tonight.

Love gleams in every line of that sculpture. This is how Jack sees me—not as a purveyor of magical healing, or a sexualized object. In this piece of art I am strong. Adventurous. Visionary. It's as if he reached down into my soul and extracted the best part of me, and then placed it on a pedestal for all to see.

He loves me.

The skilled fingers that crafted the sculpture are drumming a nervous rhythm on the table beside me. Those hands showered sleet onto forest fires, helping to save countless lives and homes. Those fingers endured blistering burns, caught me when I tumbled from the cliff, made dinner when I was hungry, brought me coffee when I was tired.

The bidding is skyrocketing, eager hands lifting one after another all over the room. I don't hear the final number because I have collected Jack's hand in mine, and I'm telling him, with my eyes, how I feel.

"You're coming with me. Right now," I whisper, grabbing my purse, wrap, and camera bag.

"Hell yes," he whispers back.

We rise together, unnoticed amid the flurry of excited comments about the sculpture, and I draw Jack out of the meeting room and down the hallway. There's another hallway branching off to the left; it's gloomy and half-lit, and I pull him into it. Then I drop my bags, grip his ridiculous beautiful coat with both hands, and drag his face down to mine.

The kiss is ice-white fire, searing through my nervous system. We are galvanized, our bodies sucked together, not a sliver of space between us. Jack cups the back of my neck, his breath eager in my mouth. I remember what he said, about yearning to be touched, and I slide my arms under his coat, around his torso, sweeping them up across his back and then down to his waist. I am unleashed, wild, free-floating, crushing myself harder into him.

Then I break away so I can look into his eyes—his sweet, hopeful eyes. "I love you."

"God, I love you," he answers, tightening his grip on me. His kisses are a frenzied staccato against my lips.

"Jack!" I slip my fingertips between our mouths. "Take me home."

"But—the benefit—"

"I don't give a damn."

He grins. "Yes, ma'am."

Quickly I pick up my things. There's a whirl of snow and ice—that odd feeling of dissolution and reassembly—and then we're in my apartment—in the living room, not the bedroom. Maybe he didn't want to assume that I planned to sleep with him. Sweet man. I'll soon dispel any doubts he has.

"Take the coat off," I order, laying aside my wrap and bags. He sweeps off the coat and tosses it aside. The dress shirt underneath is surprisingly silky to the touch, and its texture only heightens the spiraling need inside me. Jack's hands graze my waist and lower back, drifting down to my rear. He hesitates, but I press closer to him, encouraging the touch, and he cups me tighter, releasing a satisfied sigh. The slide and squeeze of his hands, shifting the slinky material of the dress over my skin—it's exquisite, overwhelming. I'm tingling all over, trembling with need.

"You have too many clothes on," I tell him.

"So do you."

Slowly we move apart, eyes locked on each other like a pair of predators circling the same prey. By the time I manage to slither out of my dress halfway gracefully, Jack has his shirt and pants off. He's just wearing boxers now, and they do absolutely nothing to hide how much he craves me.

For a second I panic. I haven't had sex in a long time; and when I did, it wasn't always great. Sometimes I didn't even feel like doing it, but I went along with it anyway because that's what a girlfriend does, right? At least that's what I thought, until Karyl assured me loudly that I had every right to say 'no,' anytime I didn't want sex.

This time I want it, a hell of a lot. But I'm no pristine frost goddess with flawless skin.

"You should know that I have some—issues," I mutter. "My nipples are kind of wonky, and there's this weird mole on my butt—" What am I even saying? Am I *trying* to turn him off?

Jack laughs. He approaches me, his fingers gliding along my arms, and he tucks his mouth against my ear. "You think I give a shit about any of that? You could be covered in scars or scales and I'd still want you."

God help me, I think he actually means it. "Do we—do we need birth control?"

"No. Elemental gods like me can't reproduce with humans."

"Are you sure?"

He draws back, looking into my eyes. "Are *you* sure? Because if you're not, we can sit on the couch and watch Netflix or something. Or I can leave, if you want."

"No, I—" I bite my lip hard. "I want this, but I'm nervous, Jack."

He chuckles. "So am I. Haven't done this in two hundred years."

"Oh. Right." Confidence flows back into my heart, warming me, loosening the tension in my limbs.

"Yeah, it's all good." He kisses my forehead. "We'll figure it out together." One of his fingertips traces the curve of my strapless bra, teasing, tempting, slipping just beneath the edge.

"For fuck's sake, take it off," I whisper.

He grins. "You don't usually swear like that."

"I save it for special occasions."

He reaches around the back and unhooks it—lets it fall. "You're so warm," he whispers, his cool palms cupping the soft swell of my breasts—and then he ducks in and kisses one, then the other. My neck arches back reflexively, and I close my eyes.

"Am I too warm?" I gasp.

"Not at all. Come here." He hooks a couple fingers into the waistband of my underwear and pulls me against him.

We're kissing again, his tongue a sweet chill over mine, his mouth deliciously soft. Another part of him is deliciously *hard*, and rubs against me through thin cotton between us. The friction is so tantalizing I can't help writhing against him.

"I'm sorry I'm not hotter," Jack murmurs against my lips.

"You're plenty hot," I respond breathlessly.

"No, I mean—human men are hot-blooded, so—"

"I get it. But you don't feel ice-cold there, just kind of lukewarm. Will I be too hot for you, inside?"

Jack laughs, gripping my hips and pressing me tighter to him. "I may be cold-blooded, but I'm not made of ice. It won't melt, if that's what you're worried about."

"Okay, we need to stop with the apologies and the questions. Just shut up and kiss me, idiot."

Chuckling, he gives me a slow, sensuous kiss, then catches my lip with his teeth and tugs gently before looking me in the eye. There's so much lush sin in that blue gaze of his, under the sweep of those dark lashes. I can't wait any longer.

"Cut these off," I hiss at him, tugging at my underwear. Sharp icicle tips emerge from his fingernails, and he slices away the panties. He glances at them where they lie on the floor, and his cheeks turn adorably pink when he sees how wet they are.

"My bed," I whisper.

On the way, he sheds his last scrap of clothing.

17

NOT ALONE

My ex Declan seemed to think I should climax from his mere presence; he never bothered to learn how to help me get there. My other ex Sam took a little more time with me, but he always finished within ten seconds himself. Not nearly long enough, in timing or physical dimension.

With those experiences haunting my mental space, I can't help a resurgence of nerves as I back toward the bed, my fingers laced with Jack's.

How will he want to do this? And how fast will it go? How much can I ask of him? And how—

Jack picks me up bodily and tumbles me onto the bed, rolling onto it himself and tangling his limbs with mine. He kisses my cheeks and my nose while I laugh in helpless surprise.

"You were thinking too much," he says, smiling.

I try to respond, but the hard length of him is tucked between my thighs, exactly where I need it, and the words on my lips fade. My hips surge, wakening a wild flutter of sensation through my core, and Jack's eyes close, a moan slipping from his mouth. I move again a few times, my hips bucking against his, until he pulls away and nudges my legs apart, kneeling between them. With his frosty shock of hair, his sharp cheekbones, and his lean muscled body, he looks like a magnificent frost faerie; and my breath catches at the realization that he loves *me,* that he is aching to please *me.*

His long fingers touch me tenderly, exploring, experimenting. He's not skilled at this, but he watches my face, keenly analyzing my reactions, and whenever he elicits a squirm or a whimper, a sexy little smile hovers over his mouth.

Part of me doesn't like being spread so wide to him, letting him look at me so openly, explore me so boldly. I'm too vulnerable now, stripped of every defense. Bared to his judgment. I'm giving him the ability to hurt my heart like others have hurt it, to sear and scar me. To reject me.

When he backs further down the bed and kisses my inner thigh, I panic. Is he about to do what I think he's about to—

A wet, sweet tongue circles delicately over me, and I want to say that he should stop, that I've never allowed anyone to do this to me before, and that I'm not about to start now—but I'm sinking into a limpid, quivering pool of bliss and I can't. I can't form words anymore. There is nothing but the gentle pressure of his fingers holding my hips, and the lascivious glide of his tongue.

There's a soft kiss, and a little suction, and that nearly does me in. But he stops, and kisses his way up my stomach, along my neck, back to my mouth. The kiss he presses to my lips is tender and refreshing, like cool water on a burning summer day. Like snowflakes on flushed skin.

He's slipping inside. It's easy, and perfect—not a hint of pain or tightness on my part, and I realize with sudden, broken joy that *this* is how it should be. How it's supposed to feel.

His head tilts back, and the beauty of him is nearly enough to send me over the edge. But then he *moves,* and I arch off the bed, wrapping my arms around his body, trying to get nearer, trying to pull him deeper into myself.

Jack braces himself on his left arm, his muscles swelling gloriously, and with his thumb he teases me closer, closer—

A breathless shriek escapes me as a piercing bolt of white-hot pleasure arches from my center through my entire body. Aftershocks follow, thrilling me senseless. Several deep thrusts later, Jack cries out and presses his forehead to mine, panting, while a delicious coolness bathes the inside of me. He shudders all over, and when I open my eyes, snow is falling in large, soft flakes from the ceiling of my bedroom, and the light fixture is coated in lacy frost. Icicles have sprouted from the bedframe and the carpet.

I don't mention any of it. I hold the cool hardness of his body against the warm softness of mine, and I close my eyes to everything else.

At some point we must have snuggled up to sleep, because when my eyes flutter open, the room is pitch black. Jack's arm is flung across my stomach. He must have reverted to his magical form, because his skin is glowing faintly, a pale light like snow beneath the moon, and the tips of his ears are pointed again. His white hair practically sparkles. I touch a lock of it, sliding it through my fingers.

Before now, I never understood how people could want to have sex all night long. I suppose technically they don't mean non-stop sex all night long— but all night long with breaks in between? That's something I think I could do.

I wriggle closer to Jack, tracing his jawline with my fingertip. Do I dare wake him? Would that be too presumptuous, too needy? Will he think I'm greedy or slutty for wanting more?

"Jack," I whisper in the dark.

"Hmm," he mumbles. "What time is it?"

"1: 35."

"M'kay. Merry Christmas." When his eyes blink open they glow with an azure luminescence. "I have a surprise for you."

"Oh really?" My hand delves into the space between us, wandering along his stomach. Something about the smoothness of his skin and the grooves of his abs is deeply satisfying to me. Then my fingers graze the part of him I was looking for, and it stiffens under my touch. "I love my surprise."

"That's not the surprise," he growls, burying his face in one of the pillows. "You'll need an overnight bag for the surprise."

"You're taking me somewhere?"

"Yes."

"But I have plans for Christmas dinner, with Karyl and her wife, and the baby."

"Oh." He lifts his head, and I can barely make out his frown in the shadowed room.

"Did you think I would be a poor little lonesome thing on Christmas Day? That I didn't have friends?"

"Not exactly." His tone is vaguely apologetic. "But could you maybe tell them that you have plans with me?"

"I think so. They have family coming anyway, so they'll have plenty of people around the table. I suppose I can let you spirit me away. Are you taking me back to your ice castle?"

"The operative word is *surprise*," he says. "Which means I'm not telling you our destination. Now are you trying to start something here, or can I go back to sleep?"

"You're grouchy when you wake up."

"I thought you knew that about me. After all, you were the one who woke me up the first time we met." He rolls onto his back with a sigh.

"Fine. Go back to sleep." I flounce over in the bed, a little frustrated—but I'm smiling, too, because I'm in bed with him, and he has a Christmas surprise for me.

Oh hell—I didn't get anything for him.

Jack moves closer, his chest pressing against my back. His cool hand slides between my legs. "Too late. You already started something." He takes my earlobe between his teeth, and I shiver with delight, curving my arm up to stroke his hair.

"You sure you're not too tired?" I whisper.

"Too tired? Impossible. I've been pining for you since I first saw you." He kisses the sensitive hollow below the corner of my jaw.

"Pining, huh?"

"Yes, pining." The chill of his breath whispers across my neck while his fingers move in slow, tantalizing, mind-melting circles. "To long deeply for, to miss, to desire to the point of pain."

"I didn't know you felt that strongly."

"I held back, because you weren't ready."

"It's hard for me, giving in." My voice is barely a murmur. "To me, caring means getting hurt. It always has." My mother, my exes, so-called friends in college, my new coworkers. A question slips out, more plaintive and pitiful than I intended. "Are you going to hurt me, Jack?"

His body tenses, and he presses a kiss to my shoulder blade. "I will do everything I can to avoid it."

It's an honest answer. No false promises, no extremes.

"Does this hurt?" he murmurs, moving his hand up to caress my stomach.

"No."

"And this?" His fingers circle my breast.

"No." I'm trembling, aching, completely unfamiliar with this side of myself. I'm still a little uncomfortable with it—can scarcely believe that I'm giving myself so completely to a man I met just days ago.

"And this." Jack's fingers return to the area they were tending earlier. "Does this hurt?"

"Hell no."

After a few more minutes, when I'm whimpering and wordless with need, Jack curves his body around mine and joins with me again. We shift our limbs, working out the best angle. This time, my release is a gentle flood, a surge of mellow delight, dreamy and tranquil in the quiet dark. Jack moans softly against the nape of my neck, his sharp teeth grazing my spine. Then he tucks an arm around my waist and pulls me tight against him, and we sleep that way until the sun glows through the cheap blinds covering my window.

Jack insists on making me an omelet with the bits of this and that he finds in the fridge. Meanwhile, I text Karyl about my new plans for the day, with apologies and promises that we'll stop by briefly to drop off the gifts before we leave.

"Girl. Of course you should go with him!" she texts back, with many enthusiastic emojis. "I'm thrilled for you. You get that cute butt!"

Blushing, I text, "I already did. Last night. Twice."

She sends a row of wide eyes and then a GIF of some anime girl jumping up and down. "YOU WILL TELL ME ALL ABOUT IT LATER."

"Maybe." After setting the phone aside, I toss some items into a bag, focusing on clothes that I can layer, since he hasn't told me where we're going. I add toiletries as well, grumbling internally over the fact that Jack doesn't sweat, or need deodorant, thanks to his supernatural sweetness and frostiness. Then I remember the faint coolness of his release inside me last night, and I wonder, for a naughty moment, how he would *taste*.

I blink the thought away. By the time I finish packing, Jack has already chilled his omelet in the freezer, and mine is fresh from the pan. He's practically bouncing with excitement, a wide smile on his face. My cheeks would be tired of grinning by now, but he seems buoyant with joy and energy. It's adorable.

"Eat up!" He passes me my plate. "It's already ten o'clock."

"It's Christmas morning, Jack. We should be taking it slow. Drinking hot chocolate or some such crap."

"Ew." He grimaces.

"Fine, a nice cold chocolate milkshake for you." Propping my butt against the counter, I take a bite of breakfast. I feel strangely, delicately happy, terrified to let myself be too joyful because then something is sure to mess it up. My skin feels warm and soft and alive, and there's a pleasant sensation deep inside me— the afterglow of satisfaction. I don't typically crave sex that often; surely, after last night, I am thoroughly sated. Still, when Jack sidles up to me with a grin and bumps his hip lightly into mine, a tremor of desire trickles through those secret spaces. And my heart pulses extra hard once or twice, a tightening surge of happiness just because he's here, because he exists, and he loves me.

We eat companionably, side by side, while Jack eyes my apartment. "You don't have any Christmas decorations."

"No. I'm not big on that stuff."

"Nothing I can't fix." Setting his plate aside, he steps forward, planting his feet with purpose and flaring out his hands. Tendrils of ice flow from his fingers, twisting together into the shape of a frosty Christmas tree trimmed with globes of snow. A flick of his hand, and rows of icicles lace themselves across the window, splitting the sunlight into rainbow shards that fleck the walls.

"It will all disappear when we leave," I tell him.

"Yeah, but it's pretty, right?" His blue eyes sparkle at me.

His grin is contagious, and I smile back. And then I feel it—that twinkling joy the songs talk about. That sense of specialness and family and holiday.

"I think you've infected me with the damn Christmas spirit." I poke his shoulder with the handle of my fork, not the tines, because he's wearing the same shirt from yesterday, and it looks fancy enough to be dry-clean only or some nonsense like that. I don't want to get cheesy egg bits all over it.

"I have another dose of infection planned," says Jack, "if you ever finish that omelet."

Putting the last bite into my mouth, I set the plate in the sink. "Let's go."

First we drive Jack's rental car over to Karyl's house to drop off the gifts and say a quick "Merry Christmas." She gives me a tight hug and then waves us off eagerly. "Go on, you two! Go have some wild holiday fun!"

After returning the car to the rental place, we spiral back to my apartment to pick up my bag.

I've pictured a hundred different places where Jack might take me. Munich's Christmas market. London. Paris. Tokyo. A tropical island—though honestly I can't envision Jack lounging on a beach in the sun. I can just see his lip curling, hear his confused tone: "*Why* would you want to lie on hot sand?"

He could be taking me to a cozy mountain cabin, or a penthouse in New York City, or back to his ice castle. We can go literally anywhere. The freedom of instantaneous travel without expense—I don't know if he realizes what a privilege that is.

Swinging my overstuffed travel bag onto my shoulder, I lock both arms around Jack's torso. He has a bag too, and he shifts it aside so it won't bump my arm. He kisses the top of my head, then my ear, and when I look up he captures my mouth eagerly, inhaling as if he wants to breathe me in.

And then we're whirling away, dissipating into whatever magical space he travels through when he spirals. When we reappear, still locked together, I have to close my eyes and breathe slowly until my body acclimates to being solid again.

"It doesn't get any less weird," I tell him. "Any idea what it does to a human body, doing that over and over?"

"No." Concern shades his voice. "I hadn't thought about it. I guess I've only done it once or twice to people—never as often as I have with you."

I press a hand to my roiling stomach. "As much as I want to travel, we might have to save it for very special occasions."

"Understood." He runs his hands along my arms. "You okay?"

"I will be." I sniff, and my eyes pop open. Past the snow-fresh scent of Jack, there's another smell—oddly familiar.

Rotting leaves, a hint of moldy sourness, and stale smoke lingering in the chilly air.

We're in a thicket of skinny trees that are still clinging to a few of their shriveled brown leaves. Through their branches I can see blocky whitish structures.

I push away from Jack and stumble out of the trees onto hard-packed dirt studded with bottle caps, crumpled scraps of soggy paper, bits of rotting boards. Ahead sits an ivory mobile home, its lower siding stained with red-brown dirt. The steps are half-sunk into the ground, and someone has set a crate on top of them to bring them up to the level of the door. The windows are boarded up, like they always used to be, to keep the light out and the heat in. A tumble of boxes, wooden slats, pipes, and dingy folding chairs clutters the space beside the steps.

A few feet away there's a metal lounge chair with blue plastic slats. In its armrest cup-holder is a clear cup, half-filled with water and discarded cigarette butts.

There's no snow anywhere, which is to be expected. Alabama doesn't generally get snow on Christmas Day.

"Jack." I speak his name very calmly. "Why did you bring me here?"

"This is your home, right? Where you grew up? Where your mom lives? I looked it up... I..." His voice trails off as he leans around to look at my face. "I thought it would be a nice surprise—humans are always wanting to go home for Christmas, right?"

My sinuses prickle, a warning of oncoming tears, and my lungs tighten into panicked fight-or-flight mode. "Not always, Jack. Not this human."

"Oh hell."

I pinch my lip between my teeth and sink my nails into the flesh of my palms.

"I'm so sorry, Emery. I didn't realize—I should have asked—"

"Stop it." I lace my fingers with his. "You were trying to be sweet. It's okay. We really haven't known each other very long—we can't be expected to know each other's baggage."

He looks at me earnestly, his eyes a soft and sorrowful blue. "I want to learn everything about you."

Inwardly I squirm, shrinking from the necessity of telling him all the sordid details of my childhood. "Maybe eventually."

"I'm sorry."

"Stop apologizing. Let's just get out of here before she—"

Right on cue, the door of the trailer squeaks open, and my mother appears. She's very obviously braless under one of the silky slips she wears like dresses.

The long, baggy sweater she's got on over the slip does nothing to conceal her chest or protect her thin legs against the cold.

My mother is all leathery skin and high cheekbones. Her lips are seamed with wrinkles from years of puckering around cigarettes. Her hair straggles out in clumps and frizzy spikes, pinned in odd places by sparkly dollar-store barrettes. A big poinsettia clip by her temple is her sole nod to the season. She's tapping a pack of cigarettes against her hand, her lighter pinned between two fingers.

"Well, fuck me," she says.

18

MERRY CHRISTMAS, EVERYONE

I never buy my mother Christmas presents. But of course Jack did—one of those gift packs with lotion and body wash and fluffy slippers. My mother squeals and simpers, stuffing her feet into the slippers at once and lathering her veined hands with the lotion. She's effusive with Jack, all welcoming smiles and season's greetings, while she barely says a word to me. Jack put my name on the gift tag, too, but Sandy knows I didn't buy it. Why should I care, when she never did? Half the time, she was too drunk to remember to buy me a gift. She'd stick a magazine and a pair of socks in a plastic bag and call it a present—or she'd have a fit of guilt the day after Christmas and buy me several large toys on credit—which we would then have to return because she couldn't afford those *and* her cigarettes.

"Sorry to drop in like this," Jack repeats for the dozenth time. "We thought we'd surprise you."

"I'll bet you did. It was your idea, wasn't it, gorgeous?" My mother prods his shoulder. "Em was never one to plan anything fun. It's always work, work, work with her. Money, money, the climate, the environment, blah blah blah. Me, I'm more the YOLO type. How about you, handsome? You like fun?"

Jack glances at me desperately. I lift my eyebrows and cross my arms. I'm not helping him out here. He wanted to surprise me? Fine. Now he gets the full, undiluted Sandy Caulfield experience, complete with inappropriate flirting. Once she gets drunk, she'll likely proposition him right in front of me, like she did with Declan the one time I let him meet her. I think Declan would have taken her up on it, too, if I hadn't shut things down quick. Knowing Declan, he probably thought it was kinky. Jack, however, looks appropriately pained. He's *so* not ready for this kind of human interaction.

"Sure, I like fun," he says feebly. "Got any board games?"

My mother squints at him, like she's trying to figure out if he's joking. "I've got 'Quick and Dirty,' 'Loaded Questions,' and UNO. Might be an old Monopoly game somewhere, but it'll be missing some cards."

Jack clears his throat. "What were you planning for Christmas dinner? I could help you cook—I brought a few things along since we just dropped in."

"Speaking of that—y'all have a car? I didn't see one."

"We got a lift," I intercept before Jack can respond. "And I assume you're doing the usual frozen pizza with a few bottles of wine? We can head out now. Don't wanna cramp your style, Sandy."

Her features sharpen. "Would it kill you to call me 'Mom'? This one," she shrugs helplessly, turning to Jack for sympathy. "No respect. She never has respected me, probably never will. Maybe you'll be good for her. You know how to be polite. Sure, you can fix us some Christmas dinner, sweetie. I got a little matchbox of a stove here, but pull out what you brought and let's see what we can do."

And that's how I end up sitting on the ugly rust-colored couch, watching dumb sit-com reruns on TV and trying not to inhale too deeply lest the cigarette-tainted air make me gag. Meanwhile, my mother and Jack converse while they work in the tiny kitchen area—or rather, my mother talks while Jack prepares the food. At first I listen anxiously, fearful that he'll give himself away—but my mother primarily talks about her favorite subject, herself, so he doesn't have to do more than throw in an occasional comment.

My mood is growing steadily darker. I did not want to spend Christmas— or any other day—in the reek and clutter of this trailer, with memories gnawing at my mind. Now that we're here, I don't see any way out of this, and it pisses me off. I was just starting to feel a hint of seasonal magic, and then Jack had to go and ruin it all with his damn dreadful surprise.

A normal human person would have asked me about my family first, would have felt out the situation before making plans. But Jack isn't normal or human, and he hasn't had a relationship in a couple centuries. I can't really blame him for not thinking it all through and not following social protocols. The idiot thought he was being sweet. He probably thought I couldn't afford to travel to Alabama, or that I didn't have time since the benefit was on Christmas Eve.

At least he had the foresight to bring food with him, or we'd have been stuck with frozen pizza or pork-n-beans from a can. The beautiful dummy packed his bag with thick steaks, and a few potatoes, and some asparagus. It's a simple meal, but delicious; and when we sit down to eat, I can't help but enjoy the flavors in spite of the stale, smoky air. There's no dining table, just a card table with metal folding chairs. My mom has had prints of "Blue Boy" and "Pinkie" hanging on the wall of the eat-in kitchen for as long as I can remember—says it makes the place more sophisticated. Unfortunately the elegant 18th century children have become so discolored and stained with beer splatters, smoke, and mildew that they look more like zombies now. There's a decayed, disturbing charm to the pictures that makes my fingers itch for a camera.

Finally I can't resist any longer—I pull out my phone and snap a couple photos.

"There she goes again." Sandy shakes her head. "Always with the pictures, and the videos. Could you give it a rest and sit down to a meal, Em? Geez. It's Christmas Day. Take a break." She turns back to Jack, still pointing at me with a sharp-nailed finger. "This girl used to work nonstop. No high school fun for her. No boyfriends, no girlfriends, no drugs or booze, no nights out—I used to beg her to do something naughty just so I'd know she was mine!" She laughs uproariously. "Always with the money-making. Always had her eyes on this camera gadget or that. 'You should recycle,' she says. Look around at this neighborhood. You think this is the kind of place that's big on recycling?" She submerges a chuckle in her glass of wine.

Jack meets my eyes as I resume my place at the table. When my mother heads to the bathroom several minutes later, he leans over to me. "Okay, this was a major disaster."

"Understatement," I reply. "Speaking of disasters, how's the fire situation?"

"I'm monitoring it," he says. "I hurt Auxesia during our last fight, so she's probably still recovering. She hasn't spread the fire any further, or started fresh ones anywhere else, so for now, the humans have it contained. I was able to shift a cold front and send some extra rain their way yesterday afternoon, before I picked you up for the benefit. I could do more if I took a few weeks to recharge."

"Like, in your ice pod thingy?"

He nods. "Every so often I need to hibernate and fully replenish my power. More often lately, it seems. The trouble is, whenever I do that, Auxesia uses the time to gain more ground and wreak more havoc."

"Doesn't she have to do something similar?"

"Yes, but it's a lot rarer for her. Humans have already tilted the planet toward global warming and eventual destruction, thanks to pollution and poor management. So her job is way easier than mine, and takes less energy. Plus she's working with the combined powers of two other full-fledged Horae."

"The sisters of hers that she drained," I recall, nodding. "So, why don't you take a few weeks off after Christmas? Seal yourself in the pod and recharge?"

"I don't want to." His fingers dance along my arm. "I want to be with you."

"I'll still be here afterward."

"Will you though?" Anxiety shimmers in his eyes. "I feel as if you might rethink this any minute and decide I'm too complicated, too much trouble, and you'd rather not be with me."

My breath hitches, because his fear is so exactly my own. "I'm afraid you'll do the same to me."

"Ha!" He shakes his head. "No. Never. I'll be your stalker until the day Auxesia finally gets me."

I was starting to smile, but his last words wipe all joy from my heart. My mother returns, making a rude bathroom joke as she takes her seat again, but I barely hear it because "the day Auxesia finally gets me" is replaying over and over in my head.

If Jack dies—if he turns into a frosty, helpless little ice wraith—the world will burn. I can't doubt that future, not after my encounter with Auxesia. And while the thought of the planet's demise terrifies me, the concept of Jack being *gone*—being less than his playful, thoughtful, generous self—that's even more frightening. His death would leave me with a raw, seeping wound that would never, ever heal. Just the thought of it is enough to kick my heart into a faster pace, triggering panic along my nerves.

There has to be a way I can help him.

And here is the truth I've been mentally sidestepping for a few days. Here, at my mother's table, in the trailer where I spent my childhood, I finally force myself to face it.

I could become like Jack.

He could do to me what Kheima did to him. Change me into something Other, something new. Someone with ice powers like his. He may not know exactly how to do it, but he must remember something about the process. If we did some research, we could probably figure it out. There's got to be a way to create another ice god—or goddess, in this case.

So what if we could figure out how to do it? Would I ask him to change me?

Would I give up my little apartment, my crappy job, and my non-existent social circle, in exchange for supernatural power and near-immortality?

Um, hell *yes* I would. No question.

I'd get to actually *help* the planet in a practical way. Sure, I might never enjoy a beach or a hot coffee again, but I've never liked sand anyway, and iced coffee is a perfectly acceptable option.

Plus I'd be with *him*—with Jack Frost—for centuries, if not millennia. I'd be his partner, his friend, his lover, and he would be mine. We could have each other's backs in the battle against Auxesia. Neither one of us would be alone anymore.

Am I honestly considering this, after knowing Jack for less than two weeks?

No, I'm not considering it. I'm absolutely certain of it, rock-solid sure at the foundation of my very soul. I've been searching for my place, my purpose, and I have found it. Like the last puzzle piece latching into place, like the final twist of the Rubik's cube, like the ultimate synthesis of lighting and framing in the perfect photo—this is the answer.

This is who I'm supposed to be. What I'm supposed to do.

The light of that certainty floods my body and vibrates through my veins, sending goosebumps all over my skin.

When I glance up from my plate, Jack is looking at me, half-smiling, his head at a questioning angle. "You okay?"

"I'm fine. I just realized something. Tell you later."

"Dessert?" My mother plunks a tin of butter cookies onto the table.

By the time we've played a few rounds of Uno and the cookies are half gone, my mother is also half gone. She's giggling and poking Jack's thigh with her toes, apparently unaware that I can see what she's doing. Finally Jack escapes to the kitchen on the pretense of washing up the dishes.

This is how I remember my mother. And I can almost guess the precise moment at which she will switch from horny to maudlin.

Right about now.

Sure enough, she looks vaguely around for Jack, then leans over the table toward me.

"Did I ever tell you," she says blearily, "about the night you were born?"

She hasn't—or if she did, I don't remember it. "No, you didn't."

"It was January. A cold, cold night. We'd had snow for a day or so, and then there was an ice storm. Knocked out power, took down the phone line. I didn't have a cellphone. So when I felt the contractions, I had no way to call anyone. I put on my coat and I wandered out into the snow in my sneakers." She wheezes a laugh. "The cold went right through my coat. I just had a little sundress on underneath, and of course my big old belly was sticking out—you were a damn heavy baby, Em. Damn heavy. Ain't too skinny now, neither, are ya?"

I roll my eyes. "Okay, Mom. Let's get you to bed now."

"No, wait." Jack steps forward, polishing a plate. There's a keen light in his eyes. "I'd like to hear this. Go on please, Mrs. Caulfield."

My mother snorts. "Miss-us Caul-field?" She draws out the name pompously. "Who is 'Miss-us Caul-field'? You can call me Sandy, sweet thing."

"Sandy," Jack says. "What happened then? You went out into the snow— you were having contractions—"

"Sure, sure, yeah. So I stumbled along. The wind was something fierce—I thought my legs would freeze. I fell into the snow, and this big old contraction just ripped through me. I hiked up my skirts, pushed a couple times, and Emery slid right out into the snow. She was a damn mess, blood and slime everywhere, and she was blue all over. I wasn't sure I wanted her, you see—no money or time for that sort of thing." My mother nods companionably to Jack, as if she thinks he'll understand and sympathize. "So I wasn't too broken up—I thought, if the winter wants her, let it have her. That's what I said, right out loud, to God or Old Man Winter or whoever might be listening."

"You actually prayed that?" Jack approaches the table, raw eagerness in every line of his body. "Then what happened?"

"Well, I had a pocketknife in the coat, and I sawed through the cord. Sat there a minute, too cold to move. And then if you believe it, these wispy blue lights gathered around Em's body—she wasn't moving, see—and they whooshed *into* her. Sank right through her skin. The next second she squalls fit to raise the Devil, and well—I dragged us both to the nearest house and they had a cell phone to call 911."

She clutches her wine glass with wavering fingers and downs the rest of it. "I'm off to bed. You two make up some kind of bed out here or whatever."

"We're going to a hotel," I say, but the words feel disconnected from my brain because *what was that story?* Is it possible that my recent meeting with Jack wasn't my first encounter with the supernatural?

My mother mutters good night and wobbles into the bathroom.

"We should stay until she's safely asleep," I tell Jack.

"Of course." He looks stunned and elated at the same time.

"What was that? The story she told?" I whisper. "That wasn't you, was it? Because that would be way too weird, if you saved my life as a baby—"

"No, no. It wasn't me. But it sounds as if your mother gave you up to the gods for dead, and that prayer enabled a couple of ice wraiths to sacrifice their lives for you."

"What? *What?*" I whisper-scream. "What does that even mean?"

"It's old magic, similar to what Kheima used to transform me," he says. "I don't remember the ritual very well, because I was so sick by the end—but essentially, the individual must be at the point of death, and their life must be yielded to the gods. It used to mean the *actual* gods—Zeus, Apollo, and all that—but now it's pretty much whoever is left, or whatever supernatural beings happen to be around at the time. When I was transformed, twelve ice wraiths merged with me, giving me their longevity, energy, and powers. It sounds like two or three of them merged with you the night you were born. Gave up their own existence to save your life."

"But—I don't have any powers."

"No, because it was only a couple of wraiths. So you came back to life, but you didn't get powers, or immortality, or any of that. I mean, I don't *think* you have immortality. It's impossible to know right now—you're still young. But

Emery, this would explain the energy I feel from you, my ability to draw power from your presence. And it explains how you found me that day in Antarctica."

"Explains it? Then why don't I feel enlightened?" I shove myself away from the card table and wander over to the sofa, where I collapse in a heap of overwhelmed brain and tired bones.

Jack sits sideways at the end of the sofa and pulls me between his legs, so my back is against his chest. Immediately I'm humming with nervous sexual energy, my breath shallower and my heart rate quicker because my rear is pressed right against his crotch. I don't know if he took up this position on purpose, to distract me or to cheer me up—but damn is it working.

He kisses the back of my neck, just below the wavy ends of my short hair. My eyes drift shut at the touch of his cool lips on that sensitive skin. "The way Kheima explained it, the magic of both the elemental gods and the original pantheon were linked to emotion. That's why worship was so important to them. When humans forsook the pantheon, the gods' power decreased, and they either left the planet or faded away. But the elementals remained, as I told you, because their magic could also be augmented from the planet itself—its fire, water, air, and earth." His mouth moves to the side of my neck, and I tip my head back, luxuriating in the attention. I deserve this, especially after what he put me through today—unintentionally, but still.

"That's one reason why Auxesia has become so violent," he says. "She chose to consume her sisters' power when they were unwilling to give it, and that negative emotion corrupted the magical energy she absorbed."

"So she made a couple bad choices, and those choices gradually turned her more evil over time."

"Exactly." Jack's palm slides along my waist, over my stomach. "And when she finally sucked away the last vestiges of their power and they faded to wisps, Auxesia took in all of the pain and hate and anger they felt for her."

"What if you were able to drain her negative energy? Not kill her, but take away everything except the last little bit of her power—and then recharge her from natural sources only? Do you think she'd be less antagonistic once she recovered?"

"Maybe. I've never thought of it like that. You see how amazing you are?" He presses a firm kiss to my cheek. "I love you. And I want to make it up to you for today—all this." He nods to our drab surroundings.

"I want to help my mother," I whisper. "I've tried, over and over, in different ways, ever since I was really young. But she won't let me."

"You can't fix people," he replies softly. "You can only love them. And sometimes, when they won't accept help, you have to let them be."

"I know that," I mumble. "Why do you think I've avoided her completely for the past few years? I had to remove the toxicity from my life."

"I'm sorry. If I had known—"

"But you didn't. We don't know much about each other, Jack. This has all been very fast."

He's playing with the button on my pants now, nudging it free. "Too fast?"

"Um, maybe..." I swallow, my hands tightening on his thighs.

He's easing down the zipper. Working his fingers into the space and running a fingernail lightly along the cotton underwear beneath.

My body melts at the touch; but then I go rigid with anxiety. "No, we can't do this here! Are you kidding?" I spring out of his lap, refastening my pants. "I won't do that with you, not here."

"A hotel then?"

"I guess." I feel strangely disappointed, and restless, and sad. This morning I had such high hopes, but as usual, Christmas is an utter disappointment.

Jack's palms sweep across my cheeks, turning my face up to his. "Tell me what you're thinking."

"I wanted Christmas magic," I blurt out. The words are silly and childish, and I'm embarrassed the second they escape.

"I could take you to another city—"

"No, I don't think my body wants to be taken apart and put back together any more today. We should just find like, a Comfort Inn or something, for the night."

Jack raises a dark eyebrow. "Uh, no. We'll be staying somewhere nicer than that. But first, we need a little magic. Is there any place in this town that you liked? Somewhere with *good* memories?"

My eyes widen. "The skating rink! Oh, but they'll be closed. It's a family-run business—they don't open on Christmas. I used to work there, you know. They were sweet people—paid me more than I was worth, honestly. And they'd let me have free skate time now and then. I was pretty good."

"Were you?" Jack's grin turns wicked. "I'm pretty good myself. Care to do a little ice dancing?"

"I told you, they're closed."

"Oh, darling. As if that could stop us."

19

COUPLE'S SKATE

I lace on a pair of skates while Jack works on getting the music going. I'm not sure how I feel about the two of us breaking into the skating rink, but I'm sure my former employers would be happy for me if they knew I'd found love. Besides, Jack has already promised that we'll leave plenty of cash to compensate them for the use of the place. He picked the locks handily with a pair of tiny ice tools, and frosted over the security cameras so no one would be able to identify us.

And now he's got the music going—a stirring rendition of "Sleigh Ride." He joins me, thunking down a pair of his own skates.

"Wait, can't you just make yourself some skates out of ice?"

He looks up at me. "I suppose, but the blades would wear down way too fast. The real thing is better. You ready to show me what you've got?"

Casting him my most dazzling smile, I swing open the gate and step out onto the rink.

I've missed this sensation—the scrape and carve of blades over perfectly groomed ice. I used to watch ice skating movies and competitions whenever I wasn't working or plowing through homework, and I'd try to copy the moves. It was probably a dangerous way to learn, but I couldn't afford lessons or a coach, though more than one person told me I should pursue skating as a career. I always thought they were just being kind. Skating was a hobby, something I did to relax, to let out stress when my mother was being especially herself. I already had my sights sets on camera work, on recording the beautiful and terrible things of the world for the purpose of preserving nature and revealing human mismanagement.

I didn't have the time or resources to devote to a career in ice skating.

But as I glide along the edge of the rink, I remember the magic of it—the sensation of freedom, of flying, and of danger, because figure skating is like high-speed dancing with a pair of blades strapped to your feet. Savage and beautiful, a blend of control and daring.

How could I have forgotten how much I loved this?

"Sleigh Ride" ends, and Lindsey Stirling's version of "Carol of the Bells" soars from the speakers.

Jack and my mother and everything else vanish from my consciousness, and I simply let go.

My legs are stronger than ever, and they remember the angles, the sweep and glide of each sequence. Swift strokes across the ice, accelerating into a spin, and my body holds itself in just the right shape as I whirl, faster and faster, spinning away all the stress of the day. Zooming out of the spin, I flow into another sequence, one I practiced countless times as a teen. A jump, landing smoothly on one blade—skimming forward, sinking into another spin, opening up to the glee inside me, to the music and the flow of energy through myself.

I've always felt so at home here, on the ice.

Was there a deeper reason for that? Did I crave the cold and solidity of it because of some latent, lingering power inside me?

The violins sing higher and sweeter, and suddenly Jack is there, winging alongside me. His face is tense, focused, but his eyes glow with admiration and feral joy. He whirls with me, following my movements, and it's better than being perfectly synchronized because I'm leading a gorgeous ice god through a whimsical dance, and suddenly I'm happier than I have ever been.

Another song rolls out over the ice, a rock version of "Little Drummer Boy," and our energy shifts—more speed, sharper movements, wilder twirls. My heart is pumping hard, my blood racing hot through my veins. I feel the song building, and in a moment of daring I try for a double axel.

A moment of spinning suspension, every muscle and bone tight, under control.

My skate strikes ice again and I wobble, but I don't fall—I skim out of the jump and grin at Jack. He loops his arm through mine and we flow round and round, caught in the beautiful synchronicity of centrifugal force, our eyes locked in wordless communion. We swirl closer, nearer—Jack's smile is gone now, and he pulls me tight against him as the music fades.

Suspended in silence we wait, our chests swelling against each other with every panting inhale.

Jack gathers two fistfuls of my shirt's hem and draws it over my head. Then he pitches it away, into the rink-side seats.

His shirt is already halfway undone; it's the work of a moment to release the few remaining buttons, and I toss it aside. It doesn't clear the rink wall, but Jack sends a blast of wind after it, whisking it off the ice.

Slow and sinuous, we dance, the metal blades slicing patterns into the smooth surface. The ice seems to glow with a pulsing azure light, and when snowflakes begin to drift from the ceiling, I'm hardly surprised. Every time Jack whisks past me, his scent floods my nostrils with frost and wind and sea. The angles of his cheekbones sharpen, matching the wicked points of his ears. Hand in hand we twirl, and then he lifts me, and I revolve in midair for a moment before he sweeps me down again. He drags me close, my spine flush with his breastbone, and when his hand wraps between my legs, I arch into the touch. He dips his face to the curve of my neck, tracing my flesh with his cold sweet tongue.

Longing is turning my legs quivery. I twist in his arms and tug him back toward the rink wall, where we emerge through the gate and stagger to the seats. Without speaking we remove our skates, fingers tugging the laces in an agony of forced restraint. When I notice Jack undoing his pants, I strip mine off as well, keeping my mind carefully blank because if I begin to think about it, I won't do this.

I'm really doing this.

The second I've kicked aside my pants, Jack picks me up bodily and carries me back onto the ice. His feet never falter or slip; it's his element, and it bends to his will and his pleasure.

I wrap my legs around his waist and crush my mouth to his, arms locked at the back of his neck. Jack groans through the kiss and shoves me against the rink wall. The acrylic barrier is smooth and cool at my back, and I pray that it can withstand the pressure as Jack pins me there, kissing me furiously, frantically. Desire licks through my body.

Jack extends those icicle claws again and tears away my panties. Damn it. I'm going to have to buy more if he keeps this up.

When his claws trace my bra strap, I grip his wrist. "It's my favorite."

"It needs to go."

"So put me down and take it off."

Smirking, Jack releases me, and I slide down to the ice. My bare feet can sense the cold, but it's not painful at all—just refreshing, like a tile floor on a summer day. Turning my back to Jack, I wait for him to unhook the bra.

"So you want me to take the bow off my present," he murmurs in my ear.

"Ew, no. I will not be objectified."

He unhooks the strap, fingers grazing my spine. "How about worshipped?"

A thrill races between my legs, through my stomach and into my heart. My breath hitches. "Well... if I must..."

At his gentle tug, the bra slides away. I am now entirely naked. At the skating rink where I used to work.

"This is by far the naughtiest thing I have ever done," I murmur, turning to face him.

"Same for me." He has discarded his last bit of clothing, too, and I nearly whimper at the sight of him. Human men have no chance at all. It's just not fair for him to look this good.

"What if someone shows up and sees us?" I whisper.

"I'll spiral us away."

"But my clothes, and my purse—"

"Okay." He nods, frowning thoughtfully. "You've got a point there. Yeah, this scenario isn't going to work. Let me get dressed again, and we'll go to a hotel where we can do this the normal way."

He takes a step toward the rink exit, but I seize his wrist and spin him to face me. "No way in hell am I waiting that long."

We collide, skin sliding over skin, curves and crevices notching together. He bears me down to the ice, cradling my skull carefully, and then he throws my legs apart and attacks me with his tongue. There's a moment of suspended, agonizing, aching need—and then a blinding surge of ecstasy zips up my spine and I scream, breathy and astonished, writhing while Jack holds onto me, drinking in my spasms with his eyes.

When my breathing normalizes again, I drag myself upright, still trembling a little, and I push him down onto his back. "Your turn."

I take a second to admire the shape of him, snowy and perfect, splayed on the blue-tinted ice. Where his body lies, lacy frost spreads in crisp curls and points, an ever-widening carpet of white.

Laying my body over his, I kiss him, lazy and soft, with long strokes of my tongue into his mouth. His length is pinned between us, and it pulses when I run my nails over his chest. When I break the kiss, he looks up at me with glazed blue eyes. "Emery."

"Hm?"

"Please."

Why is that simple plea so hot? Why do I love the shape of his face so much? Why are his hands so perfectly firm and gentle on my waist as I settle, easing down onto him—why is the contour of his throat so perfect? I have to lick his neck, so I do, and his skin tastes like fresh snow.

"I love you," I whisper.

"Goddess," he moans softly, and I don't know if it's a swear or a name for me. "Say that again."

"I love you."

We move together, our rhythm like the waves of the sea, ebbing and surging, billows piling and tumbling one over another, crest upon crest, until it all crashes down in a creamy froth of foam and slips away into a quiet rush of shared breaths.

I lie on top of Jack, my legs still shaky from my second climax. I've never had two in such close succession before, and I feel washed clean. As his hands sweep lazily over my back, tracing my spine and shoulder blades, I feel cherished, too.

"I love you," he whispers against my hair.

For a second I'm terrified that I might cry.

And then the music—which I became deaf to during our lovemaking—changes to "Grandma Got Run Over By a Reindeer." Which makes us both burst into helpless laughter. We disentangle ourselves and get dressed, still laughing; and before we leave, Jack sweeps a sheet of fresh, flawless ice over the rink, concealing all the scratches and swirls we etched in its surface. On our way out he plops a roll of cash onto the front counter. It's more money than I've ever seen at once, but I don't comment.

Since he still doesn't have a phone, I call us a car, and we head for the nearest hotel that Jack deems suitable. He's a bit of an elitist about it, and I have to stifle the urge to talk to him about privilege and wastefulness. But when you're a powerful ice god keeping the entire planet from being burnt to a crisp, I guess you deserve a few nice things. A soft, comfortable bed in a four-star hotel seems reasonable from that point of view.

When we get into our room, we don't make love again, but we snuggle into the big king-sized bed and watch a dumb, darling little Christmas romance on TV. I feel so safe, and happy, and warm—which is odd, considering that my bedmate is so cold-blooded.

Once, while flipping through the channels during an ad break, we catch a glimpse of an update on the fires in Colorado and the Southwest.

Jack's fingers tighten on the remote, and he changes the channel quickly.

Has he been ignoring a warning signal so he can stay with me?

I eye his pale, crisp profile. I know he senses me watching him, but he won't look at me.

"Jack," I say quietly. "Is there anywhere else you need to be?"

He draws in a long, deep breath and gathers me closer. "No."

And I let the subject drop. Let him be selfish for just one night.
It is Christmas, after all.

20

BATTLEFIELD

My tastes are anything but patrician. When Jack asks where I want to eat breakfast the next day, I tell him Waffle House, because that's another place I enjoyed visiting when I was younger. My mother used to take me there as a treat whenever she got a little extra money. When we enter, the thickly twined smells of bacon and sticky syrup and black coffee engulf my senses. The hiss of hot grease and the chink of plates mingle with the murmur of diners and the merry calls of the staff.

I'm thrilled to see that Ms. Shara still works at this Waffle House. She used to throw an extra piece of bacon on my plate occasionally, or slip me leftover baked goods when she thought I looked particularly sad and underfed. She's plumper and grayer now, and somehow that only makes her dearer and more beautiful to me.

"Well, butter me up and call me a turkey!" she shouts when she sees me. "Emmie Caulfield!"

"Emmie?" Jack mouths at me, smirking. I ignore him and wave to Ms. Shara. "How are you?"

"Just fine, honey, just fine. You good, darling? You look good. You look happy."

And I can reply wholeheartedly, "I am happy."

"Mm-hm." Ms. Shara winks at me and then does a pretend double-take at Jack. "And who is this fine thing?"

"This is Jack." Why can't I stop smiling? I never smile this much, or this widely, not even with Karyl.

"A pleasure to meet you, Ms. Shara." Jack gives her a little bow.

"Well, look at you with your nice manners!" Ms. Shara beams at him. "Not one of these slouchy-pants kids who comes in here muttering and grunting their order. No, this one's good people. I can tell. Well, get yourselves into a booth there and I'll be right with you."

By now I'm used to people eyeing us when we're out together. We make a beautiful couple, and that, mingled with the subtle magic of Jack's presence, makes most people take a second look, or a third. But when we're nearly done with our meal, a woman walks into the restaurant and seats herself at the counter, staring unabashedly at us. Jack's back is turned to her as he munches strips of cooled bacon, but his forehead contracts a little, and he shifts in his seat, angling his head as if he's listening for something.

"I've got a weird feeling," he begins.

"Like someone's watching us?" I nod pointedly behind him.

He twists to look—and then he turns very slowly back around to me. His face has gone rigid, with blue shadows sketched under his eyes. "That's Auxesia."

My jaws freeze mid-chew. "No." I thought she looked vaguely familiar; I've never seen her clothed, looking so normal. She's wearing skinny black pants and a big fluffy coat trimmed in faux fur. And she's staring at me.

"What does she want?" I whisper.

"I don't know. But we need to leave before she—"

194

Suddenly the grill explodes in a tower of flame. The cook jumps back with a scream, his hand smoking. Ms. Shara seizes his wrist and plunges his hand into a pitcher of ice water.

"Time to go." Jack slaps some cash onto the table and hustles me from the booth and out the door. He walks fast, away from the restaurant and into the empty lot next door, pulling me along. We push through a thin belt of trees. When I cast a look over my shoulder, Auxesia is stalking steadily behind us, just a few yards away.

"Jack!" His grip on my arm is beginning to hurt. "Let go."

"Sorry." He releases me. "You need to run, Emery. Run as fast as you can."

"And leave you here with her? No way. She looks like—" I glance over my shoulder again. "She looks murderous, Jack."

"Yeah. She's probably here to kill me, and you too. Especially you."

"Because I give you more power."

"Exactly. In her mind, anything that gives me an advantage must be destroyed." He grips my upper arms. "I'll fight her. You have to run, now. Don't stay with me out of some stupid loyalty, okay? One of us should survive."

"If she kills you, the whole world is toast anyway," I tell him. "Jack, I need to stay. I need to."

Before he can reply, walls of flame spring up around us. Jack hisses angrily and blasts a hole in the fire with a stream of sleet. He conjures an icy chain with a wicked blue blade at one end and twirls it over his head. When it snakes out, it catches Auxesia in the shoulder.

She screeches, hurling bullets of fire at us. I can't help it—I squeal with terror and crouch down, but Jack intercepts the attack with a wall of ice. His jaw is locked, mouth grim and eyes burning blue. An icy wind flows around him, lifting his hair and whipping his clothes against his body. Again he hurls the chain, but Auxesia has conjured a pair of flaming hooked knives, and she knocks the incoming blade aside.

"Let me do this, Jack," she calls. "Give her to me, and I'll spare you a little longer."

"No!" he yells back. The chain stiffens into a spear that sings through the air, slicing Auxesia's wall of fire and impaling her through the stomach. The spear melts the next second, but she roars with pain and anger. The fire barrier thickens and grows until I can't see her anymore—she could be anywhere. And now the circle of flame is tightening.

"We need to spiral," Jack says. "Hold on to me."

But a fireball sails into the circle just then, forcing us to jump apart to avoid it. I land near the wall of flame, and the fireball surges into a towering column, spreading and separating me from Jack.

He roars my name, sending out a blast of furious, frigid air that quenches every bit of the flame and turns the entire field to slick ice. Ice crawls up the branches of the tree belt we passed through, glazing every twig.

Auxesia is in her flaming inhuman form now, and the ice melts beneath her feet. Her fire lowered for a second when Jack's blast rushed over her, but it returns full-force within seconds. With a stamp of her foot, she drives a line of flame between me and Jack again.

"You can't keep this up," she says. "Give in, Jack. Our dance is at an end. The time of Earth as you knew it has ended. If you yield, I will make your deaths quick."

"That's such a cliché villain thing to say," I scream at her. I'm shaking with terror, but I'm mad, too. "A quick death is a shitty incentive."

"You'd prefer a slow death then? Noted." Auxesia forms a fireball and flings it at me.

Jack throws a spinning disc of ice, and the fireball strikes it, hissing into steam. For the next few minutes I can barely see what's happening as the two elementals battle in a rapid series of attacks and defensive moves. A tornado of Auxesia's fire is sliced apart by Jack's frosty blades. Ice bombs dissolve against a sheet of flame. A gale of knife-like sleet is forced back by a wave of fiery air. Walls of ice and runners of flame race along the ground, chasing each other, cutting each other off, never quite touching me.

There's a hideous beauty in the way they dance—Jack's lean agility and Auxesia's fierce grace. They blast into the air, hurling ice and fire, and I cover my head against the aftermath, the ice pellets and sparks raining down around me.

I have felt helplessness like this before, and I hate it. My fury and fear merge into a swelling storm inside me, but I have nothing to contribute to this fight—nothing to throw, no way to reach Auxesia. I couldn't even touch her without burning myself. I'm totally dependent on Jack to save me. As much as I detest guns, I wish I had one right now. Maybe a well-placed bullet would take down the fire bitch attacking my boyfriend.

A violent blaze of heat crackles above me, like a small sun has exploded in the sky. Something crashes to the ground a dozen feet from me. A pale figure streaming smoke. His muscles surge as he tries to rise—his blue eyes lock desperately with mine—and then he's swallowed up in the orange fire streaming from Auxesia's palms as she descends. She's spraying him with incessant flame, torching him. His screams splinter my brain.

I don't care about myself anymore—I lunge for Auxesia, catching her in a full-body tackle, smashing her face-first into the ground.

197

My flesh sizzles and ignites. Flames gnaw my stomach, my chest, my neck, and I'm shrieking with the agony of it, with the pain slicing jagged along my spine, into my brain. Auxesia throws me off, and I roll desperately, crushing the flames—but the agony doesn't stop. I lie on my back, rigid and gagging for air.

There's a flash of icy blue, and then a roar of continuous flame.

Jack isn't screaming anymore.

I try to whisper his name but my jaw is fixed wide as my insides scream voicelessly for oxygen.

Auxesia leans over me. "A slow death, granted." She flicks at my chest, and something crumbles away, something charred that used to be me.

A shadow passes over Auxesia's glowing features—a hint of regret? Or maybe it's just the play of the flames and smoke over her skin.

"It had to be done," she says. With a shower of sparks, she disappears, and I am left with only pain.

21

ANGELS

The pain is knives stabbed into every square inch of my flesh, flexing and tearing when I move. But in the worst places, there is no pain, because the nerves have burned away.

I am dying. My stomach is a smoking wreck, and my chest—I know my breasts are gone, and I suspect my ribs are exposed. My fingers are crumbling into charcoal.

My lungs spasm and flutter, struggling to suck in air.

I can't call for Jack. But when I turn my head, slowly and painfully, I see him foggily through my smoke-inflamed eyes.

He is charred black all over, except where angry red peeks through. A faint mist of blue is seeping from him, leaking into the surrounding air.

He's dying. Fading.

Now that Auxesia is gone, ice wraiths are beginning to gather around Jack. I don't know what mystical sense enables them to know that he's injured and dying, but they keep coming by twos and threes until there are at least two dozen of them quivering helplessly in the air around him, mewling and mourning.

If Death were a reaper, he would be leaning over me now, skeletal hand outstretched to claim my soul. I could give in and yield it—endure through the last moments of agony and then sink into nothing. Part of me wonders what lies beyond the brink of death, if anything. I have always wondered, and now is my chance to actually know. It's enticing to the artist in me, though my scientific half keeps muttering that there's nothing Beyond, nothing, nothing—I will simply dissipate, an echo in the universe, while my body decays and returns to the earth. Maybe a tree will grow from the ground fertilized by my remains.

My thoughts are muddling, growing slow and sluggish as my ruined lungs yield the fight.

No.

No, I have to hold onto something—there's a way out of this—what did Jack say? He was nearly dead when Kheima transformed him. You have to be nearly dead for it to work. And then you call on the gods, or whatever supernatural beings happen to be nearby...

I inhale, razors and smoke, and I rasp out words. "Hey! Wraiths—frost fairies—over here."

A few of them whirl and sweep toward me eagerly. I don't think they realized I was still alive. Their love for Jack kept them from noticing my existence at all.

One of the wraiths lays a tiny frozen hand against my cheek. Another trails icy fingers along my temple, crying softly.

"I need more of you," I gasp. "A lot more. I call on the gods—I yield myself to their will and their—their service. I—damn it, there are no rules anymore, okay? I don't know the ritual, and I don't know Greek or Latin, so if there's a magical spell, I can't say it." My ravaged torso heaves; every phrase is a burden, and acid tears stream from my eyes, stinging my raw skin.

I have always made big, impulsive decisions. Like my decision to apply for the Antarctic expedition, and my choice to stay behind and keep filming when my team left. I'm making my biggest and most impulsive decision to date, and yet it doesn't feel far-fetched or wild at all. It feels like the natural progression of who I am, and who I want to be.

This is my darkest moment. Impossible to come out of it unchanged. But I will crawl, and I will rise, and I will *become.*

"Hear me, ice wraiths—gods, whatever is listening." My voice carries the strength of the end, of desperation. "I accept the burden. I will be the champion you need. Only save me, so I can save him."

All the ice wraiths are turning toward me now, drawn by my voice. They surround me, a cloud of azure faces and ghostly limbs. One moves forward, and I recognize it as one of the first wraiths I met, on the night I went running. The creature looks into my eyes, and wordlessly we make the bargain.

The wraith dives into my chest—I feel the shock of cold down to my very spine. A ripple of tinkling music races around the circled wraiths; they are singing, high and soft and full of hope.

Another approaches me, sinking into my body, yielding its life-force to me. And another.

They are not dying for me. They are giving themselves to a greater cause, becoming part of a larger whole. Yielding their power so I can save the man we all love, so he and I can save the world.

I close my aching eyes, but the faint, faraway singing continues. A fresh influx of sparkling cold washes through my body every time another wraith merges with me. Over and over it happens, until I lose count of how many of them are now a part of me.

The cold inside me is like the still, frozen heart of the Antarctic waters. It is the majestic white of icebergs and the black quiet of space. It is the wind across moors and the autumn breeze in city streets; it is snow on the tundra and sleet in the mountains. It salves the scorched parts of my body, flowing into my muscles and expanding them, reconnecting severed tendons and tissues, spreading cold fresh skin over gaping wounds.

My eyes flick open and I sit up, half-sobbing, spreading my newly formed fingers across my stomach.

I'm whole.

And I'm new.

The few remaining wraiths are still singing, joyfully now, shrill and delighted as they circle above me. Their voices blend with a billion whispering threads attached to my consciousness—but I don't have time to listen to any of it, or to think about my new body. My sole thought is Jack. Jack. *Jack.*

The blue mist is still rising from his burned body, and I fling myself over it and him, as if I could press the energy back inside him. I cling to him, and I focus as hard as I can on the ice palace where I first found him—the icy cocoon in that blue, breathing room. I need to take him there, right now, and hope that he doesn't fall apart for good on the way.

But I don't know how to spiral.

Focus, Emery. Focus.

A knot begins to form in my chest—an ember of blue light, glowing stronger and stronger the harder I think of the ice palace. I nurture the glow, expanding it, feeding it, and suddenly with a blast of wild snowy wind, I'm gone—I'm spinning—*focus*, Emery—*ice palace*—I picture it as clearly as I can and I *pull*, dragging together the bits of me and of Jack with all the power I now possess.

We spin onto the floor of the icy blue bedroom, and Jack is still intact. I haul him onto the bed while frantic sobs lurch from my chest. My tears are sleet, flowing down my cheeks and chin and throat.

I don't recognize Jack's face anymore. It's all burnt off. His fingers, his privates, his toes, all gone. His messy, snowy hair is gone—crispy blackened skin and raw red flesh have taken its place.

I'm crying harder now, my fingers hovering and trembling over his body. As I weep, ice builds around Jack's ruined form, encasing it fully, from the soles of his blackened feet to his blistered skull. It seals up like a coffin, and my heart cracks, a chasm wide and deep.

But then—oh, then—the room begins to pulse. Deep blue fading to white, then swelling blue again.

Like a rhythm. Like a heartbeat.

He's alive.

He's alive, and he's healing.

Auxesia failed. She didn't kill Jack, or me.

I survived. I transformed. And I saved the love of my life.

And now—that fire bitch had best run to the farthest ends of this wretched planet because I am going to finish her.

BURNING HEART

There's nothing more I can do for Jack now. I slip out of the healing room and close the door, watching the clockwork snowflakes whirr and latch, locking him in.

It will take him weeks to recover, and I don't know what he'll look like when it's done. Can his regenerative magic bring him back from *that*?

Even if he's scarred, even if he's no longer beautiful in the same way, I am his. It's the sweet, bright, shining soul of him that I love, and that same sweet soul will glow no matter what its casing looks like.

My Jack. I will love him no matter what.

But right now, Auxesia needs to be my focus. She'll be low on energy after everything she spent to take us down, so I need to strike her soon. I have to figure out where she's hiding to heal herself, and I must attack her there. But I also need to take five, and figure out who the hell I am now, and what I can do. There's got to be a mirror somewhere in this place.

As I cross the great hall, something brushes my back, and I whirl, heart jolting.

Another brush across my upper arm, near the elbow.

Oh. My. God.

It's my hair.

My hair has grown—it's waist-length now, falling in perfect snow-white waves. I tug a few locks over my shoulder, trailing my fingers through it. My fingers are pristinely shaped, slim and stone-white, with pearlescent nails. On impulse I twitch them, mentally exploring the nail beds—and five arrow-sharp icicles fly from my fingers, rocketing across the hall and arcing down to the floor, where they shatter into crystalline bits.

Cool.

Since my clothes burned away, I'm entirely naked. I need to find something to wear—something of Jack's maybe, or clothes that Kheima left behind when she dissipated. Gingerly I press my fingertips to my chest, wondering whose energy I'm carrying now. Was Kheima one of the wraiths who yielded their energy to me?

My fingers rest between my new breasts—pure swells of white flesh with tiny pale-blue tips. They're very similar to my original breasts, but a little larger and more symmetrical. Part of me revolts at the idea that I've been remade into this Greek goddess ideal of beauty; but a stronger part of me is simply glad to be alive. And yeah, I'm glad to be gorgeous. Plus it looks like I won't need to shave again, because except for my long hair, my lashes, and my eyebrows, I'm perfectly smooth all over. That is an unexpected bonus. Mentally I calculate how much time that will save me in the shower—and then I wonder if I'll even need to shower again. An experimental sniff reveals that I'm fragrantly snow-scented like Jack—permanently winter-fresh.

A grin spreads across my face, effervescent joy bubbling up inside me. I twirl in the center of the hall, and when I leap into the air, I'm buoyed up by an eddy of snow and wind. It's startling at first, and I nearly fall—but a little experimentation lets me control the flow and ebb of my own little snowstorm.

I am a goddess.

I am free.

I can go anywhere now, do anything. I can change the damn world.

The glory of it swells in my soul, too big to contain, and I sweep out of the great hall, skimming through corridors and bursting into rooms, whooping and squealing at the top of my lungs. A few ice wraiths flit out of archways to watch me pass. They're clearly startled by my appearance—I assume they usually hang around here, so they weren't among the group that surrounded Jack and me after our burning. It doesn't take them long to accept me, though, and soon they're zooming along with me, voicing tiny cheers of their own.

Finally, I slow my skating and ask them, "Do you know where Jack keeps his clothes? Or are there any girl clothes around here? Like, cool dresses or whatever?" Because I think my confrontation with Auxesia calls for a truly spectacular gown.

The ice wraiths lead me deep into the palace, to a suite of rooms swathed with indigo shadows. When I touch the light fixture in the bedroom, it flares to life, revealing a grand four-poster bed draped in lacy curtains, like flexible frost. Darting through an archway, the wraiths illuminate the space beyond, and I gasp at the treasures inside. Dozens of gowns and outfits from every era, with the most modern clothing toward the front. There's nothing newer than the late eighteenth century, but I don't mind. I can make do with these for now, and later I'll spiral home to get my things—although my repertoire of mild businesswear, jeans, and hoodies doesn't seem splendid enough for this body.

Between two sections of clothing I find a broad mirror, framed in twisting vines. Cautiously I approach it.

My face is still mine; but it has definitely been upgraded. My skin is practically poreless now, frosty and smooth. My brows are dramatic black arches, and my eyelashes are thicker and darker. I still have three studs along the edge of my left ear, and a stud and a hoop in the right one. But the tips of my ears are sharp and blue-tinted now, like Jack's. I'm firmly in faerie mode, looking like some tall elven ice queen—which means I am probably invisible to humans as well. And I have no idea how to switch to my human aspect. So I won't be talking face-to-face with Karyl or anyone else for a while.

I'll have to email Karyl after I spiral back to my place for my things. I can't text her, because my purse and its contents burned to a crisp in that Alabama field. Maybe I can tell her Jack and I are traveling the world together. She'll worry a little, but honestly she's the only one who will care that I'm gone. I can quit my job via email; the thought gives me a shiver of satisfaction.

Before any of that can happen, I need to choose a dress. This immense closet would be Karyl's dream; she'd go rabid for all the vintage fashion.

The farther back I walk in the closet, the more ancient the clothing gets. Historians would love to see these pieces. I make a mental note to talk to Jack about donating some of them to museums. I don't think he's holding onto them out of affection for Kheima; he probably just hasn't bothered to move them. Just in case, I'll approach it tactfully when I get the chance.

For a second my energy falters, and the weight of loneliness descends on my shoulders. With Jack unconscious in the regeneration room, and only the wraiths for company, I am truly alone down here, under vast layers of ice, at the world's end.

How did Jack handle the loneliness for so long?

No wonder he was so eager to have me in his life. My heart turns tender and sore at the thought of my sweet, cheerful Jack fighting alone, holding back fiery destruction with his own two hands, returning wounded and weary to these beautiful hollow halls. My fingers tighten on the crisp brocade of an Elizabethan-era gown.

He won't have to struggle alone anymore. I'm here now.

I wander further down the row until my fingers slip into the folds of a long dress—shimmery and simple, a Grecian column of white that pins over one shoulder and falls in glimmering ripples to the floor.

This is the one. I know it from the second the fabric glides across my skin, flowing into place along my legs. There's a slit up to my thigh on the left side, which is perfect for strenuous movement—like fighting a fire goddess.

I don't bother with undergarments, and I leave my feet bare.

Strength and power oscillate through my body, tangible energy welling just under the surface, chafing to be released. But I need to remember that I'm not invincible. If Auxesia is deep in some volcano, it's going to be tough to access her. If I go striding into a volcano, I'll melt, or burn to a crisp. Just the thought of heat is enough to make my skin crawl.

I'll have to draw Auxesia out somehow.

My attention swerves to the myriad of fine threads tugging at the edges of my consciousness. This is how Jack knew where the biggest, most dangerous fires were, and where he needed to introduce cold fronts to balance out extreme heat. If I can find a spot where Auxesia has set fire in motion, and wipe that entire area clean with my powers, she'll probably come to investigate, and that's when I'll get her.

I crash clumsily to earth somewhere in the middle of Saskatchewan—my chosen area for the first major test of my powers. Jack said his transformation involved a dozen wraiths, but I'm fairly sure more than that went into me. What does that mean for my power levels?

Maybe I should wait and do this when Jack awakens. But by then, Auxesia could have healed herself and burnt the world to a crisp. No, I have to act now. Fires are burning throughout the Midwest, threatening homes and crops, gnawing at beautiful old forests. For some reason the thought of those decades-old trees being charred to stumps infuriates me more than the loss of human buildings.

My new form allows me to do something about that anger. The plan is to send a cold front from Saskatchewan across the border into the Midwestern states, hopefully blotting out or reducing some of Auxesia's fires.

I leap into the sky, borne up in a storm of snow and fury. The sky around and above me soars infinite, clear and cold and borderless. It is magnificent, and I am the queen of its scope, the guardian of its future.

I am so far beyond lobbying and research and grants and benefits now.

Magic builds inside me, bright energy and purifying cold, ready to burst from my body.

Gritting my teeth and spreading my arms, I release it all.

The magic explodes from my chest and my hands, a titanic ring of icy air blasting outward. Clouds form instantly, racing away toward the south, carrying cold rain in their bellies. Frigid wind pours from me, and I close my eyes, reveling in the sensation of power, so much power—it kicks up my hair and twists through my dress, surging around my body.

The energy is leaking out too fast now—I can feel it ebbing away, and I close myself off from the flow, sinking back down to earth. My limbs are faintly weak, but I feel refreshed, too—sated, like I did after sex with Jack.

I'm not sure exactly what that release of magic will do, but it's bound to get Auxesia's attention. She'll try to find its origin. So all I have to do now is wait for her to locate me.

The Twilight Motel in Prince Albert, Saskatchewan seems like a decent place to lay low. Experimentally I walk into the lobby, Grecian gown and pointy ears and all; but the pasty man at the desk seems doesn't notice me. So I really *am* invisible, which is cool and also extremely weird. When the desk clerk steps outside on a smoke break, I check myself in under an innocuous false name and snag a room keycard. I have the tiniest bit of guilt about not actually paying, but hey—I'm trying to save the world here. I think I deserve one freebie.

There's a computer at the end of the lobby with a sign tacked to the peeling paint: "Business Center, Paying Guests Only." Front-Desk Guy is still outside smoking, so I step over to the computer and email Karyl about my fake trip with Jack. I tell her that my phone fell in the toilet and died, but that I'm ordering a new one soon. Better that than the truth, that my purse, wallet, ID, and phone are in a smoking crater somewhere in Alabama.

Front-Desk Guy saunters back inside, so I have to postpone my resignation email to the conservancy. Just as well, because I need some rest after all the energy I expended. The hard little bed in my self-assigned motel room isn't great, but after everything I've endured lately, I'm pretty sure I could zonk out on a slab of rock.

I jerk upright out of a dream, my heart banging wildly. A quick scan of the room reminds me where I am, what I've done, and who I'm waiting for. The trace of cigarette smoke in the musty room is oddly soothing, maybe because it's so coarsely familiar in a world where my own body feels alien to me.

The TV on the dresser is also familiar in an ugly, prosaic sort of way. Grabbing the remote from the nightstand beside me, I power on the TV and begin flipping through channels. The smush of the button under my thumb is familiar too, and my breath slows—until I land on the weather channel, where a man is gesturing at a map of the Midwest. His face is lit up with the morbidly thrilled expression newscasters wear whenever there is a disaster to talk about. "We're getting reports of an unusual Arctic blast surging into the Midwest, bringing record low temperatures for a number of States. Ice storms and heavy snowfalls have left thousands of homes without power. We're looking at some really stunning temperature drops here—for example, in Amarillo, Texas, the high just yesterday was ninety degrees, and today, as you can see, it has dropped below zero. The bitter cold is expected to hang around for a few days, with temperatures breaking records set in the early 2000s and the 1990s."

"Oh god," I whisper, and then I clamp my hand across my mouth.

Oh my god. *I* did that.

Ice storms. Thousands of homes without power. Record low temperatures.

Slowly I tug the thin motel blanket up to my chin, stunned by the power of unbalanced magical energy. I thought I'd be sending in some rain to help with the fires, not causing a huge Arctic weather anomaly. I'm going to have to be a lot more careful about the use of my energy, until Jack wakes up and teaches me how to control it. This job is going to take more finesse than I thought.

And it will require balance, on both sides. Which means I can't kill Auxesia. Much as I'd like to, I can't destroy her entirely, or there will be no one on her side to maintain the balance, to restore the heat of the world where it's needed. If I kill her, the Earth might slip into another Ice Age, which could be just as devastating as a fiery inferno.

I need to wear her down—to drain her power to its dregs. I have to suck out all the roiling negative energy she's been feeding herself for so many decades. Maybe, just maybe, its absence will allow her to contemplate her place in the cycle, her responsibility to the people and animals of Earth. Maybe while she recuperates she'll have time and space to regret her plan for global destruction. Maybe she could come around to a healthier point of view.

But that can only happen if I manage to face her successfully. I spent a lot of power on that Arctic blast of mine, and I'm not sure how much I need to defeat her. I've never fought anyone in my life. When Jack battled Auxesia, he made it look so easy—skating around her, erecting frosty barriers and shooting out ice missiles. I don't know how to do any of it.

My throat tightens, and my fingers scrunch the blanket into desperate fistfuls.

Oh hell. What have I done?

Auxesia is going to come here. She's going to find me, and I'm not ready. What was I thinking, trying to face her without Jack?

Not that I had a choice—he was too far gone to help me. And I couldn't wait. Since Auxesia believed we were out of the picture, she was probably planning a grand globe-burning for the next week or so. But her plans will have changed by now. She'll have realized that most of her fires on this continent are out, and not by natural or human means.

I can't be here when she arrives. She'll burn this motel to the ground, along with everyone in it. I'm lucky she didn't do it while I was asleep.

The cold wraps me in a vicious embrace when I step outside. Two cars sit in the strip of lumpy parking lot belonging to the motel. A single streetlight blooms yellow atop its stalk, casting a sickly circle onto the salt-stained snow at the edge of the lot. Ahead is the main road, bare and black, rimmed with bristly dark trees. Instead of walking toward it, I circle the motel, heading for the fields behind it. Here at least, the snow is clean, not grayed and blackened with road salt. My feet break through the crust of half-hardened snow and sink to mid-calf in the thick brown meadow grass underneath. I probably should have worn shoes after all; just because I'm impervious to cold doesn't mean the soles of my feet are invulnerable to spiky stalks and prickly weeds. But I don't want to waste any energy on flying until I absolutely have to.

Something pops in the air in front of me—a winking speck of light, there and gone. There's a glow at the edge of my sight, and my stomach lurches into my throat; but when I whirl to face the glow, it's not Auxesia. It's a pair of fire sprites, like floating embers with eyes. If they once looked vaguely human, like the ice wraiths do, the semblance has long since faded. They are pulsing lumps of heat, flickering with low flame, staring at me with amber eyes that swell and recede unnervingly.

Maybe they are scouts, sent by Auxesia, here to figure out what's going on and report back. If so, she can't be far behind.

Summoning my courage, I speak out. "Well? Where is she? I'm not just going to stand here all night. Go and get her." I want to say more, about vengeance, and a reckoning, but it feels awkward because what if they can't even understand me? "Do you understand? Go get Auxesia!"

A flare of heat at my back. "No need."

I spin, clenching my fists.

Auxesia's flame is low, barely clinging to her form. She still has ragged gashes where Jack's ice weapons sliced through her.

"How is this possible?" she growls. "You were dead."

"Wrong. I'm not dead, and neither is Jack."

Her scarlet eyes scan my form. "How did you transform?"

"None of your business."

"And Jack—he's probably hidden away in his disgusting ice hole. I should go and drag him out and finish him off. I'll cut off his head this time." Sparks whirl around her as she prepares to spiral.

Without thinking, I reach out and grab her wrist.

Pain beyond thought sears through my entire being, scorching my nerves, razing me to the bone. I scream, but Auxesia screams too, the high keening shriek of a being in mortal agony.

I hurl her away from me, panting and staring at my blackened hand.

Auxesia snaps upright, sailing toward me over the field. The tips of her toes don't touch the snow crust, but still it melts in her wake, and the dry grass sparks into flames.

She opens her mouth, and the glow in the back of her throat warns me one second before she vomits a flood of liquid fire.

I'm dead.

Am I dead?

No.

Somehow I managed to throw up a shield—a huge chunk of ice between her and me. The lava she spewed at me is eating it away. It's a glass-thin sheet now, and I skate upward into the sky, lobbing chunks of ice at Auxesia. My battle style is not as sophisticated as Jack's, but it's more effective than I expected, probably because the fire goddess is still exhausted from fighting Jack yesterday. One of the ice chunks strikes her head, knocking her to the ground, and another crashes against her shoulder, driving her onto her back.

She's down. I won't get another advantage like this.

I land and plunge forward through the crunchy snow and the brittle grass, flinging out my power, shaping it with my thoughts. Pinnacles of ice shoot up from the frozen ground, curving over Auxesia's crumpled body, securing her to

214

the ground. She ignites, trying to melt through the bonds, but I keep hurling more and more energy toward her. Power explodes from my hands in clumsy bursts, layering the fire goddess in sheets and slabs and whole blocks of ice, until her fire fades to a weak glow, barely visible through the pyramid of ice.

Approaching, I place my hand against the outer wall of the prison I've made.

I can sense Auxesia's power, fluttering feebly. She's weakening fast, the last eddies of her energy burning away.

She is dying.

I can't kill her. But I do need to drain her of everything that she has, until there's only a flicker left.

With a blow and a thought, I crack the ice prison, sloughing off layers and shards until I can see Auxesia's face. I leave the last layer of ice in place, along with a heavy chunk on her chest, to hold her still; and I sit down beside her.

The scarlet light of her eyes is a dull amber now, and her flaming hair is all but quenched, a subtle glimmer across her scalp. She tries to vomit fire again, but she can only cough out a wisp of smoke.

"Bitch," she wheezes.

The word is so caustically familiar, so weirdly human, that I almost smile. "You started this."

She turns her face away.

"I'm not going to kill you," I tell her. "Not gonna lie—I want to, because of what you did to Jack and me. You've caused so much damage, ruined so many lives. But you're the last fire goddess, the only hope for balance in this world. So I'm going to let you live, for now. I think it will take you a long time to recover from this, and I hope you'll take that time to think about what you used to be."

"What I used to be?" coughs Auxesia. "Idiot child. You know nothing of deities and their roles."

"I'm not an idiot child. And unless I'm mistaken, this form makes me one of you now."

Her lips curl in a sneer. "You're a poor excuse for an ice goddess. You can barely control your powers. Do you know what havoc you wreaked, blasting the midsection of the United States with your cursed ice?"

"Okay, that was overkill." I wince. "I was trying to get your attention."

"Mission accomplished."

Wry humor is not something I'd have expected from her. It surprises me into a half-smile. "Look, we don't have to be enemies. Despite what you've done, I know you have a role in this world, a part to play. Jack says that at some point, before his time, you worked with the frost deities—a kind of push and pull, give and take, to maintain the earth's climate. Can't we get back to that?"

"The human masses work against everything we do." Her voice is a series of harsh pants, and smoke leaks from the corners of her lips. "It's as if they are actively trying to immolate themselves and their world, the fools. I was only going to give them what they desire—a blazing end."

"I won't deny that they tend toward self-destruction," I say. "But perhaps they could be taught. If we work together, if we educate them while in our human forms, then maybe eventually they will learn. In the meantime—"

"In the meantime we flit about the planet, fixing their mistakes?"

"Jack and I will have the lion's share of that task," I remind her. "Our powers are uniquely suited to combat global warming. All you have to do is bring the seasonal warmth when and where it's needed, and help us even out the weather patterns. Besides that, you could take human form and enjoy yourself for a while. Take a vacation. Goddess knows you need to de-stress."

Auxesia gives me a confused glare. "You're very strange. You should be finishing me off right now. I'd welcome the relief."

"A death wish?" I raise my eyebrows. "I thought you wanted a new world."

"I don't know what I want," she says in a vicious whisper. "I have existed for so long, I don't know who I am anymore. I thought perhaps birthing a different world would be something—new. Something worth existing for."

I scramble to my feet, incensed. "You can't destroy all the life on a planet just because you're bored and purposeless!"

"Well, when you put it like that." Her face contorts in a snarl, which quickly melts into a look of pure anguish and exhaustion. "Please stop torturing me with your inanities. Either kill me or release me."

"I'm actually going to leave you right here." I brace my hands on my hips. "When I spiral, the ice holding you will dissipate. And then you can slink back to your volcano and think about your life choices. I tend to believe that people can't change—that once they go bad, it's game over. I've known too many permanently shitty people to think otherwise. But if you'd like to surprise me, and redeem yourself, have at it. Just be warned—if you come after us again, we'll have to give you a longer time-out."

"Insufferable creature," she snarls. "Do you think an altered body and a white dress gives you the right to speak to me like an equal?"

I lean in, propping my elbow on my knee. "I'm not speaking to you like an equal, honey. I'm your damn superior."

And with a swirl of ice and wind, I vanish.

23
THIS
BEAUTIFUL BURDEN

For the next five weeks, I am alone.

I pop back and forth between Antarctica and my apartment, tied to the world only through email. Occasionally I have to pop into stores at night to steal food and other necessities. I'm invisible, so if the security cameras catch anything, it'll be hella mystifying to whoever sees the groceries disappearing off the shelves. I quickly discover that I have the power to decide whether or not the items I'm carrying remain visible once they're in my hands. It's a nice perk, being able to extend the magic to whatever I'm carrying.

My apartment is too new to really feel like home anyway, so I spend most of my time in the ice palace—partly because the cold refreshes me, and partly because I want to be near Jack. And also because the palace is filled with incredible treasures tucked away in closets and corners. There must have been dozens of frost beings living here at one time, and all of their things have simply been left behind, perfectly preserved. I "adopt" a number of the most delightful items and set myself up in the room next to Jack's. It's easy enough to tell which space is his—there's a long, low bookshelf stocked with novels and art journals beside the bed, and there's an adjoining room filled with blocks of stone and ice, with carving tools scattered around. A few of the blocks have been partially shaped, but Jack was too busy finish them. It's immensely flattering that he made the time to finish the statue of me.

My room is sleek and spacious, with a ceiling of frosty white detailed with a network of deep azure vines. There's a plush sofa, huge white floor cushions trimmed with twinkling crystals, and side tables with mosaic tops of glossy colored tiles. And there's a gleaming bathroom as well, although there's no tub, and the shower water is permanently frigid. That suits me well enough, because the thought of steaming in a bath is completely abhorrent to me now. In fact, the only reason I need to shower is if I get really dirty—say, covered in ashes and grass from a battle with a fire goddess.

Parts of the palace have been magically hewn from the depths of the unmeltable ice and the continental bedrock, but other parts are crafted of stone, marble, brick, or wood. The beings who lived here have added onto the palace and repaired it over the centuries, until it is a labyrinth of rooms and a mishmash of interior design styles. Only the front section, where the great hall and the regeneration chamber are located, has a classic, synchronous beauty befitting the domain of an ice god. The rest is very much a medley, and the range of decor helps me feel more at home. The ice wraiths are certainly trying to welcome me in their own way; they tend to follow me around while I explore, and if I want privacy I have to firmly tell them to go elsewhere.

I'm very frustrated that I can't figure out the lighting here. It appears to be magical, sometimes reacting to my touch or to my entrance into a room. Maybe ancient frost spirits merged with the palace fixtures, and *they* power the lights. It's as likely as any other theory I've concocted. There's no electricity anywhere, so if I want to watch any TV shows or play any games or work on my laptop, I have to charge all my devices at my apartment and then spiral them along with me to the palace.

I haven't spiraled anywhere besides the palace, a grocery store, and my apartment since I defeated Auxesia. I can go anywhere I please, but I know Jack will want to join me when I explore the world; and besides, I want the freedom to interact with everything in human aspect instead of slinking around as an invisible ice being. And for that, I need his help.

Between my two homes and the surface of the Antarctic world, I have plenty to keep me occupied. Editing the footage and photos from the Antarctic trip takes up some of my time, and when that's all turned in, I photograph some of the ancient objects in the palace and sell them as stock images. I'm out of a job now—might as well make a little money where I can. I still haven't found an actual treasury in this place, and until Jack wakes up, I have to be able to buy food.

Until Jack wakes up.

If he ever does.

Each day I slip into the regeneration chamber to look at him, but the layers of ice over his body are too thick and frosty for me to see anything clearly.

All I know is that he isn't dead, because the blue heartbeat glow of the room is as strong and steady as ever.

For now, it's enough to know he's alive.

One evening I'm in Jack's room, which I frequent almost as often as mine—tucked into a nest of fleecy blankets, skimming through one of his art books, when there's a scuffing sound in the hall.

I startle so hard the book falls out of my hands, landing upside down on the bed.

Jack stands in his bedroom doorway, stark naked and perfectly whole. Not a scar on any part of his perfect body. The curves of his shoulders and the swells of his pecs have an icy sheen to them, like a snowbank in the sun.

All of his fingers and toes and other bits are back. His hair falls in snowy, sparkly waves around his temples and cheeks. As I watch, a few flakes of broken ice shake loose and tumble to the cold tiles of the floor.

He's so beautiful—just like I've imagined him a hundred times since I sealed him away.

Clinging to the doorframe, he stares at me.

"Emery," he whispers. "You died. I—I died."

"No," I reply softly. "The frost wraiths saved us."

He takes a step forward, absently brushing crystallized snow from between his newly formed fingers. "You saved me."

"I asked the frost wraiths, and they gave themselves to me. They transformed me."

"Are you all right? The change—going through it alone—oh god, what about Auxesia? How long was I out? What has she done? It feels—" He hesitates, his eyes turning distant. He's tapping into the threads of consciousness that attune us to the world. "It feels quiet out there. Peaceful."

"I wouldn't say peaceful." I grimace. "The humans are perfectly capable of creating climate trouble without Auxesia."

"I mean, yes, but it's different. Wait, what do you mean, 'without Auxesia'?"

"I challenged her, right after I transformed. Fought her, and drained her. She's not dead, but it's going to take her a very long time to recover. And I don't think she'll be as powerful or as evil anymore. Even if she is, it'll be okay, because you have me now—we're in this together—"

Jack charges me, crashing onto the bed and clasping me in his arms. "Alive. You're alive. You actually survived that hellfire, you beautiful warrior goddess—*look* at you!" He pushes me back to arm's length. "I can feel the power just rolling off you. How many wraiths merged with you?"

"I'm not sure," I murmur. "A lot more than twelve, I think."

"Nick's icy balls." He breathes the curse so fervently it sounds like a prayer. "Have you had any trouble with your powers?"

I wrinkle my nose at him. "I kind of set off a record-breaking wave of Arctic weather across the Midwest. Ice storms, power blackouts—yeah."

"Did anyone—" He hesitates.

"No one died as far as I know," I say quietly. "A lot of inconvenience and expense, though."

"That's all right. And even if you did harm someone by accident, well— Auxesia has been the cause of far more deaths. Defeating her was certainly the greater goal."

There's a shadow in his eyes, but I don't ask if he ever lost control of his powers, or what harm came of it—because every bit of that is in the past. The only thing we need to think about is the future. Our future, and the future of our precious Earth.

Jack's expression is still distant, haunted, so I rise and do a slow twirl in front of him. "What do you think of the new bod?"

He smirks. "Icy hot. But I liked your old one."

"I can't figure out how to switch back to human form," I admit. "I haven't been able to do more than email with Karyl. I called her once, but I forgot that in this form I'm inaudible to humans, too. I had to hang up and text her instead. She's starting to believe you kidnapped me or you're beating me, because I won't show her my face."

He draws back, scandalized. "We can't have her thinking that. I'll show you how to do it. It's like a switch in your mind, or the unlock pattern on your phone—but you have to set it first, for it to work. Usually the trigger is a particular memory from your human life—a moment when you felt especially grounded in yourself, secure in who you were."

"No wonder I couldn't switch," I mutter. "Not sure if I ever felt that way."

"You're kidding." Jack stands up, and I notice that although he's still taller than me, the difference in our heights isn't quite as dramatic now. "I've never met someone so sure of their goals and purpose."

"Sure of goals, maybe, but not necessarily confident within myself. I work hard, but I've always had to struggle along. Some people seem to have everything handed to them. *They* have innate self-confidence, and it shows. The first moment I felt completely, solidly sure of myself was on Christmas Day, when I decided I wanted to transform and be your partner in this."

Jack's lips part as if he's about to reply, but then his eyes widen. "You did it. There you are."

"What?" I dart to the dressing table mirror. Sure enough, my reflection is the old Emery—or close enough. I still look like I've had a significant makeover, but I'm not quite as sharp-edged and sparkly, and my ears are rounded. "Oh my god. I did it."

Jack slips his arms around my waist from behind. He's in his human aspect now, too. "Now switch forms again, and I'll change with you. Think of the moment you first transformed. Ready?"

Closing my eyes, I concentrate on those first moments of terror and triumph, when I knew that my transformation was real, and I was alive. When I knew that I could save Jack.

"Good," he whispers in my ear. "Now again, to human aspect and then back, this time with your eyes open."

We switch to human form and then to our frosty godlike aspects.

"You'll have to be careful not to switch inadvertently," he says. "Or you'll disappear right in front of whoever you're talking to. It's happened to me before. We'll practice until you feel comfortable, so you can see Karyl face-to-face again."

"Speaking of practicing and feeling comfortable..." I watch my cheeks flush faintly in the mirror. "If you're feeling well enough, we could—test out this new body."

Jack meets my reflection's eyes, and his tongue glides over his lips. He was already growing hard against my back, and now his desire is stiffly unmistakable.

I revolve between his arms until I'm facing him, and I tilt my mouth up to his, but I don't kiss him right away. Our noses brush lightly, cheeks grazing, breath whispering over sensitive skin. The almost-kissing is exquisitely torturous, and the air between us fairly glitters, icy and electric. Then Jack makes a sound—a desperate whimper of need, and I relent. Sinking into the kiss is deliciously gratifying. Jack devours my mouth, tasting its new flavors, and my eyes flutter shut because the taste of *him* is so familiar now, comforting and carnal, but with that edge of sparkling magic.

He breaks the kiss abruptly, his eyes glittering with a new idea. "I think we should go somewhere special. Somewhere beautiful and cold, like Prague or Budapest. You know, to celebrate your transformation, and our—what would you call this, anyway? Are we married?"

"You could say so, I guess. Bonded for life."

"Only if you want to. I can always move elsewhere, give you space—"

"No." Pressing both hands against his back, I pull him against me. "No space. I've had my space for five weeks, Jack Frost, and I didn't like it. I want you *here*, with me, I want you—" I suck in a breath and set my mouth to his ear. "I want you inside me."

A shiver runs through him, and I smile, biting my lip.

"Yes," he breathes, kissing me quick and fierce. "But later I'm taking you to Prague. The architecture—the snow on the rooftops—" another kiss— "you're going to love it. We'll stay as long as you want—I have a place there. You can film, and take pictures—"

If it were possible to burst with joy, I would be exploding into colorful fireworks right now. My love for travel, and art, and film, and Jack, all wrapped up in one package—it's almost more than I can handle.

I need release. And he can give it to me.

"Don't be gentle," I whisper, looking into his eyes.

A wicked light sparks in his gaze. He seizes me and whirls us both into the air, across the room, crashing onto the bed. I'm tearing off my clothes, and he's already naked and rigid and wanting me—our kisses are teeth and fury and claiming. We are so painfully alive, raw and craving, healing up those scorched places in our souls, the parts that bled when Auxesia tried to burn us away. I'm trembling with desperation to get him inside me, to grip him tighter. He's here, all of him. Mine. Safe. The words pound over and over in my head, a reassuring echo of each thrust he makes.

Mine. Safe. The joy of it throbs through my every nerve—swells immense and unbearable and almost—almost—

And then something bursts in my brain—a white light, shards of ice exploding into stars that turn into suns that turn into supernovas—my legs jerk and quiver with the intensity of the sensations rocketing through me. My ragged inhale leaves my throat in a wild scream, and Jack answers with a broken roar of his own.

We collapse side by side, gasping, and I press my cheek against his chest. "That was amazing."

"Hell yes," he says, still panting.

"Sex has flavors, doesn't it? I never realized it before. But it can be good in lots of different ways. Our first time was beautiful, and the second was gentle and soft—and the time at the skating rink was daring and wild—and then there was *this*." I push myself up on my elbow. "We get to do *this* again and again, as much as we want? For real?"

Jack's white teeth flash. "Incredible, isn't it?"

I curl up against him with a little wriggle of sheer delight.

Later we spiral to the surface of our continent—our beautiful Antarctica, where we are king and queen—and we walk the land. It's a clear day, with a brisk wind that tosses and twirls my long white hair. The dance of the snowy waves around my face mirrors the exuberant dance of my heart.

I've been liberated. Empowered. I've slipped into the skin I was meant to fill. My intensity, my passion, and my ambition were always a little *much* for my fellow humans. But now, all that intensity is permitted—in fact, it's encouraged. Jack's relief shows in the ease of his shoulders, the bounce of his steps. He's glad to have a true partner, one that he didn't deceive or enslave, one that believes in the cause as he has come to believe in it. I revitalized his passion for the world, and now I'm stepping alongside him to share this beautiful burden.

We pause on the crest of a ridge, looking out over the black rock and white ice and crystal-blue waters of our domain; and my mind slips back to the day when the blizzard scoured this land and drove me down into Jack's cave. The hint of frost magic inside me led me straight to him. As if it was fate.

Except I don't believe in Fate, or gods, or an afterlife.

Except maybe I do.

I slip my arm through Jack's, leaning my head against his shoulder.

He wraps his arm around me. "I don't think I thanked you yet, for saving my life. For doing this—changing your entire world, for me. You rescued me from—I don't think I could have gone on much longer without—"

I lay my fingers over his lips. "Did I rescue you, or did you rescue me?"

He beams at me. "I guess we rescued ourselves *and* each other."

"And I think that's called a healthy relationship," I say softly. "But I wouldn't know—I've never had one. Until now."

EPILOGUE

10 YEARS LATER

"Meryl!" I catch my daughter's shoulder as she breezes out the back door of Karyl and Sarah's house. "Wear your coat!"

She turns, and my breath stops for a minute because her big blue eyes are so exactly like Jack's. "But Mom, it's so hot!"

"It's freezing cold outside, and normal human kids wear coats." I hold out the offending garment, and she slips her arms into the sleeves. "Remember, human aspect only. No vanishing or spirals."

"I know, I know."

"Remind your brother."

"Yeah, yeah." She flounces away into the snowy backyard.

"Oh god, the attitude," I mutter.

"And she's only eight." Jack's low voice at my ear sends a tingle of delight along my spine. "Go easy on her. She's doing really well keeping our secret."

"I know, but if Karyl and Sarah ever found out—"

"They haven't so far, and this is our second Christmas with them."

"It's so damn stressful this time, though. Staying two nights, being in the house all together—especially with Alex. You think a six-year-old is going to remember to stay in human aspect when he opens his gifts?" I groan, pressing my face to Jack's shoulder.

"It's fine, Emery. He did okay last year, and if something happens, we'll deal with it. Do you honestly think Karyl would betray you if she knew? Or Sarah?"

My mouth twists. "No, but it would blow their minds. Wreck their reality."

"And?"

"And we've talked about this, Jack. They might let something slip to a neighbor, a relative—"

"We can't keep the kids isolated. They need to have friends, and Karyl's kids are the best."

"Yeah, they are." I smile, thinking of the little humans running around the yard with my kids.

My kids. Two words I thought I'd never say, because procreation between humans and elemental gods wasn't possible. Turns out that procreation between two frost elementals is definitely possible, though somewhat different from human processes. When my belly began swelling a year and a half after my transformation, Jack and I were both shocked. Meryl arrived only six months later, which apparently is full-term for our kind. The birth was a lot quicker and tidier than human births, which was a good thing because Jack had to help me through it.

Meryl was a cosmic shift, a lightning bolt to the life I was growing used to. Jack was instantly enamored, and my resistance melted within a few days, yielding to a love so deep that I couldn't imagine not having wanted her.

And then, a couple years after that, we had Alex. My darling Alex, with eyes so pale blue they're nearly white, and a heart as big as Antarctica.

Karyl bustles up to us, carrying three steaming mugs. "Cocoa?"

The thought of pouring hot liquid down my throat is revolting. "Um, wow, that's so thoughtful!" I accept the two mugs, setting them down on the hallway table. "I'll just let these cool off a bit."

Karyl cocks her head, smirking. "Uh-huh. Okay. This from the girl who used to burn her tongue all the time because she couldn't stand her tea or coffee getting cold."

"Tastes change," I murmur.

"Right. The kids getting along okay?"

"Yeah, they're having a blast."

Karyl is still watching me more closely than I'd like. "And there's another example of tastes changing. Because I remember you insisting over and over that you'd never have kids. That you wouldn't want to bring helpless children into an overpopulated, dangerous, messed-up old world like this one."

"Yes, but—these kids are different." I watch Meryl dancing past the back door with Karyl's daughter Darla, and my heart throbs with pleasure. "These kids have the power to change the world."

"Yes, they do." I can feel Karyl's eyes on me.

Jack's grip on my hand tightens.

"They have power," Karyl repeats, her tone unmistakable.

My head whips toward her. She's looking at me seriously, her dark eyes wide with meaning. Behind her, red-headed Sarah stands in the kitchen doorway, holding their sleepy two-year-old Wendell in her arms.

"We figured it out last year, right at the end of your visit," Sarah says. "When you were getting ready to leave, Wendell was crying, and Alex made a snow pacifier for him. I nearly keeled over with shock."

"After that it wasn't hard to see the other clues," Karyl says. "Where you met Jack, the way he looks, and the way you disappeared for a while before coming back all pale-ified, your sudden decision to live 'overseas'—we put two and two together. Mostly. Now it's time for y'all to fill in the blanks. If he vampirized you without your permission, Emery, I swear—"

"It's nothing like that," I reassure her. "Why didn't you tell me you suspected something?"

"We wanted to wait until we were sure," Sarah replies, shifting Wendell onto her hip. "Jack, darling, I saw you 'shovel' our driveway early this morning. Wish I could clear it with a snap of my fingers."

I whirl on Jack. His cheeks are already flushed a guilty pink. "Jack! You promised me you would shovel it the human way!"

"It would have taken so long—I thought everyone was still asleep."

Slowly I face Karyl again. This woman has been a true sister to me, for years. She taught me everything my mother never bothered to. She comforted me after my breakups and helped me see the toxic pattern in my choice of men. We have encouraged each other, celebrated each other, supported each other. Besides Jack and the kids, she's the most important person in my life.

"Do you want us to leave?" The words clog my throat; I can barely force them out.

"Leave?" Karyl exclaims. "Hell no. You're going to sit your asses down and explain every damn thing."

"Language," says Sarah. "Your son is right here, Karyl."

The conversation that follows lasts for a full hour and resurfaces throughout the day—after the opening of the presents, and during the Christmas dinner, and between the board games. With his secret unveiled, Jack indulges his creative side and crafts delicate ice sculptures for each of the children. I manage to take some videos and pictures of the festivities, but inwardly I'm twisted into anxious knots, even after we sit both families down and discuss a plan for secrecy. I'm not sure it's enough. I can't be sure that Karyl still looks at me the same way.

Finally my kids are settled in sleeping bags in their friends' rooms upstairs. Karyl and Sarah retreat to their own room, claiming exhaustion, but I'm guessing they want to debrief, to unpack everything Jack and I have told them.

I sit on the couch, glaring at some glittery Christmas movie that's still playing on the TV. What if Karyl and Sarah's kids tell someone about us? Any adult they told would probably chalk it up to youthful imagination—but who knows?

Long fingers compress my shoulders, kneading away the tension. I tilt my head back, looking up at Jack as he stands behind the couch.

I still can't believe I get to see him every day. The angles and contours of his face are a constant delight to my artistic soul, especially when he's in his supernatural Jack Frost form, as he is right now. When he leans closer, the sweet fragrance of his breath wafts across my lips, sending a tingle of delight along my body.

"They won't betray us," he whispers. "And if by some chance they did, by intent or accident, we have power. We can disappear. We can spiral. We have money, places we can go. We'll be fine, and the kids will be fine."

"Thank you," I murmur, right before he kisses me.

"I'll continue this massage," he says. "But I need you to pull that neckline of yours down a little lower—it's the least you can do as payment."

I tug at the loose neck of the sweater until the arches of my breasts are clearly visible. "Like this?"

"Mmm." Jack pushes my hair aside and kisses along the curve of my neck, each press of his lips a sparkling seal of his love. "Would you like to take a walk with me?"

"It's late..."

"It's Christmas."

"Fine." I twine my fingers through his and follow him to the back door. We step into the delicious, refreshing cold, easing the door shut behind us.

The backyard is large and completely fenced in, with a snow-covered shed at the far end. Jack leads me toward it.

"I think you have devilish intentions, sir," I tell him.

"The very worst intentions." Jack pulls me around the corner of the shed, into the shadows behind it, and shoves me against the rough wood. When he lifts my arms above my head, pressing them to the wall, manacles of ice lock into place around my wrists. "Lady Frost, Goddess of Ice, Queen of the Snowy Sea, I intend to ravage you, here and now."

"Is that so?" I can barely breathe as he trails both hands over my body. Every sweep and squeeze of his fingers lights me up, inflames me with unbearable anticipation. Intimacy isn't just pleasurable for us; it has a mutually regenerative effect on our bodies and our abilities. Still, I value it most for the spine-tingling climaxes that only seem to get better the more years we spend together. "You know I could break these cuffs easily."

"But you like being at my mercy," he says, looking into my face while his fingers slide along the inseam of my pants.

Oh god. I do. I really do.

I'm about to reply, but just then a constellation of sparks explodes behind Jack, leaving a tall dark-haired woman standing in the snow. She's in human aspect, wearing a long red dress.

"Auxesia," I whisper.

Jack quirks an eyebrow. "Is this some new kind of roleplay—"

"No, god no! Auxesia is right behind you."

The manacles around my hands shatter. Jack whirls to face the fire goddess, holding one hand behind his back while a sword of blue ice appears in his fingers. We've had cautious dealings with Auxesia over the past ten years, while she grudgingly worked with us to lessen the harmful effects of global warming. The humans think it's because they've been trying harder, and they deserve some of the credit; but most of the improvement is due to the powerful partnership between me and Jack Frost, as well as Auxesia's reluctant cooperation. But Jack still doesn't trust her. Understandable.

"I seem to have interrupted something," she says stiffly. "My apologies. Far be it from me to keep you from rutting in the snow like a pair of Arctic foxes. You can put your sword away—both of them." She glances at Jack's crotch.

He chuckles, and the ice sword disappears. "I assume you have a good reason for disturbing us on Christmas Day?"

"I felt your presence, you and your young," she says. "There's another one coming, yes?"

"Another?" I frown.

"You are carrying a third child. Did you not know? I can sense its energy."

Jack whirls, his face lighting up—literally glowing, like starlit snow. "You're pregnant again?"

Wonderingly I place my hand over my stomach. "I didn't realize."

"Yes, well... the two of you will need some form of birth control." Auxesia's lip arches. "You can't be spawning frost babies every few years. The entire earth will be swarming with them by the time Emery is two hundred. The balance will be thrown off. And we all know how keen you are to maintain the precious *balance*."

"And we appreciate your help with ensuring the balance," I say. "Our family planning is our business, but don't worry, we don't intend to overrun the world with our 'spawn,' as you so delicately put it. And if you're so concerned about evening the numbers, why not find someone of your own to 'spawn' with?"

Auxesia's scarlet eyes widen. "I don't—I cannot—"

"Why not? Find a nice human man who makes your heart flutter, and convince him to turn into a fire god. Then you can make your own little fire-babies."

"But—who would I—" She swallows, and her cheeks flush a dark red. "I don't know how to do that."

"Easy. Get yourself an apartment and play human for a while. Meet some people, see what happens. I'm just saying—if you're worried about the balance."

She stumbles over a few half-formed words and then disappears in an explosion of sparks. "Merry Christmas," I call after her.

Jack frowns deeply. "I don't think it's a good idea for her to be birthing fire-babies. You realize she's probably going to seduce some hunk of a human guy into signing up for god status, and he won't be ready for the responsibility, and we'll have some stupid meathead hurling fireballs around the globe for fun."

"Or she might find someone she actually loves. And maybe having a few kids will keep her busy—distract her if she starts having globally destructive thoughts again. Also since when did you become the pessimist? That's my job."

He grins. "They say married couples adopt each other's traits over time."

"Oh god, that's terrifying. So in a few hundred years I'll basically be you, married to myself?"

"Well, when you say it like that, it's not cute."

"Good. I abhor cute."

"Really? Because you seem to like our kids, and they are pretty damn cute."

I bite back a smile. "I am forced to like them, enslaved by my own maternal instinct."

"Right." Jack crowds me back against the shed again. "You're so cute when you're being curmudgeonly."

"Curmudgeonly? Who says that? And also I am not cute."

"You're going to make some very cute noises before I'm done with you." His blue eyes promise all kinds of sensual mischief, and I can't help myself— my smile grows wide enough to rival his.

Thick, soft snow drifts lazily from the dark sky as Jack Frost leans in, his lips brushing my cheek. "Now, goddess mine, where were we?"

ACKNOWLEDGEMENTS

I'd like to thank my wonderful Patreon members for their encouragement and support! Honestly, you all are the BEST.

Some of my subscribers took me up on the offer to be listed here in the "End Credits!" Go ahead—check out their websites or social media handles and follow them! Whether you're a writer, a reader, an artist, or all three, a supportive network is a beautiful thing.

Astra Crompton http://www.astracrompton.com/
Sarah Underwood @s_e_c_underwood
Amalie R. Frederiksen @ARFrederiksen
Stephanie Saroiberry @steviesadberry
Chesney Infalt @chesneyinfalt on Twitter & Instagram
Johanna Randle @RandleJohanna
Carol Beth Anderson https://www.carolbethanderson.com/
Kayla McGrath @_KaylaMcGrath
Darby Cupid @darbycupid
Lily Grasso @feyspeaker on Twitter and Instagram
Lydia V. Russell @fey_girl63
Haley Walden http://www.authorhaleywalden.com

BONUS SCENE

Note: This story takes place shortly after Auxesia's defeat.

It's been a long day. Jack and I spent hours refreezing the edges of glaciers and shifting ocean currents with gigantic pulses of power. I should be exhausted, and I suppose in some ways I am—my magical energy is lower than usual. But there's something uniquely invigorating about a full day's work when it actually makes a difference, when you know that you've done a really good thing. Jack's approach to the work has been fairly hit or miss, especially since Auxesia kept distracting him with wildfires; but I've been keeping more careful track of things, creating metrics by which we can judge our results and estimate where the next adjustments should occur. I've set up a sort of control room in the ice palace, just for that purpose. It's outfitted with a generator and computers and lots of screens so I can have multiple programs open at once. I'm peering at a chart of ocean currents when an icy gust of wind surges into the room, whisking my long hair around my shoulders.

Jack follows in the wake of the wind—I can see his tall form out of the corner of my eye, but I don't turn because if I look at him, I will be distracted.

He approaches behind me and trails his fingertips along the slope of my neck. "Still working?"

"Mm-hm."

"A pity."

"It's important, Jack."

"Of course it is." He collects my frosty hair in his hands and twists it aside, pressing a cold kiss to the back of my neck, right over my spine. Another kiss follows, a little lower. And another.

A tingle of delight races along my nerves.

And then Jack drops my hair and turns away. "Too bad you're working on such very important things. I guess I'll leave you to it."

I spin in the chair and leap up. "I—I guess I could take a break."

He's halfway to the door, but he turns, his beautiful mouth widening in a devilish smile.

Of course. That was his plan, to tease me and pretend to leave, so I'd want him even more.

He approaches me, and my breath catches again because I still see myself mentally as plain old human Emery, not frost goddess Emery, and I can scarcely believe that this beautiful frost faerie loves me, wants me, craves my body and my soul. He's unbuttoning his shirt, throwing it aside. That expanse of pale carved abs, blue-shadowed and fairly glittering, never fails to tempt my fingers, and this time is no exception. I reach out, eager to trace every slope and plane of his body, but Jack catches my wrists with a lightning-quick movement.

"No, baby," he says. "Not this time."

He sweeps my arms upward and crowds me back against the wall, pinning my wrists together. A pair of icy shackles grows from the wall, locking my arms in place above my head. With a twitch of his fingers, Jack creates an icy chain that slithers around my ankle, drawing my right leg aside; and he does the same with my left leg, until I'm splayed open so wide my flimsy white dress rips along the thigh.

"Damn you. I liked this dress." My words float from my lips with my shallow, quick breaths. I'm wildly excited, my skin tingling all over; and the crease between my legs is growing slippery already.

"I'll buy you another." Jack extends icy fingernails and comes so close I can taste his sweet breath. "Hold very still, darling." He cuts careful slits in the fabric across my chest, grazing the thin, sensitive skin of my breasts with the tips of his claws. My nipples tighten to eager buds, and I try to take shallower sips of air when all I want to do is heave in great bursting breaths.

"You know I can break these cuffs," I whisper. "It would be easy."

"But it would spoil the fun." He braces his forearms on either side of my head, his chest skimming mine and his mouth whispering over my lips. "You break them, and I'll leave you wanting." He lightly scrapes the hair away from my face with his icy claws. And then he traces his cool, sweet tongue across my lower lip.

"Oh god," I whimper. "You're the devil."

"And you like it."

"This is—different—from what we usually do."

"I know. But it's something I've always wanted to try." He backs away and sends a whispering trail of cold air along my skin, peeling away the fabric he shredded. Within seconds I'm naked from the waist up, fully exposed to his view.

With a single claw, he dents the trembling flesh below my navel, and he draws a line gently up my stomach, through the valley between my breasts, and along my throat.

Then he backs away again. "Close your eyes."

I obey, and he seals my lids shut with a lacy blindfold of frost. The next second a tendril of icy wind coils around my thigh, sliding under the fluttering skirt of my ruined dress. It passes lightly across my center, a tickling breath, and I flinch, trembling harder. "Jack," I breathe.

"You're so beautiful." His voice is strained, wonder and barely repressed desire. "I don't think I'm cut out for this slow teasing crap. I just want to hold you."

"Come here," I beg. "Come to me, Jack. Come into me."

He swears fiercely, and the sweet chill of his presence grows stronger, nearer. I smile, because I have reclaimed the power.

Then he closes his fingers around my hips, and before I can prepare myself his tongue glides over me—a long slow lick that makes me cry out and jerk against the icy shackles.

He has gotten so much better at this. Lapping and swirling, kissing and nibbling—I'm nearly sobbing, I'm shuddering, desperate—he rises, and I can feel the planes of his body sliding against mine as he stands. He's naked, his hard length pressing in just the right spot, and he kisses me, swirling that same naughty tongue through my mouth. I attack him with my kisses, tugging his lip with my teeth in a vain effort to keep him close. He's distanced himself again, and I hate it.

"Jack, if you don't touch me now, I swear you'll regret it."

Another flick of frosty wind across my folds, a crisp touch of curling frost, and I'm quivering again, nearly there—so close—

243

"Jack, please."

"Screw it," he says, and the shackles and my blindfold splinter into snowflakes as he crashes against me. My arms drop around his neck, and he hoists me up, shoving me back against the wall and entering me in the same swift motion. The sudden contact finishes me—my neck arches back and my eyes close as orgasmic power pulses through my body. The entire wall shatters and I fall backward through it, with Jack's body still locked to mine. I'm bucking under the force of the glittering pleasure jetting through me. Snowy chunks of the broken wall rain down around us as Jack shoves into me again, and again, and again. When he comes, a wave of icy magic explodes from him, blasting through the room.

We lie tangled in the ruin we made. My muscles feel melted—I'm a slushy puddle of sated limbs and a pounding heart that's slowing, slowing, sinking into the afterglow of truly supernatural sex.

Jack is just as limp as I am, but he manages to mutter, "Emery, I think we broke your computers."

"Probably just the monitors," I said. "We can buy more of those. The hard drives are fine."

"I'll help you fix it," he says. "And then—we should probably not do that in your office again."

"Probably not." I nuzzle my face into the hollow of his throat, where I can inhale the fresh snowy scent of his skin. "But it was fun."

MORE BOOKS FROM REBECCA F. KENNEY

The DARK RULERS adult fantasy romance series

Bride to the Fiend Prince
Captive of the Pirate King
Prize of the Warlord
The Warlord's Treasure
Healer to the Ash King
Pawn of the Cruel Princess
Jailer to the Death God
Slayer of the Pirate Lord

The WICKED DARLINGS Fae retellings series

A Court of Sugar and Spice
A Court of Hearts and Hunger
A City of Emeralds and Envy

The PANDEMIC MONSTERS trilogy

The Vampires Will Save You
The Chimera Will Claim You
The Monster Will Rescue You

For the Love of the Villain series

The Sea Witch (Little Mermaid retelling with male Sea Witch)
The Maleficent Faerie (Sleeping Beauty retelling with male Maleficent)

The SAVAGE SEAS books

The Teeth in the Tide
The Demons in the Deep

These Wretched Wings (A Savage Seas Universe novel)

The IMMORTAL WARRIORS adult fantasy romance series

Jack Frost
The Gargoyle Prince
Wendy, Darling (Neverland Fae Book 1)
Captain Pan (Neverland Fae Book 2)
Hades: God of the Dead
Apollo: God of the Sun

Related Content: *The Horseman of Sleepy Hollow*

The INFERNAL CONTESTS adult fantasy romance series
Interior Design for Demons
Infernal Trials for Humans

MORE BOOKS
Lair of Thieves and Foxes (medieval French romantic fantasy/folklore retelling)

Her Dreadful Will (contemporary witchy villain romance)

Of Beasts and Bruises (A Beauty & two Beasts retelling)

Made in the USA
Columbia, SC
18 January 2024

bd233a8d-a909-49ef-bcb4-7fac33dc7d97R02